HOT ROUTE

BOSTON BLIZZARD SERIES
BOOK 1

C.L. ROSE

HOT ROUTE

C.L. ROSE

Edits and Proofreading: Breanne at Breezy Book Edits

To my husband.
Thanks for helping with…research.

PLAYLIST

1. Dirty Thoughts - Chloe Adams
2. FU In My Head - Cloudy June
3. The Man - Taylor Swift
4. Confident - Justin Bieber f. Chance The Rapper
5. Ur Perfect I Hate It - Mickey Valen f. Emilia Ali
6. Church - Chase Atlantic
7. Wannabe - Austin Giorgio
8. The High - Bryce Savage
9. Fallin' (Adrenaline) - Why Don't We
10. Thinkin' Bout Me - Morgan Wallen
11. Whiskey Glasses - Morgan Wallen
12. Thing for Ya - Chri$tian Gate$
13. A$$A$$IN - Beauty School Dropout
14. Curiosity - Bryce Savage
15. EAGER - Britton
16. Yours - Russell Dickerson
17. Ride - Chase Rice f. Macy Maloy
18. Snooze - SZA
19. Under the Influence - Chris Brown

PROLOGUE
MADS

"WHAT DOES IT SAY?"

My best friend Dia hovers over my shoulder as I try to bargain with my Jurassic Era laptop.

"Hold on. I can't get the email app to load," I tell her, debating on setting the entire apartment ablaze so I can use the insurance check for an upgrade. I'm fresh out of college with a mountain of student loans, so barring any acts of blatant vandalism and fraud, I'm stuck with this piece of junk for a little while longer.

"Aha!" I yell excitedly as the app loads fully, showing me exactly what I'm looking for. "Oh my God, I've never been so nervous. This email has the power to crush my dreams."

"What an amazingly positive attitude you have. It's simply contagious," Dia deadpans. "Just open it and read, bitch. I have a dick appointment in twenty minutes, and I need to know if I can bang Trent without the guilt that comes with leaving you here heartbroken."

"Wow. If I was sitting here crying my eyes out, you'd still go?" I say, feigning offense.

"A girl has needs," she replies. "And his eggplant is literally the size of an eggplant. Now read."

I open the email and take a deep breath before relaying it to her aloud.

"Dear Miss Rodgers, I hope this email finds you well. I'd like to congratulate you on being accepted to our internship program. You are one of four interns that will be coming to work for us in the Journalism and Content Creation department here at Tailgate Media's Boston location. Over the next year, you will learn the valuable tools needed for an opportunity to interview for a full-time position with us. This is a paid internship. We have discussed those figures previously, so you should have everything you need. Please contact my assistant Dani at the phone number below for the details on the job. I look forward to working with you. Sincerely, Jacob Shane."

I take about three seconds to gather myself before I scream excitedly. Dia launches herself at me, hugging me tightly.

"I knew you'd get it! Nobody knows all that boring sports shit the way you do! Plus, you're hot as fuck and the male viewers are going to jizz in their pants when they hear you talk about all of it!" Her smile fades slightly. "I'm going to miss you."

"I'm going to miss you, too," I tell her, not wanting to think about how I'll survive without my other half. "But bitch...I'm fucking chasing my dreams in Boston!"

ONE
MADS

"IS THAT EVERYTHING?" my mom says as I carry the last of my bags down the stairs.

"Sure as shit hope so," grumbles my dad as he not-so-gracefully jams a suitcase into the non-existent space in the back of my mid-sized SUV. "One more grain of rice and this car is going to bust like a can of biscuits."

"Calm down, Dad. It's not that much stuff. Just the necessities for a one-year trip across the globe." I wink.

Dia shoots me a glare. "Stop saying shit like that! You're not going across the globe. You're not even going across the country. It's not that far." I know she's trying to convince herself of that more than me, so I wrap her in a tight hug, inhaling her minty shampoo, hoping I can burn it into my memory for those days when I'm missing her.

"I'm only a FaceTime away." I pull back slightly, dropping my forehead to hers. "Call me anytime. Day or night." I try my best to hold back my tears, but it's no use. Dia has been my other half since we were in diapers. We've never spent more than a week apart.

"This mascara was thirty-six dollars and your selfish ass has me ruining it," she jokes, sniffling. I do my best to wipe the black from under her eyes, but I'm just making it worse. She smiles through her tears and playfully shoves me away.

"Okay," she takes a breath and smooths out the non-existent wrinkles from her black tank top. "Time to go do big girl things."

I hug both of my parents once more and smile when my dad hands me a wad of cash.

"For snacks or whatever," he shrugs, acting tough but I can see the unshed tears in his eyes. I've only seen him cry a handful of times in my life and the look on his face right now is making me feel so many different things. I'm sad that I'm leaving them behind, but I'm chasing this dream that I've had since the first time he took me to a pro football game when I was eight years old. I fell in love that day.

"Wow! It's so big!" I squealed, my eyes bouncing from one thing to another as my father led me by my hand to our seats. We made our way to the bottom of the stairs, him ushering me to the middle of the very first row on the thirty-yard line.

Directly in front of us stood a woman in a black pencil skirt, her white silk button up tucked into her waistband. She settled a small device into her ear before taking a microphone from a younger man standing by her side. Just then, players began trickling out from the tunnel in their uniform pants and t-shirts, taking places on the field to stretch and warm up.

"Excuse me! Jonathan!" the woman said loudly to a player jogging by. He stopped abruptly, smiling as he made his way to her side. "Can I have a quick minute? Just a few questions," she asked, her confidence radiating from her small frame as she looked up at him.

"My pleasure, Molly," he replied, standing close enough to hear her, but far enough to look her in the eye as they spoke. Even though he was at least a foot taller, I could see that he respected her.

"You've been looking strong this season, coming back from an ACL tear. How has your recovery affected your ability to run those

precise routes you're known for?" she asked before turning the microphone to him.

He paused, thinking before he answered.

"I have a great team of doctors and physical therapists who tailor made my rehabilitation plan specifically for that. I think my knee is as strong as ever and I feel great when I'm cutting or juking defenders. The injury was a setback, but I'm grateful that I had the opportunity to learn my body better as I healed."

The reporter smiled as she pulled the microphone back in front of herself.

"Thank you so much, Jon. Good luck today."

"Thanks, Molly," he said, ending the interview before jogging off.

I stood there in awe as my little mind imagined a future where I could make grown men stop in their tracks to talk to me about the game. I wouldn't be the weird girl who knew how many touchdowns my favorite players had on the season or the number of career wins a head coach had under his belt. I would just be normal here. They'd see me and respect my knowledge and love of sports.

For the entire four quarters of football that followed, I thought of the perfect post-game questions for the winning team. And I smiled at the thought of a time when I'd be the one asking them.

I'm brought back to the present as my mom steps forward, wrapping her small arms around me. I inhale her comforting scent as I commit it to memory for those nights where I'm sure homesickness will find me. Thankfully, I'll be staying with my cousin Sarah at her apartment until my internship paychecks start coming in, so at least I'll have a little familiarity. But every girl knows there's nothing like a hug from your mom sometimes. My throat tightens at the thought.

She steps back, her expression hardening before launching into one of her famous Diane Rodgers pep-talks.

"You are a strong, smart, independent woman. You're stepping into a male dominated world and there will be times when people try to make you second guess whether you belong. Don't you let them put doubt in your head and heart. Nobody is more qualified for this job than you. And I can't wait to turn on my television one day soon and see you commanding the sidelines."

"Thank you, Mom. For everything," I say, tears filling my eyes. I give her one last hug before hopping into my dad's waiting arms. Words fail me because what do you say to the man who taught you everything? The one who sat in front of the computer, pausing game replay videos and breaking down each play into words a young girl could make sense of. We spent hours learning the history of the game and trying to stump each other with facts and statistics.

All I can manage is a choked "I love you, Dad."

I owe these people everything for fueling my dreams of becoming a sports journalist.

"Okayyyyyyyyyyy. Get the hell out of here so I can move my stuff into your room and claim my spot as your parents' new favorite daughter," Dia chides, although I know she's using humor to mask her emotions.

Classic Diamond.

I roll my eyes before smacking one last kiss to her cheek and getting into my car. Turning the key, it makes a small sputter before the engine roars to life. I smile triumphantly as I fasten my seatbelt, hearing my father mumble something about *that pile of shit car belonging in a junkyard.* That's a problem for future Mads who gets big girl paychecks. I just need to make it to Boston and I'll be golden. At least for now.

"Bye! Stay out of trouble!" I yell from the window, waving to the three most important people in my world as they get smaller and smaller before disappearing from my rear-view mirror.

Now, there's nothing left to do but look forward. And the future looks pretty amazing.

I've been on the road for about five hours and my legs are dying to get out and stretch. Taking the I-90 from Chicago all the way to Boston isn't exactly the most scenic route and I'm bored out of my mind. I'm about a quarter of the way through Taylor Swift's full discography and while that's kept me busy, I need a break from driving.

I'm sobered by the thought that I'm actually on my own. I know I'm in Cleveland, but I've never been to Ohio before and I'm a little nervous being in a strange place by myself. Mist fills my eyes as I realize that this is my life now. Just me, chasing a dream that I may never reach without the people I love holding my hand along the way.

As doubt creeps into my head, I'm on autopilot as I mindlessly follow the highway signs. Before I know it, I'm waiting at the stoplight off the exit to Downtown Cleveland. Pulling into a parking space, I feed the meter with enough change to buy myself about thirty minutes. Even though I've never been here, my destination is lit up with bright lights in front of me.

Pulling up my hood, I let my feet bring me exactly where I need to be. As the entirety of the Cleveland Rockers' stadium comes into view, something inside me settles. Just like our field at home, it's huge. A big Jumbotron sits atop the stadium, replaying game highlights and interviews from seasons past. People are walking by, paying me no attention as I sit on a bench painted in their team colors of purple and orange before closing my eyes.

I listen to the sounds of the game replays and cheering fans on the screen as my body relaxes. This is where I belong. I love all sports, but football is my safe space. The chaos of the game is home to me.

With a renewed excitement for whatever the future holds, I walk back to my car. As I merge back on to the highway, I can't help but feel butterflies in my stomach while I crank up the music and head toward my new home.

TWO
MADS

I GET out of the shower, reaching for one of the fluffy white towels supplied by room service. I arrived in Boston last night, opting to stay at a hotel instead of showing up on Sarah's doorstep with all my shit on a weeknight. I know she was expecting me, but I didn't want to wear out my welcome before I even moved in by waking her in the middle of the night when she had to work in the morning. Plus, I have a meeting with Jacob Shane this afternoon to sign the contract for my internship.

I dry my body before gently using the towel to squeeze the excess water from my thick, brown hair. Wiping the steam from the mirror, I look at my reflection.

"You, Madison Rodgers, are about to make all your dreams come true," I say out loud. "If any of those boys tell you you shouldn't be there, you kick them right in the taint!"

It's not exactly my mother's pep-talk vibe, but it does the trick. I puff up my chest, spin on my heel, and head out of the bathroom. Opening my garment bag, I pull out my most professional looking outfit and lay it on the bed. I check the clock and realize that I still have about thirty minutes to relax before I need to start getting ready for my meeting. I've already researched transportation and know my way to the T, so I won't have to spend unnecessary time trying to find parking.

I sit on the bed, scooting my way up to the pillow before grabbing the remote and turning on the television. I decide to set an alarm on my phone to alert me when I need to get dressed so I don't get carried away watching TV or accidentally fall asleep. Sitting back against the headboard, I flip to BSN just in time to see an interview with some of the star players of the Blizzard, the city's pro football team.

Standing to the right of Tanner Lake, their starting quarterback, is wide receiver Blaze Beckham. This will be his third year in the NFL, and he's already broken a slew of season records. Last year, he had 1,970 receiving yards. Everyone had the Blizzard winning the whole thing, but they lost the AFC championship game in overtime after a blown pass interference call. Vegas still has them as a clear favorite to win the championship this year.

The interview continues, cutting to highlights of Lake and Beckham working their magic on the field. It's almost like they share a brain with how seamlessly they play together. As soon as the ball is snapped, Tanner goes through his progressions, finding an open Blaze almost every time. It's not that defenders don't try to cover him. He's just that fast.

The camera cuts back to the interviewer as he continues peppering the players with questions about the team as well as their personal lives. Tanner gives virtually zero information, which isn't surprising. He's notoriously private. But Blaze seems to be an open book. He's all over the gossip blogs with a new woman on his arm every weekend.

"Blaze, you were recently seen leaving a Beavers hockey game with the team owner's daughter, Jessie Young. Is there something going on between the two of you that you'd like to tell us about? Perhaps an inter-sport love connection?"

The interviewer flashes a hopeful smile while he waits for Blaze to give him the scoop.

"I know my love life is often a topic of discussion around here, but I'm sad to say that I have no tea for you, Brad. Jessie is a great friend and that's all."

The interview ends and it moves on to top highlights from last night's hockey and baseball games. But I am left daydreaming about how unbelievably attractive both Tanner and Blaze are. I swear, being fine as fuck is a prerequisite for making the Blizzard roster. I've snuck a peek at Tanner's issue of ESPN magazine, where he bared it all for the camera on several pages, more times than I should probably be comfortable admitting.

Whatever. I am a red-blooded American woman who can appreciate a good set of abs and a firm butt. Don't make it a thing.

My mind wanders to what Blaze would look like under all that padding. I've seen him in photos wearing street clothes, but I think this might be the first time I've really considered that he probably has the most amazing body. He's done interviews where he has talked about his strict eating habits and private personal chef. He obviously takes good care of himself, and I'm sure that shows when he's naked.

Unable to help myself, my fingers start flying across the phone keyboard, typing *shirtless photos of Blaze Beckham* into the search bar. The moment the results begin filling the page, my jaw drops. I had no idea that he was the face of so many ad campaigns. Most of which have him in very little clothing. One is from a popular underwear company. The photo is of him standing in nothing but a pair of black boxer briefs, thumb tucked into the waistband, pulling it down slightly. His other hand is gripping the back of his neck, and he's looking into the camera with intense brown eyes. His dark brown hair has that freshly fucked look. He probably rolls out of bed looking like this every day.

My mouth instantly becomes dry, and my breathing goes

shallow. I'm still sitting here wrapped only in a towel, but my body feels like it's on fire. Looking around as if the room is full of other people instead of completely empty, I cautiously undo the towel where it's tucked into itself above my breasts. I pull it apart and coast my fingers downward, past my belly button, stopping at the shaved mound of my pussy. I gently rub soft circles over my clit and moan at the contact.

Continuing to look at the photo of Blaze, I imagine he is standing in front of me, that thumb ready to pull his briefs down so I can finally see his mouthwatering length. I lower my fingers to find that I'm soaking wet. They easily slide inside as I breach my entrance, my breath hitching as I curl my fingers forward, brushing my g-spot.

It's been over two months since I've been able to orgasm. I've tried my full arsenal of toys multiple times, none of which have gotten me to the finish line. I was starting to think my preferences and past experiences in the bedroom had desensitized me to *normal* stuff. But here I am, with just my fingers and a shirtless photo of Blaze Beckham, ready to fall over the edge. I just need *one. More. Min—*

The loud screeching of my phone alarm has me ripping my fingers from my body like they're on fire. The screen is black, asking me if I'd like to *Stop* or *Snooze* while I jackknife up into a sitting position, breathing like I just ran a marathon. I stop the alarm and toss my phone aside, throwing myself back onto the pillow with an arm covering my eyes.

"Holy fuck," I say to myself, still breathless and reeling from how quickly I was writhing on a hotel bed while looking at a not-even-fully-naked man. I mentally high-five myself because *progress*.

Now that I've been cockblocked by my own phone, I peel myself from the bed and get dressed for the meeting. The throbbing ache between my legs subsides slightly but doesn't fully go away. It never does. But now isn't the time to focus on that. I have a contract to sign.

THREE
MADS

MY KNEE BOUNCES up and down rapidly as I sit in the cold, hard chair outside Jacob Shane's office. I already have the internship, so I have no idea where the nerves are coming from, but I feel like a rubber band about to snap at any second. My palms are sweating, and my teeth are abusing my lower lip as I wait impatiently. What if they hate me? What if I can't hack it in the real world of sports journalism?

"Mr. Shane is ready for you," the receptionist says, snapping me from my preemptive self-loathing. "You can head right in." She smiles before returning to her work.

My mask of confidence quickly slips back onto my face as I stand, smoothing my black pencil skirt and heading through the door into Jacob's office. The walls are covered in framed jerseys, all autographed. Behind the desk is a collage of photos of the man himself with various athletes and other high-profile celebrities.

This is the big time.

"You must be Madison," Jacob says, standing.

"It's very nice to finally meet you, Mr. Shane. Thank you so much for the opportunity," I say before reaching out to shake his hand. He's different than I thought he would be.

First, he's wearing jeans and an old Boston College t-shirt. Not what I expected from the owner of a company that's worth a cool four-hundred million. He waves a hand, gesturing for me to sit before he mirrors me. But where I'm stiff as a board with my back straight and legs crossed at the ankles, he has his socked feet propped up on the desk between us while he leans back in his chair. Grabbing a ball from a miniature Stanley Cup replica in front of him, he begins tossing it in the air while I silently wonder if this is a normal occurrence around here.

"So," he begins, "there have been a few changes to the terms of the internship, and I just want to run them by you before you sign anything."

I uncross my ankles because my anxiety is giving me two choices. I can either allow my knee to resume its bouncing or I can climb up the fucking walls right here.

"Okay," I answer, confused as to what could've possibly changed since the last time we spoke.

Jacob leans forward slightly, pushing a folder my way. "We recently had to part ways with one of our full-time reporters. Without getting into the dirty details, she was caught in a compromising position with someone who worked under her. That's against our policy. So, we have an opening in the media department and would love to make it a competition between our new interns. But we need to move fast. The timetable for hiring is one-hundred and twenty days, which means you won't have the full year to intern here. We will need to make a decision in the next four months on which of you would be the best fit for a full-time position here at Tailgate Media. Is this something you'd want?"

I stare at him, dumbfounded for a second before quickly recovering. This is huge. My dream job is so close. All I have to do is block out any distractions and put my heart and soul into the next few months.

"Sir, this is all I've ever wanted," I answer him honestly.

"I'm confident in my ability to take on whatever you want to throw at me." I might sound cocky, but I don't care. I want him to see how ready I am to make this internship my bitch.

He nods his head before handing me a pen. "Happy to have you on board, Madison. All I need now is for you to look over the contract and sign."

I open the cover and scan the paperwork inside. I have most of the details from speaking with Jacob's assistant Dani prior to today, but honestly, this thing could say that I need to go streaking through Fenway in the middle of a baseball game as part of my job description and I would still sign it.

I flip to the next page, where it talks about salary and notice that the amount is considerably smaller than we had discussed. But since I am here no matter what and don't want to ruffle any feathers, I let it go. I can get a part-time job to supplement the income so I'm able to pay my portion of the bills at Sarah's. This internship is only twenty hours a week, so I'll have some extra time on my hands for a second job. It's a small sacrifice in the grand scheme of things.

Picking up the pen, I sign my name next to the flag and close the folder before handing it back to Jacob. I try not to let it show that butterflies are currently tickling the inside of my stomach. It's official, I am on my way to becoming the next big thing at Tailgate Media.

As if he can hear my inner thoughts, Jacob stands, smiling before extending a hand to me across the desk. "I have a good feeling about you, Miss Rodgers," he says while we shake hands.

I can't help the smile that blooms across my face at his praise.

"I won't let you down, sir."

FOUR
MADS

"SO, TELL ME ABOUT YOUR MEETING," Sarah says, standing in my doorway while I unpack my suitcase into the empty dresser.

"I went in there expecting to just sign my contract and get ready for the next year of my life, but Jacob hit me with a bomb right off the rip. I guess they had to fire one of their reporters, so they're looking to hire a replacement quickly. They want to make it a competition between the four of us and at the end, one of us will be a full-time employee at Tailgate."

"Oh my God, it's totally yours! You're going to kill it, Mads!" she squeals, throwing herself dramatically onto my bed. I try to be humble and hide the excitement from outwardly showing on my face, but it only lasts a moment before I'm grinning ear to ear. "Remember when we were like, eight years old and my dad and I came to visit while they had their fantasy football draft? All I wanted to do was hang out with the cute neighbor boys, but you insisted on sitting in the living room with them while they made their picks. They ended up kicking you out because you were scoffing over their shoulders the entire evening."

I laugh, remembering that night as if it were yesterday. "Uncle Jimmy took a quarterback with the first pick. And not even a good one. If memory serves, he was benched by week three and was cut shortly after."

"I swear, you're such a freak. How do you remember all that?" She says jokingly before turning to her side and propping herself up on her elbow.

I chuckle. "No clue. But it's a cool party trick."

Remembering the rest of my meeting, I continue. "While I was looking at the contract, I noticed that I'm going to be getting paid less than expected. I think I'm going to need a part-time job for the next four months or so to be able to afford to live here. So, if you know of anybody that's hiring, send them my way."

"Actually," Sarah replies, face scrunched like she's thinking, "Tyler's mom owns a company that staffs personal assistants to high-profile people in the city. She asked me if I wanted to work for her, but I thought it would be best if I didn't mix business with pleasure when it comes to my boyfriend's mother. That could get ugly if something goes sideways. But I know the demand has grown since she opened and she has been looking for more employees. I can definitely set up a meeting with her and get you working quickly. Most of the people that need assistants use them for odd jobs and don't have them work all day, so it would be kind of perfect for you."

I thank her as she gets up from the bed and skips to the doorway. It's easy to see how we are related. Not only do we look similar, but we share our mothers' signature bubbly, positive personalities. Well, we're positive as long as we remain caffeinated. Coffee is life in our family.

"Hey, Sarah?" I say, making her turn around before she leaves the room. "Thanks. For everything."

She winks at me. "Of course."

I'm left alone in the room with my mountain of clothes

and a whole room that needs to be decorated with pieces of home. I abandon the dresser for now and move to another bag with some of my personal items. First, I set a photo of myself and Dia on the nightstand. It's from a music festival we went to last year. We're both smiling with our faces painted and glitter all over our bodies. I remember it like it was yesterday, drinking ourselves silly until we stumbled to our tent for the night. We laughed until our sides hurt, which is definitely the norm for us.

A feeling of sadness washes over me as I remember just how far apart we are. Normally, after something big happens, we grab some Ben and Jerry's and stay up all night watching movies and doing makeovers. Not that I think Sarah would object to that kind of girly fun and I do love hanging out with her, but nobody is Dia.

I look at the clock and notice that it is probably past my best friend's bedtime, so I shoot her a quick *I miss you* text and return to setting up my room. Before I know it, it's one in the morning and I'm practically dead on my feet. I slide under the covers and sleep takes me quickly. I'd say my first day in Boston was quite a success.

FIVE
BLAZE

"BECKHAM, WHAT THE ACTUAL *FUCK*!?" My agent, Mac yells through the phone. I pull the device away from my head because he may have just blown my eardrum. "I told you I needed you to be on set for that commercial shoot at six this morning. Why did I get a message from the director at nine saying you never showed? Do you have any idea how much money you just screwed us out of? Let alone the fact that they probably won't want to work with you again because you aren't reliable!"

I pinch the bridge of my nose while I actively will my body not to puke. I suppose staying up all night with a random cleat chaser was probably not the best idea when I had to be up early the next morning, but she promised me she could suck a golf ball through a garden hose and I wasn't about to deny her the opportunity to show off that skill on my dick.

"Mac, I'm gonna need you to lower your volume just a few notches. I think I'm dying," I groan, letting my head fall back on the couch.

Why the fuck is it so bright in here?

"You're not dying. You're hungover," He deadpans.

"What the ever-loving fuck were you thinking? Partying the night before a shoot with the biggest shoe brand in the world. The brand that you signed a five-million-dollar contract with, might I add."

I hear some ruffling on the other end of the line and I'd bet every dime I have that he's rifling through his desk looking for some Tums. I have a gift for making his ulcer flare up. I couldn't tell you why the grumpy old prick still puts up with me. Oh, yeah, I can. Because signing a five-million-dollar endorsement is not an irregular occurrence for me. Not only am I the top-paid receiver in the National Football League, but you can't walk down the street in this city without seeing my face on a billboard or the side of a bus.

He must've found his antacids because I'm treated to his loud, open-mouth chewing before he continues. I can't decide whether the sound makes me want to cry, puke, or punt one of these couch pillows into the fucking sun. But he's already not very happy with me, so I keep those thoughts to myself.

"You need to straighten up, kid. Stop drinking and chasing women every time you have a night off. Not that you *had* last night off. You should've been in bed early, resting for your early call time."

I get why he's annoyed. I'm an amazing football player, but all the other stuff? The off-the-field part of being a pro athlete? I have a hard time keeping track. There's always a photo shoot or appearance to be made. I spend long hours eating prepared meals from Tupperware containers while being carted from one location to the other. And now, I've started my own brand of athletic wear, which will just add more to my plate.

I sit up, wincing slightly when the pounding in my skull returns. "I think I need some help keeping my shit together," I tell him. "Maybe I need to hire someone to take care of my schedule."

"Actually, there's a fairly new agency in Boston that

matches people up with personal assistants. I've worked with them before and haven't heard any complaints. I can get someone to come every day and make sure you know what's going on. And if you have any extra tasks for them, that'll be up to you."

I scoff. "No thanks. Last thing I need is some stranger hanging around twenty-four seven, all up in my business. Just tell them I need help keeping my schedule straight and that I'll possibly have them come along to shoots and appearances, so I don't have to eat cold lunches out of plastic containers all day."

"Whatever," he replies. "Just do me a favor and remember the advice I gave you about not sleeping with anyone who works for you."

"C'mon Mac. If I didn't know any better, I'd think you wanted me all to yourself," I joke.

He tells me someone from the agency will be contacting me before we end the call. Now that I've given myself an accidental day off, I can chill here and let the remnants of last night leave my system before hitting the gym with my teammate Dalton this evening. I can't help but think about how my life is right now. All I do is play football, work out, and party with random women when I have some free time, which is limited these days.

As glamorous as it looks from the outside, I'm getting to a point where I'm starting to think that there must be more to life than this. Most of my teammates and old college buddies are in serious relationships. Some of them are even married with children. And here I am, missing important appearances because I was trying to get my dick wet with a woman whose name I can't even remember. All this stuff was cute when I was a rookie, but maybe I need to think about what my future will look like when I'm no longer able to play the game I love.

"Fuck that. Live it up while you can, Becks," I say to myself before drifting off to sleep.

SIX
MADS

AS I PULL through the gates of the massive housing complex, I almost go off the road several times, looking at the row of homes that I am driving past. Grabbing my Gucci dupe sunglasses from the center console, I slide them onto my face. There is no way I'm driving through this place and not pretending like I'm one of the Real Housewives of Boston. So what if I drive a busted down Chevy that sounds like the RV from National Lampoon's Christmas Vacation? It's called *staying humble.*

"I bet Maury Povich lives here. Fucking *love* that show," I say to myself as I continue driving toward my destination.

Double checking the paper that was given to me by Tyler's mom, I pull up to the address in front of me. The house is huge. As a matter of fact, this isn't a house. I would say it's a mansion, but I feel like maybe there is a better word for it. A castle? A Kingdom? I don't know, but this is easily the biggest house I have ever seen. Surely, there must be more than one person living here. I'd be willing to bet it's a senator and their family or something like that. I really hope I don't get stuck wiping snotty noses and changing diapers. I just want to schedule some meetings, run some errands, and get my paycheck.

I shake my hands out after putting the car in park. Taking a deep breath, I try to calm my nerves as I double check to make sure I don't have lipstick on my teeth. That would be embarrassing. I step out of the car and take a moment to get another look at the massive dwelling I'll be spending at least half of every weekday in from now until I'm done with my internship.

"It could be worse," I say to myself. "Be thankful you're here and not riding on the back of a garbage truck." Not that I have anything against garbage trucks. I'm just not built for that kind of manual labor.

Sucking in one last deep breath, I reach out and ring the doorbell. I hear some loud footsteps, what sounds like grunting, and then the door swings open abruptly. The man standing before me completely steals every last breath from my body. He towers over my five-foot-five frame. His messy brown hair is in direct contrast to his perfect face.

Say something cool, idiot. My brain wills me to stay calm for just one moment in my socially awkward life.

"You're not Maury Povich." *Oh my God. I want to die.*

"What?" he says, eyes wide as saucers.

"You know. Maury. *'You are* not *the father!'*" I say, using a deep, manly voice.

He looks at me blankly for a moment. "You were expecting Maury Povich? Wow. Sorry for the letdown. I'm Blaze Beckham. I play —"

"Wide receiver for the Boston Blizzard," I interrupt him like an absolute cantaloupe, remembering how I almost got myself off looking at his shirtless photos a few days ago.

Please, God, just let me say something normal, and I promise you I will never ask for another thing as long as I live.

I shake my head, trying to get myself together. "I know who you are. And I wasn't expecting Maury Povich, per se. I wasn't given a name of who I would be working for. I was just caught off guard."

Blaze quirks a brow. "They didn't tell you that you'd be my new assistant? That seems a little weird. What if you hated me? What if you were a Miami Rage fan? You're *not* a Miami Rage fan, are you?"

"No," I say, walking past him, through the door. He follows, shutting it behind us.

"You're Madison Rodgers. Right?" he says, eyeing me nervously.

"You'd better hope so," I chide. "Otherwise, you just shut yourself inside your super expensive home with someone who could very well be a serial killer."

"Let me see your ID," he says, holding out his hand.

I go to grab my wallet from my cross-body bag, realizing it's not in its usual spot on my hip.

"My bag is in the car. But look," I continue as I pull my name necklace out from under my shirt, showing him.

"Mads, huh? That your nickname?" Captain Obvious asks, standing down now that he knows I'm not some stabby Rage fan trying to up their odds of making it to the playoffs.

"Yep, that's me." I shoot him a smile.

"Tell me about yourself, Mads."

"Well," I begin, "I graduated college last spring with my bachelor's in Communications. I was offered an internship at Tailgate Media, so I moved here to Boston for that. Right now, I'm living with my cousin in Eastie until I hopefully get hired on there full-time. I needed some extra cash for expenses, so here I am. At your service."

He smiles warmly. And by *warmly*, I mean that my panties just melted clear off my body. *Stay professional, Madison. Forget about the fact that you fucked your fingers to this man less than seventy-two hours ago.*

Professional? Yeah, right. I'll be lucky if I get through the rest of today without slipping and calling him Daddy.

I...ill...II...II.0 2I0 3I0 4I0 5I0 4I0 3I0 2I0 1I0...II.0...II...II...II...

BLAZE

Son of a motherfucking bitch.

I was supposed to get an assistant. I mean, this girl techni-cally *is* an assistant, but she's also the sexiest little thing I've ever seen. And Mac specifically told me not to sleep with the people who work for me.

Maybe just the tip?

No! I need to get my shit together. I am the most eligible bachelor in Boston. I had a threesome with a mother and daughter last weekend. I can literally go to the grocery store, point to a random woman like I'm picking a grapefruit, say "I'll take that one.", and be railing her into next week within minutes. I do not need to fuck my new assistant.

Mads stares at me wordlessly with her beautiful green eyes while I try to stop my brain, which has gone fully rogue at this point, from thinking about how well her tits would fit in my hands. Or my mouth.

"Are you okay?" She asks.

"Yeah. Totally," I reply, trying to sound collected. "Just, uh, got a lot going on. Which is why you're here. I wanted to be the one to fill you in on everything. I started my own clothing line recently and we've gotten a huge response from the fans," I say proudly. "Initially, it was just going to be online. I have an e-commerce website where people can go to make purchases from my current line. But since we're doing so well, we've decided to do a pop-up shop in Boston before the season kicks off. We've rented a space for this coming week-end. I'll be there signing things and hanging with the fans. They'll be able to get a full boutique experience, enter some giveaways, and make purchases that day."

"Wow. That's amazing!" she says, smiling. "How can I help?"

"Well, I honestly just need you to be an extension of me," I reply, immediately cringing internally at how weird that sounds. I continue, "If I'm hanging with fans, the last thing I'll be thinking about is all the boring stuff. I get so excited to be with them that I'll forget to eat or not notice that I'm low on photos to sign for them. So, if you notice anything like that, just give me a hand."

She nods confidently. "That's easy enough. Make sure there are enough photos for the fans and shove something in your mouth if it's been too long." It's her turn to cringe now as I laugh quietly.

"Sounds like you'll do just fine." I wink, causing a blush to erupt over her cheeks and neck. God, she's fucking adorable. A little harmless flirting is okay as long as I don't cross any major lines. All I have to do to keep her around is not fuck her or fall in love with her. The love part is easy, but not burying myself balls deep inside this girl is going to take some effort.

SEVEN
MADS

> Mads: You are never going to believe who my new boss is.

> Dia: I was literally there when you opened the email.

> Mads: No, not from Tailgate. I got a part-time job as a personal assistant. I went to go meet the guy earlier and it's Blaze motherfucking Beckham.

> Dia: Who?

> Mads: How are you from this planet?

> Mads: <image>

JUST LIKE I knew it would, my phone rings one second after I texted Dia Blaze's underwear ad. "Hello, Diamond," I greet her.

"Man meat!" she yells so loudly, I have to hold my phone away from my ear to avoid permanent damage.

"Umm, what?" Sometimes I forget that my best friend has absolutely no filter and some of the things that come out of her mouth make sense to her, but zero to anyone else. Myself included. I've known her my whole life and she still confuses the fuck out of me sometimes.

"That fine specimen is your new boss?" she says. I can tell by her voice that she's jumping up and down. I've seen her do it a million times. She gets so excited that she has to move her body to stop from spontaneously combusting.

"Yeah," I reply. "He's the star receiver for the Boston Blizzard."

I hear a loud *whoosh* and know she's abandoned her jumping in lieu of throwing herself on the oversized beanbag chair in her living room. "You should totally fuck him."

I scoff as though that's the most ridiculous thing I've ever heard. I definitely won't be telling her how I defiled that very underwear ad in my hotel room last week. "Dia, he's my boss. I can't fuck him. Also, look at him. Guys like that…they don't date girls like me."

She sighs, annoyed. "Okay, first of all, do not put yourself down. You're hot as fuck and you're dirty in the sack. A guy like that should be so lucky. Plus, I didn't say *date him*. I said you should *fuck him*."

"Why don't you come here and fuck him yourself?" I say, ignoring the pit in my stomach as I speak the words. Blaze is so hot and I'd prefer all of the fantasies I have of him naked to include *only me*. Even though I'm probably playing with fire thinking about him like that at all. But nobody has to know, right?

"Eh," she replies. "He's too pretty for me. He looks like the kind of guy that would make sure you're comfortable before he fucks you gently. Like he'd grab an extra pillow for under your hips even if you didn't ask for it. You know I only like guys who treat me like garbage, fuck me, then never call again," she jokes.

I hope she's wrong. Because the Blaze from my fantasies wraps my hair around his fist while using my body to get what he needs. He says dirty things in my ear until I fall apart under him. *There's that ache again.*

"Anyway, can we please stop talking about how my boss fucks. I won't be able to look him in the eye Monday when I start." Yeah, right. Now that's all I'll be thinking of. "How are you?" I ask, changing the subject.

"I'm good. That new dance studio in the city opened on Friday. I tried out one of their advanced ballet classes and the owner pulled me aside asking if I'd ever considered teaching."

Dia is an amazing dancer. We both started ballet classes when we were still in preschool. Where I was completely uncoordinated and just didn't enjoy it, she flourished. Dance became her outlet. As we got older, she immersed herself into being the best ballerina she could be, hoping it would open doors for her in the future. And it did. Right before we graduated, she was offered a full scholarship to the New York School of Dance. But her parents got into some legal trouble and she had to decline the offer in order to go straight to work to earn money to help them out. It ended up being a futile effort because their problems were much larger than any of us knew. Thankfully, she hasn't talked to either of her parents in years. But the opportunities for her to further her career as a professional dancer were all but gone by the time she was out from under their hold.

"That's amazing, D!" I reply. "What did you tell her?"

She sighs. "I told her I would consider it. On one hand, I think it would be cool to teach people, but I also wonder if they would think I was a fraud. I abandoned a career in dance, so do I really have a right helping people on the way to their own?"

"You're not a fraud," I reassure her. "And that studio would be so much better with you on their staff."

As confident as she is, and as much as she uses humor to mask her real emotions, I know Dia feels like a disappointment with the way that her life has turned out. What she doesn't see is where she had to claw her way out of in order to be where she is today. Most people would have quit and given up on everything. She should be a statistic, but instead she is thriving. I couldn't be prouder of her.

She blows out a breath. "Maybe I'll go back and see what they have to offer."

"Atta girl," I reply.

"So, you start both jobs Monday? How will that work?"

To be honest, the situation couldn't be more perfect. Blaze said he doesn't need help with the things he's got going on until later in the day most times. He also mentioned that he would probably need some help on the weekends, but those are my days off from my internship. Thankfully, there will be no overlapping.

"Well," I begin, "I'll be at Tailgate from nine to one every weekday. Then, I'll go home, change, and grab some food before heading to Blaze's at three. I'm actually looking forward to seeing the daily life of a professional football player. This might be helpful when it comes to my internship. Not many people get to see what I'm about to."

"I hope you mean his dick," she says, causing me to roll my eyes. One thing about Dia; she never lets a heavy conversation stay heavy. And I love her for that.

"Sorry to tell you, but that particular piece of *man meat* is off limits."

"Yeah, yeah," she chides, "I read a book like this once. If he asks you to be his fake wife, just promise me you'll say yes."

I bark out a laugh. "In the unlikely event that Blaze Beckham fake proposes to me, I promise I will accept."

"Thank you," she says. "Okay, I have to go get ready for my shift at the club. I love you."

"Love you most," I say before hanging up. As always, I feel better after talking to my best friend. Now I can spend the rest of the night focusing on preparations for the week. I'm starting two brand new jobs and I'm excited to learn everything I can about the world of sports journalism. This internship could open so many doors for me if I pour my entire heart and soul into the next four months. I can't let anything distract me from showing Jacob that I'm the right choice for the permanent position. Even if that distraction is six-two with deep brown eyes and a perfect body.

EIGHT
MADS

SO FAR, day one of my internship is going well. It's only four hours a day, so it has flown by. There was a lot of paperwork to fill out when I first got here this morning. That was surprising, considering all the stuff I had already filled out with Jacob. But I met my new supervisor Janine, and I think we'll get along really well. I love how this company employs as many women as it does men. It's intimidating in the world of sports journalism to be a woman who is completely outnumbered. But Tailgate Media seems to be very progressive, and that makes me even more hopeful that I have a future with this company.

It's nearing the end of my day, so I tie up the loose ends on the emails I was assigned to send out to various agents and start to tidy up my cubicle. Tomorrow, I think I will bring some things to personalize my desk. Everybody else here has so much personality in their little nooks. Maybe I'll bring some of my signed memorabilia because who doesn't love showing off just a little bit?

"Great work today, Madison," Janine says, leaning a hip on my desk. "You really got a jumpstart on those emails. Hopefully, we get some hits on them so you guys can start learning the ropes when it comes to interviewing professional athletes."

"We'll get to do that?" I'll ask, shocked.

She smirks. "Well, one of you is going to be doing it and getting paid the big bucks for it sooner or later, so we may as well just throw you in the deep end, right? It can be nerve-racking speaking to such big personalities. Pro athletes can be a little intimidating sometimes."

I decided this morning that I was not going to tell anybody that I was also working for the city's biggest football star. I didn't want anybody to think I got this job because of Blaze. I didn't even know him when I earned my position here. Plus, I know people can turn on the charm when they want something, and I would guess meeting Blaze Beckham would gain me some fake friends really fast. I want no distractions while I'm here, so I'm going to keep to myself as much as I can.

"Thank you again so much for all of these opportunities. I can't wait to learn everything you know," I say, as I shove my water bottle into my tote bag.

She stands to her full height, smoothing out her jacket. "It was so nice meeting you and I will see you bright and early tomorrow."

"See ya!" I reply, waving at her before heading toward the exit. I have to run home and change into more comfortable clothes before heading to Blaze's house. I can't help but feel butterflies in my stomach. He seemed very nice, but Janine was right. Pro athletes are intimidating.

An hour later, I pull into Blaze's driveway and park my car. As I get out, I chuckle at my piece of crap sitting next to a brand-new lifted truck and a blacked-out Mercedes. I wonder if both of these cars are his. It's not like he doesn't make enough money to have ten garages full.

Walking to the entrance, I ring the doorbell and wait for him to answer. A few seconds later, the door swings open.

Like I didn't just see him a couple days ago, all the breath leaves my lungs. He really is the most beautiful human being I have ever seen, with those intense brown eyes that almost put me in a trance every time I look at them too long.

I school my expression and give him a shy smile and wave. "Nice to see you again, Mr. Beckham." *Why is it so hard for me to act like a normal functioning adult when I'm near him?*

"Mr. Beckham is my dad, Baby Doll. Call me Blaze."

I laugh nervously as I walk through the door, which he closes behind us. I feel like I didn't get a good chance to look around last time I was here, so I take a moment to scan my surroundings. Through the door, is a large entryway with a big table. There are fresh flowers sitting in the center of it, which surprises me because this is supposed to be a bachelor pad. Shouldn't it smell like old socks and have crusty clothes laying in random places? We walk through an archway and enter a very large, very modern kitchen. The appliances are all stainless steel, and I can literally see my reflection in them. The marble countertops shine brightly, and there is a large bowl of fruit in the center of an island. I turn to the right, where I see a huge white dining table with lush, padded chairs. It could easily seat ten people. A dark-haired man is sitting there, chugging from a reusable water bottle. He's completely shirtless and extremely sweaty. *Okay. This is the best job I have ever had.* When he lowers the bottle and raises his head, I recognize him immediately. Trying to remain cool, I keep my trap shut and let him introduce himself. He stands, sauntering toward me with a cocky smirk. "Hey there, beautiful," he says. "I'm Dalton Davis. Star running back for the Boston Blizzard."

Before I can reply, Blaze sidles up next to him. "Nope. Off-limits," he says to his friend.

"Dibs," Dalton says quietly out of the corner of his mouth like I'm not standing three feet away.

"Dude. No," Blaze argues, grabbing him by the shoulders

and turning him back toward the table. "Sit. Or *leave*."

Dalton huffs out a breath, but relents, sitting back at the table.

Blaze looks at me before shaking his head. "Sorry about him. He has no filter."

I look over at the table, where Dalton is sitting with his palm propping up his head. If I didn't know any better, I would say that he's pouting. He looks like a little kid whose dad just took his lollipop and threw it in the garbage.

"We were just working out downstairs," Blaze says. "We're going to go back down and finish up. I've cleared a space for you in my office and set up a computer. I didn't know if you would want to use it or not, and it's no big deal if you don't, but I thought you might want to have a space of your own here. There's also a new iPad in there for you because those are easy to throw in a bag when we're on the go. Office is the second door on the left down the hallway. When I'm all done working out, I'll come up and show you around more."

I can't say I'm not shocked that he put so much effort into having me here. He must really need extra help if he's gone this far to make my job easier.

Dalton makes a big production of hugging me, much to Blaze's chagrin, before they return to the basement. I walk down the hall, finding the office. Much like the rest of the house, everything in here is neat and tidy. A large desk sits in one corner. There isn't much on it besides a laptop and a few pieces of paper. In the other corner, there's an identical desk. Sitting on it is a brand-new Mac desktop and an unopened iPad. I walk over and take a seat in the fluffy white chair. The desk is set up with all kinds of office supplies in pastel colors. Honestly, if I had designed my own area, I wouldn't have done it any differently. It's like he already knows me.

Pushing that thought from my head, I open the iPad box and start the setup process. When I get done with everything

I can do in here, there's still no sign of Blaze, so I grab my phone and start scrolling Instagram. I should probably feel uncomfortable and out of place, but strangely I don't. I don't know if it's the house, or the extremely attractive man who lives in it that's making me feel this way.

BLAZE

"Bro, *that's* your new assistant?" Dalton whisper-shouts as we descend the stairs to my home gym. "You should see the girl they sent me last month after I strained my quad. She looked like the female version of Adam Sandler."

I eye him skeptically as we reach the basement. "I swear to God if you even *think* about hitting on Mads, I'll tell everyone you have syphilis. And they'll believe me because you're, well, *you*."

He feigns offense, placing a hand over his heart. "Damn, Becks. You wound me. I'll have you know, I always wrap it up. I may be a man-whore, but I'm a *smart* man-whore."

I roll my eyes, pretending he isn't right about Mads being an absolute knockout. The last thing I need is him going after her, fucking her, breaking her heart, and making things weird as fuck for me. "You act like you didn't have that actress from *Wavelength* begging to suck you off two nights ago. She's a dime, man."

"Okay, first of all, she didn't beg. She asked once, very politely. Who am I to tell America's sweetheart no? I don't need that kind of karma. Spot me," he says, laying down on the bench.

I step up to the bar, hovering my hands under it in case he needs it while he lowers the weights to his chest. He bangs out ten reps, then sets the bar back on the rack before sitting up.

"I'm just messing with you, Becks. If you want her for yourself, just say that."

This guy is a fucking handful.

I sigh, frustrated. "I don't *want her for myself*. I just want her to be able to come in here and do her job. That's it." I'm a goddamn liar, but that's definitely not something I'm willing to admit out loud. Truthfully, she's hot as hell and I'd love to bury my face between her legs. But Mac is right. I definitely need to keep things professional. Mads is the key to me keeping my shit together so I can focus on what's important. Football.

"Ten-four, buddy. Whatever you want to tell yourself," he says, wiping down the bench before throwing the towel into the hamper. I grab my water bottle and finish its contents. My arms feel heavy and kind of sore, which means I probably overdid it a little bit today. But the regular season starts in two weeks, so I've been trying to take everything up a notch. Players like Dalton and I don't get many reps on the field during preseason games. It gives our second and third string players an opportunity to see the field while also protecting the starters from injury before the season kicks off. I'll admit, it's hard to watch from the sidelines, but I understand the importance of keeping us healthy.

We head back upstairs, anticipation running through me the closer I get to Mads. *What's that about?*

Entering the kitchen, she's nowhere to be seen, so I say my goodbyes to Dalton and head down the hall toward my, or *our*, office. I pause at the doorway, watching her scroll through her phone. She hasn't noticed me yet, so I take in the delicate slope of her perfect nose. The rosy color of her soft cheeks. A strand of shiny chocolate brown hair escapes from behind her ear, falling into her eyes. I fist my hands at my sides, stopping myself from walking over to tuck it back. *What the fuck is happening to me?*

Realizing I need to get my shit under control and keep this

relationship strictly business, I clear my throat softly and enter the room. She startles slightly before her face relaxes into a smile when she realizes it's me.

"Sorry," she says, standing from the fluffy desk chair I had the designer pick out for her. "I didn't want to interrupt you, so I figured I'd sit here and scroll Instagram until you gave me some work to do. The thirst traps are on point today."

"The fuck is a thirst trap?" I reply, confused.

"Blaze, you're a professional athlete with *those*," she says, gesturing toward my midsection. "Please tell me you use them to your advantage on social media."

I smirk before lifting my shirt just enough for my abs to come into view. "You mean these?" I reply, unable to wipe the cocky grin from my face. I flex the muscles subtly, just because. Her green eyes lock on to my exposed skin and I swear I hear her breath hitch. Maybe it's wishful thinking, but she almost looks turned on.

That makes two of us, Baby Doll.

She shakes her head as if she's trying to clear it of whatever thoughts she's having before she brings her eyes to mine. "You have a lot of fans that are women. Why not use your body to gain followers?"

I raise a brow, not really sure where she's going with this. Thankfully, she continues.

"I'm not saying to strip naked and show them all your... goods," she says, cheeks heating. *God, she's cute.* "But you'd be surprised at the views you could get from a few shirtless Reels of yourself working out. Toss a shirt from your clothing line on at the end of it and you just brought all that attention to your brand." She shrugs like that isn't the most brilliant idea ever.

I walk over, putting an arm around her shoulder and leading her out of the room. "Well, first let me give you a tour of the place. Then you can teach me everything you know about the art of the thirst trap."

NINE
MADS

"SARAH! I'M HOME!" I shout from the entryway. Setting my keys into the decorative bowl on the sofa table, I look around to see an empty room. Sara is usually home by the time I get home from Blaze's, but the place is completely silent.

I sit on the couch and grab the remote, flipping to ESPN. It isn't long before Blaze's face fills the screen while they talk about how he's already on track for a record-breaking year. We're officially into the regular season and he's on top of the ranks for targets, receptions, and receiving yards. He's also second in yards-after-catch. He's even more impressive than I expected. And seeing it in person? He's amazing.

Things have been great off the field, as well. We had his first pop-up shop the second week I was working for him and it went great. Watching Blaze interact with his fans is the most wholesome thing I've ever seen. He truly loves and appreciates them for getting him where he is. Most superstars get annoyed with people coming up to them on the streets, begging for autographs and photos. Not Blaze. He feeds off their energy and is always happy to take the time with them.

One thing that *does* drive me crazy is the way that some of his female fans feel like they have free rein to put their hands on him. The first time I watched one of them sneak her hand under the hem of his shirt while posing for a photo with him, I was shocked. And when I asked him about it, he gave me a non-committal shrug like it was just something that wasn't a big deal.

Why it bothers me so much is not something I'd like to unpack right now…or ever.

I mean, I get it. He's hot as sin and I'd love to run my hands over his body. But doing it without asking is just desperate.

Why am I still thinking about this?

I snap out of my thoughts when Sarah busts through the door, giggling maniacally. She stops in front of the couch but continues bouncing on the balls of her feet like a toddler whose cool aunt just sugared them up before sending them home. I stare blankly, waiting for some type of explanation as to why she's acting like a lunatic, but she just continues hopping in front of me.

"Okay, I give," I say, raising a brow. "What's going on?"

"Pow!" She yells, punching her left fist out between us. It takes me a moment to focus because she's jumping higher now, but once my eyes lock on, I gasp.

'Oh my God!" I yell, standing and grabbing her hand to get a better look at the ring on her finger. "You're getting married?"

"I'm getting married!" she screeches. We probably look ridiculous, but I don't care. Sarah spent four years in a toxic relationship before she found the strength to leave. When she met Tyler a few months later, she was so afraid he'd hurt her that she pushed him away. But he hung in there and waited until she was ready to let him prove that he wasn't like her ex. They've been inseparable ever since and I couldn't be happier for them.

"Tell me *everything*," I say, dragging her to sit next to me on the couch. She turns to face me, grabbing a throw pillow and hugging it in her lap. She's glowing. If I didn't love her and Tyler so much, I'd be jealous. It's always been our dream to have the big, lavish ceremony where we would promise forever to guys who were totally obsessed with us. We used to wear our mom's dresses and heels, picking wildflowers and weeds from my back yard to make bouquets for our pretend weddings. I still have that dream. And I know I'll find it one day, but my main focus right now is landing the job at Tailgate, so I'm more than happy to let Sarah have her time to shine with me by her side.

"Well," she begins, "he had this whole elaborate plan where he would take me to watch the sunset at the docks. He even had fairy lights and blankets set up ahead of time. But you know me. I was hangry and refused to go anywhere without eating first. So, he rushed to Mister Burgers, but the drive thru line was like, ten miles long. I could tell he was really frustrated, so I asked him what was wrong. And he just blurted it out. Said he couldn't wait another minute to ask me to be his wife." She smiles, eyes glassy with unshed tears.

I slap a hand over my mouth as I try to stop the water-works, but I fail miserably. "That is the cutest thing ever! You guys should totally have Mister Burgers cater your wedding." I'm half joking, but I can't say I would be mad if they actually did. Their fries are, by far, the best I've ever had.

She purses her lips like she's actually considering it, which makes me laugh. "I'm so happy. I feel like I don't deserve Ty. He's so good to me and I just want to be a good wife to him."

I grab her hands, pulling her eyes to mine. "Sarah, you are *perfect* for him. I've seen the way he looks at you like you're the only person in his world. You deserve all of this." I allow my tears to flow freely, happy for my cousin.

"Thank you," she whispers softly.

"Let's celebrate!" I yell obnoxiously, running to the kitchen to grab the bottle of champagne we bought earlier this week for our Sunday morning mimosas. I rip off the foil and unwind the wire before resting the bottle on my bent knee and working the cork loose. It pops somewhere into the corner and I quickly fill two glasses before walking back to the couch.

"So," she says, grabbing the champagne and taking a sip, "Ty did suggest that I move into his place so we can start saving up for the wedding. I know you and I planned on re-signing the lease here together when it goes up at the end of the month, so I didn't want to make any decisions about that without talking to you first. Maybe we can talk the landlord into a month-to-month lease, and I'll keep paying my half here until your internship is over. I don't want—"

"Sarah," I interrupt, "I can find a smaller place. Between my internship and my job with Blaze, I'm sure I can find a one-bedroom close to the city. You need to be with Tyler right now."

She looks up at me, reluctance clouding her eyes. "Are you sure?"

"Of course," I reply. Honestly, I have no idea how I'll find a place to live in the next two weeks, but I won't be the reason she doesn't enjoy these first days with her new fiancée. Even if it's a tiny apartment, I'll be fine for now. At least until I land this permanent job and the paycheck that comes with it.

She tips back her glass, finishing the bubbly while kicking her feet wildly. "I'm getting married, bitches!" she screams with her hands cupping the sides of her mouth.

I run to refill her glass, pushing my living situation to the side for now. That's a problem for tomorrow.

Tonight, we get wasted.

TEN
BLAZE

"HMMM," Mads says, tapping her finger against her plump bottom lip while she thinks. "I think you need to change the trunks. Those ones are too long." After she took some time to get comfortable with her job here, we finally decided it was time to dive in on trying to boost my social media presence.

My eyes go wide. "If I go any shorter, this'll go from thirst trap to porno faster than you can say 'wardrobe malfunction'. I don't even *own* shorter ones."

She pauses, a sly smile taking over her face. "Off," she says, pointing to my lower half. When I don't react fast enough, she snaps her fingers, catching my attention. "Lose the trunks."

She can't be serious.

"Mads, I'm not wear—"

"Do you want me to teach you how to make a thirst trap video or not?" she whines, stomping her foot on the pool deck. She reminds me of a little baby bear when she's frustrated. Cute as fuck but could still probably rip you apart.

I raise a brow at her, hoping she'll relent, but she doesn't. So, I turn my back to her before whipping my shorts to my ankles like she asked.

"Jesus fuck, Blaze!" she yelps, causing me to turn around abruptly, cupping my hands over my junk. She's got both hands glued to her face, eyes completely hidden. "What are you doing?!"

"What you told me to do!" I reply. "You literally said *lose the trunks.*"

"I didn't know you weren't wearing underwear!" She's squealing at this point. I can't help the laugh that bursts out of me.

"Why the fuck would I be wearing underwear with swim trunks?" I ask. "Do you wear underwear when you swim?"

She shakes her head, hands still covering her eyes. "No."

"Then why would you assume I did?" I say, pulling my shorts back up while she continues to hide.

She huffs a frustrated breath. "I don't know. I wasn't thinking."

I walk over to her, still chuckling as I try to pry her fingers from where they're smooshing her nose and eyes. "You can look now. The big bad monster is back in his cage."

She opens her fingers just enough to peek at me. When she sees that I'm clothed, she drops her hands and smacks me on the arm.

"Ow!" I say, even though she definitely didn't hurt me. "What was that for?"

"Next time you decide to free Willy, give me a heads up first." She's totally flustered, and I can't say I hate the blush that's now covering her face and neck. I know she didn't see my dick, but she had to have gotten an eyeful of my ass before she realized what was going on.

"My bad, Baby Doll." I'm not exactly apologizing because, *sorry, not sorry.* But I do her a favor by not teasing her about her reaction. "Seriously, let's finish this."

"Fine," she relents. "Forget the shorter shorts. Just get in the pool. I'll start rolling and you can pull yourself out from the side. Dry off and then put on the shirt."

I follow her directions, jumping into the deep end before popping up and swimming to the side wall. When she gives me the signal that she's recording, I flatten my hands on the pavement and lift myself from the water. Once I'm out, I make a show of bending over for my towel before slowly rubbing the soft fabric over my chest and abs. When I'm dry enough, I grab the shirt from my newest fall release and pull it on. I finish by looking into the camera and giving a charming wink.

"That should do it," she says. I don't miss the breathy tone to her voice.

I busy myself by drying my legs as she works her magic, choosing the right song and filters for the video. She's in the zone as she concentrates on turning the fifteen-second recording into something that'll hopefully gain exposure for my brand. Mac will probably shit a brick when he sees it, but I don't give a fuck. Mads is a female football fan and I trust her. She knows what sells a lot better than any of us do.

"Done!" she says, excitedly. "Want to see it?"

I walk over to her, looking over her shoulder as she presses play on her phone. It doesn't even look like the same video we just shot. It begins with me lifting out of the pool. Everything is in slow motion, rivulets of water languidly making their way from my chest to the waistband of my shorts. Snooze by SZA plays in the background and I have to admit, the video is hot as fuck. As I smooth the shirt over my chest, the camera zooms in on my logo before cutting back up to my face, just in time to catch my wink before the screen fades to black.

"Wow," I say, amazed at how she took a random video of me in my back yard and turned it into *that*. "You're fucking amazing."

Her big eyes sparkle as she smiles brightly.

Fuck, she's pretty.

"Thanks," she replies. She looks proud. And she should

be. I know my way around social media, but certainly not enough to be able to edit videos like she just did. I can tell bringing her on as my assistant is already turning out to be a good choice. Could be life changing if she agrees to continue sharing her knowledge and skills with me. It's not exactly part of her job description to do this, so I'm lucky she didn't tell me to go fuck a cactus when I asked her to help me post a thirst trap video.

"Holy shit!" she says, startling me.

"What?"

"It's been up for three minutes and look how many views and likes it already has!" She turns the phone to show me the video, which she posted to my TikTok account. I watch as hearts continue to rise up the screen, the comments section moving so fast I can't even read it. I've posted here before, but I've definitely never seen this kind of engagement.

She turns, looking over her shoulder at me with a smile. "I told you this would work. I'd bet my paycheck that your web sales will increase considerably within the next day or two."

"You'd better be careful, Baby Doll," I chide. "Keep this up and I'll tell Jacob he can't have you for that permanent position." I'm half joking, but I'm also not ruling out doubling whatever Tailgate Media offers her to work for me full-time.

She sighs. "That would mean they'd have to choose me for it first."

"Why do you think they won't?" I can't imagine, with her talent and hard-working attitude, that she wouldn't be a shoe in.

"It's—It's not a big deal," she says, softly. "Don't worry about it."

I don't want to pry, but I also can't stand the thought of her thinking negatively of herself. She's been an incredible help to me since she's been here, and I know she's pouring every ounce of herself into her internship. "Tell me," I say, gently so she doesn't think I'm pushing.

"There's one other girl, but between you and me, I don't think she's ready to be a sports journalist yet. We work primarily with hockey and football teams, and she doesn't quite have an understanding of either game yet. And she always seems so nervous and timid. She'll get there, but she needs time."

I stay quiet while she pauses, thinking.

"The other two interns are guys. They're constantly cutting me off when I speak. They'll try to mansplain things to me like I couldn't do the job in my sleep. When I try to speak louder, they look at me like I'm some wannabe 'cool girl' who doesn't really deserve to be there. I knew it would be like this, but it's just exhausting."

I make a mental note to be more aware of the female journalists I work with. I'd never purposely treat them differently, but I also don't want to be unaware of it. It's not the 1950's. Women are out here killing it in a male dominated world, and they can't even do their jobs without getting shit for it. I might only be one athlete, but I'll do what I can to make a change in this industry. Even if it's a small one.

"Listen to me, Mads," I say, using my thumb and forefinger to lift her chin so her eyes meet mine. A jolt of electricity shoots down my arm when my skin meets hers, but I ignore it. "You're smart, badass, and you deserve that job more than any of those fuck heads. If Jacob Shane can't see that, he's dumber than he looks."

She swipes at a tear that escaped her eye before a confident mask covers her face. "You're right." Her bright smile warms my entire body.

"That's my girl," I say. "Now, let's go eat. All that hard work checking out my naked ass must have you famished."

ELEVEN
BLAZE

"TELL me again why *we're* doing this?" Dalton says, heaving a large box into the bed of my truck. "Last I checked, you have enough money to pay someone else to do shit like this. Look!" he says, shoving his hand in my face. "That's a blister starting. I can't have blisters. Next to this face, my hands are my biggest moneymakers."

I sigh. I swear, being his best friend means living in a constant state of annoyance. "I already told you. Mads offered to do it, but her car is too small, and I don't want her lifting these boxes. They're heavy."

We had our first pop-up shop for my clothing line during the preseason and it went so great that we scheduled another one for this weekend. We play on Thursday night this week, so we have the weekend off. We rented out an empty boutique in the city for Sunday, where we'll set everything up for people to come shop in person. I'll be there signing autographs and spending time with the fans. It'll be my last chance to really interact with them before the harder part of our schedule picks up.

Mads has been such a huge help. I thought she'd need some time to learn the ropes and find her way around my busy life, but she fits in like she belongs here. Not only has she been getting my social media engagement up, but her knowledge of football has come in pretty clutch for me, too. Last week, she asked to watch game tape with me and pointed out that I was taking a false step, making me slower off the line. I worked on it with my wide receivers coach and I'm seeing a huge increase in my speed.

She had the idea to bring some of my inventory to the house so she could make sure we have everything we need before we have it delivered to the boutique on Friday. Last time, open space to set up was more limited than we expected, making it difficult to sort through everything before hanging it on the racks. I don't have a team that's dedicated specifically to these tasks because the pop-up shop was only supposed to be a one-time thing. This line was initially only supposed to be offered on my website, which it will go back to after this weekend.

To be honest, it's been amazing working so closely with Mads on this. We always have fun together and we make a hell of a team. Right now, she's clearing space in our office to empty these boxes and take inventory of the items we'll be selling this weekend. I tricked Dalton into helping me bring everything from my brand headquarters, which is really just the one-room office space my website is run out of, to my house by telling him I was going for ice cream while I was out. Since he's basically a toddler in the body of a grown man, he came along, no questions asked.

Pulling up the driveway, I shift into park so we can transfer everything into the office. We make quick work of unloading the truck while Mads goes through each box, one by one. By the time we're done and Dalton makes his exit, she's on the office floor, up to her eyeballs in hoodies, hats, and water bottles.

Stepping over the piles, I make my way over to her, but I notice immediately that something is off. She's been less talkative, which I chalked up to her being busy, but now that I'm looking at her, I can see something is weighing on her.

"Hey," I say softly, taking a seat next to her on the floor. "Everything okay?"

She sighs. "Yeah. Just some stuff going on."

I have an overwhelming urge to fix whatever it is. I know I won't be able to focus on anything when my favorite girl is upset. Maybe it's her internship. I have done plenty of interviews with Tailgate Media. I know Jacob Shane well enough to talk to him if someone is giving Mads a hard time there.

I wait for her to elaborate. I don't want her to feel pressured into telling me, but I also need to know so I can help her. Thankfully, she takes my silence as an opening.

"My cousin, Sarah is getting married," she says, flatly.

"You don't like the guy?" I'm a little confused because I could've sworn she's spoken highly of him in the past.

She looks up at me, her pretty green eyes full of sadness. "No, I love Tyler. They're so perfect for each other."

Now I'm even more confused.

Thankfully, she continues. "The lease on our apartment is up next week and she's going to move in with him. I can't afford the rent on my own and the place is too big for me anyway. I've been looking for a one-bedroom for the last week, but everything I've found is way out of my budget. If I don't come up with something quick, I'm going to be homeless. I'll have to quit my internship and leave Boston." As she finishes the last sentence, her voice breaks and tears start streaming down her cheeks.

"Come here," I say, grabbing the hem of her shirt and pulling her into a hug. She buries her face into my neck, her body shaking as she quietly sobs. I inhale the scent of her shampoo and if I never smelled another thing as long as I lived, I'd be perfectly fine with that. "Shhhh. It's going to be okay."

She looks up at me and I decide right there that there's no

way I'm letting her leave. I push a strand of tear-soaked hair behind her ear, which earns me a small, watery smile. I might be crazy for what I'm about to do, but if losing Madison Rodgers before I even get a chance to really know her is the only other option, I don't care.

"Move in with me."

She stills in my arms for a moment, her teary eyes becoming wider as my offer hangs in the air between us. I don't want to beg her to say yes, but I will if it comes down to it. All I know is that I can't let her go. Aside from making my life easier, I've found myself counting down the minutes until she walks in my door every day. I know working for me is just a means to an end for her and that her internship is why she came to Boston in the first place, but I wish I could be the reason she stays.

"Blaze, if I can't afford a two-bedroom apartment in Eastie, what makes you think I could even cover a fraction of what it costs to live here?" she says, her feisty little attitude still showing itself from underneath her sadness.

I chuckle, pulling her back into me because for some reason, holding her close just feels right. "Maybe you forgot the part where I'm a wildly successful and extremely wealthy pro athlete," I say, trying to lighten the mood. She huffs a breath and I continue before she can argue. "It's just me here in this big house. Pretty sure there's like, five vacant bedrooms. Plus, it'll take some stress off me knowing someone is here taking care of the place while I'm on the road." That last part is a complete lie. I have a housekeeper that comes to check on the place if I'm away for more than a night, but I need to make it look like Mads is doing me a favor. Otherwise, I know she won't feel comfortable staying here rent-free. I decide to hammer that point home, just in case. "It would really help me out, having you here."

Please, Baby Doll, just say yes.

She sniffles, taking several moments to think. I know she

wants to agree, but I also know she isn't used to being given anything in her life. I want nothing more than to change that because she deserves it, but this has to be her own decision.

Finally, she pulls herself back and I immediately feel the loss of her warm body against mine. I grab a random hoodie from beside me and start folding it to stop my hands from reaching back out to her.

"Okay," she says, softly. Straightening her back, she eyes me before she continues. "But you have to let me help around the house." I open my mouth to argue, but she cuts me off. "I'm not kidding, Blaze. If I'm staying here, I want to earn my keep. In addition to my duties as your assistant, you're also going to let me take care of some household chores. I'll clean up, cook any meals that your chef doesn't prepare for you, and I get to do the grocery shopping."

I try to play it cool even though the knots in my stomach have me ready to laugh and puke at the same time. "Alright, roomie. You've got yourself a deal," I say with a smile. She rolls her eyes playfully, grabbing the hoodie from my hands and shaking it out.

"You're folding it wrong," she winks.

Fuuuuuuck. What did I just get myself into?

TWELVE
MADS

TODAY IS the final pop-up shop for Blaze's clothing line. As fun as it's been to work with him on preparing these events, I have to say I can't wait until it's over. Between my internship, packing my stuff at Sarah's so I can move into Blaze's, and making sure today goes off without a hitch, I am exhausted.

I never thought fighting for a position with one of the country's top media conglomerates would be the easy part of my days, but the work I'm doing at Tailgate has been a breeze. After a week or so of emailing agents and publicists, I was able to secure some pretty decent interviews. It only took me a few of them to find my groove and shake off the nervousness of being around famous athletes. I suppose being in such close proximity to the biggest one on the planet when I'm not in the office helps with that.

I still haven't mentioned to Jacob, Janine, or any of the other interns that I am also working for Blaze. I checked and it doesn't go against any company policies, so I didn't feel like I needed to divulge that information. The last thing I want is for Jacob to offer me the permanent position because he thinks I have an in with the Blizzard. I want the job more than anything, but I want it because I earned it, fair and square.

"Where do you want these?" Sarah asks, face hidden behind a giant box. I guilted her into helping me today by reminding her that she's about to be blissfully indisposed with her new fiancée after the weekend and I'll likely only see her when they come up for air.

Dramatic? Yeah, probably. But it beats interviewing and hiring a staff for just one day. Blaze's line will be going back to his website after today.

"Right over here," I reply, leading her to the racks along the side of the boutique. I thought it would be best to have items along the wall that fans will line up at while they wait to meet Blaze. As a kid, I probably came close to sending my parents into bankruptcy with all the candy and trinkets I roped them into buying while we stood in the checkout line at the grocery store. This is that, but with adults.

As we start unboxing the deep blue crewnecks that sport Blaze's logo, the bell above the back door rings. I look over to find the man of the hour looking absolutely delicious in a pair of gray sweatpants and a black hoodie.

"You're drooling," Sarah whispers, crouching down beside me to untangle our mess of hangers. "I don't blame you. Those pants are as good as lingerie in my eyes. Like, seriously, Tyler *who*?" she jokes.

I frantically wipe my mouth and realize that she was fucking with me. She laughs in response. Kicking my foot out to hopefully shut her the fuck up, I wave to Blaze. He sees me immediately and I take off in his direction because there's no way I'm letting her speak openly in his presence. Sarah would throw me under the bus in a heartbeat for my reaction to the way he looks today.

"Looking good as always, Baby Doll," he says with a grin. I give him a quick hug, trying not to press my body to his, even though every instinct in my body tells me I should. As close as we've gotten and as good as it feels to have his attention, I'm still trying my best to stay professional.

"Thanks," I reply, looking around the space proudly. "We've been setting up since yesterday and I think it turned out better than last time. I wanted to—" I stop speaking when I realize he's staring at my shirt. He swallows thickly, his Adam's apple bobbing in his throat.

"You're wearing my hoodie."

Shit. Is he mad?

I look down nervously. I was so hot from running around earlier that I forgot to grab something warm to put over my tank top. My car wasn't big enough to transport the rest of the boxes this morning, so I drove Blaze's truck and he brought one of his other cars after he was done at the gym.

"Uh, yeah. Sorry," I apologize, going to grab for the hem to take it off. "I found it in your back seat. It was cold out—"

He reaches out and grabs my hand, lingering for a moment before letting me go. "No. Wear it. Please."

I smile, looking up to see something in his eyes that I've never noticed before. If I didn't know any better, I'd call it heat. But that can't be right. I'm his assistant. That's it. Blaze Beckham can have anyone he wants. I'd be stupid to think he sees me in that way at all, no matter how good it would feel if he did.

BLAZE

I'm doing everything I can to connect with my fans today. As grateful as I am that they chose to spend their Sunday standing in a long ass line just to see me, I can't stop staring at Mads. The sight of her in my clothes is making me fucking crazy. She looks like...*mine.* It's covering all the good stuff and it's about three sizes too big, but she couldn't be any sexier to me. I imagine gripping onto the hem, bunching it above her ass as I pound into her from behind.

I snap out of my fantasy just in time for the next fan to reach my table. She's tall and has legs for days in her tight jeans and formfitting jersey. My number twenty-two stretches across her large tits, which are straining against the fabric. Normally, this is exactly the type of woman I get hard for. But as I look at her bright-white smile and clearly bleached blonde hair, I feel absolutely nothing going on below the belt. *Weird.*

Thankfully, the woman can't read my thoughts because she smiles sweetly. She's a fan, so of course I extend my hand to shake hers.

"Oh my God, Blaze! I'm your *biggest fan,*" she says with a high-pitched giggle. "Can I get a picture with you?"

I nod politely, standing from my chair and rounding the table. She hands her phone to her friend before stepping up next to me. I try to keep some distance between us as I bring my hand behind her, hovering it, but never touching her.

"Smile!" the friend with the camera says. Just then, the woman next to me turns, wrapping her arms around me waist tightly and leaning her head into my chest. I used to love this shit, but as soon as I hear the shutter of the camera, I back away like she's on fire. As she goes to pull a piece of paper from her pocket, no doubt her phone number, I see a small black blur running through the back door.

Fuck.

I don't even give the fan a chance to hand me the paper before I thank her for coming and send her on her way. I wouldn't call her anyway. Apparently, I'm only interested in one woman. And it looks like I have some damage control to do.

"I just need a quick break," I tell the people standing patiently in line. "Everything in the shop is fifty percent off until I get back." I leave the cashiers with the customers and run out the back door after Mads.

I step into the slightly chilly fall air and look around until I spot her sitting on a stack of old milk crates. She sees me immediately and quickly schools her expression. But I already saw it. I step up beside her, casually leaning against the wall next to her perch.

"You ran out of there faster than Dalton after he breaks a tackle. Have you ever considered a career in the NFL?" I joke, thankfully getting a small smile in return as she looks up.

"Doesn't that bother you?" she begins. "The women just putting their hands all over you like that?"

I can't stop the cocky smirk from blooming across my face. "You jealous, Baby Doll?"

"No," she scoffs. "And stop calling me that. It feels...*dirty* now. You probably call all the girls that."

Yep. She's definitely jealous. *Why do I love it?*

"No can do, Baby Doll. The nickname stays. And I promise you I've never used it on anyone but you." Her eyes lock with mine and the corner of her mouth turns up slightly, but my girl fights her smile. It's fine. If she wants me to work for it, I will.

I reach out my hands and she grabs onto them, a jolt of electricity zapping me where we're joined. If she feels it, she doesn't react as I pull her up to stand. As much as I want to push her up against the cold brick of the building and taste every part of her, I know I can't. I've all but abandoned Mac's warning about sleeping with my employees because I'm starting to feel like that's inevitable with Mads, but I've got to play the long game here. I'm lucky she agreed to come live with me. If I move too fast and break her professional boundaries, I'll lose her.

"Let's get back in there before I lose more money," I chuckle, interlocking our fingers and pulling her back into the shop. "You can sit next to me and beat the female fans off with a stick."

THIRTEEN
MADS

I'M EXCITED as I make my very first grocery run since moving in with Blaze. I'm honestly still surprised he agreed to let me do this, but I made him think it was a dealbreaker for me. It wasn't, really. I just wanted to feel like I was earning my keep. I hate the feeling of having things given to me that I haven't worked for.

The past week should've been a weird transition for me, considering it's not my house, but I can tell he wants me to feel like it is. My first night there, he abandoned his strict diet so we could order pizza from my favorite spot. It's the same one Sarah and I used to get delivered to her house as teens because their delivery drivers were always cute. We'd make her mom answer the door while we peeked from behind the curtains, giggling like idiots.

When I told Blaze that story, he immediately called and placed our order, refusing to let me get a glimpse at the driver when he arrived. Instead, he held the pie box out of my reach until I told him he was hotter than any delivery boy I'd ever seen. We ate a large pizza by ourselves that night and watched playoff baseball until we fell asleep on the couch like we've been friends our whole lives.

I have to admit that I'm already starting to feel things for him. Confusing things. I know he's my boss and I need to keep things somewhat professional, but being around him is so easy. He makes me laugh and I just feel so comfortable when he's around. I find myself rushing out the doors to get home at the end of my internship every day, just to see what he's doing.

As I push the shopping cart through the produce section of the grocery store, I take another quick look at Blaze's shopping list. I'm down to the last few items and I'm noticing a theme.

I'm also noticing a difference in penmanship. Everything I've crossed off so far has been typical of the meals I've seen him eat. Things like chicken breast, potatoes, carrots, and applesauce pouches because Blaze is really just an overgrown child. Everything tracks. But as I look at the two items in my hands, I'm thinking I've been bamboozled. I'm holding an eggplant and one single banana.

I decide to give Blaze a call because I smell a prank, but staying true to age-old grocery store traditions, there's no service. I guess I'd better grab everything that's been scribbled down, just in case.

There are two things on the list I still have to grab. I make my way over to the cucumbers, grabbing the largest one I can find because, if I'm going to embarrass myself while checking out, I'm going big.

The last item makes it all clear as to who we can blame for this whole debacle. Magnum condoms.

Fucking *Dalton*. In the weeks that I've known him, we've spent a good amount of time together. He's always at Blaze's house, digging through the refrigerator or flipping through the latest releases in the theatre room. We banter back and forth like we've known each other forever. He even saddled me with an annoying nickname, which solidified that we will officially be friends forever. His words, not mine.

I return all my penis-shaped foods to their original locations and run to the pharmacy on the opposite side of the store. He wants to have a prank war? Game. Fucking. On.

"Excuse me," I say to the young pharmacy assistant standing at the cash register. "Can you help me with something?"

When I pull in the driveway, I see Blaze's truck in the open garage. I should call him out to help me carry these bags in because there are a lot of them, but my inner strong, independent woman reminds me that I don't need a man. I can do this myself. And I can do it in one trip.

Opening the trunk of my car, I start carefully hanging the bags from my arm. After the first five bags, it's heavy, but I can make it from the car to the door. At least, I think I can.

After I've loaded both arms to the max, I grab a bag in each hand and realize I miscounted and there's one lonely bag remaining. I'm not coming back out for just one thing, so I do what any normal human being would do. Just as I bend my head into the trunk, I hear the front door open and the sound of footsteps coming closer.

"What are you doing?"

I pull myself from the trunk, shopping bag hanging between my teeth, to see Blaze staring at me like he's never seen a person grocery shop before.

"Jesus, Mads. Let me help—"

"Mmm-mm. Hmmphfhpp!" I yell, turning my head from his grabby hands.

He raises an eyebrow. "Seriously? Were you listening to Olivia Rodrigo on the way home again?"

I growl as I trudge past him, wearing about a hundred pounds worth of grocery bags. As I approach the door, I know I'm fucked. My hands and mouth are full, and the door is closed. I hear Blaze slowly walking up behind me and in a moment of quick thinking, I bring my foot up and try to turn the doorknob. I immediately regret my decision when the loop of my shoelace wraps around the knob.

Frantically, I start yanking my foot with intentions of unhooking myself, but it only makes the knot tighter.

"Madison, how the fuck?" Blaze scolds, coming up behind me. Knowing there's no way in hell I'm letting go of these bags, he reaches for my foot at the same time I yank. At that exact moment, my shoelace breaks, and I go falling backward, all my weight crashing into Blaze. We both topple to the ground, my back to his front, as the bags I was carrying like a pack mule scatter everywhere.

One minute, Blaze is laughing hysterically while I wiggle around, trying to get off of him. The next, we're both completely silent as I feel something very large and hard pressing against my back.

Oh. My. God. He's hard.

He clears his throat, breaking the spell I'm under. I scramble to my feet, doing everything I can to avoid eye contact. My willpower is obviously shit, because when I look at him, he's staring back with a cocky grin.

"You done?" He says, a low chuckle coming from his lips as he blatantly adjusts himself.

I side-eye him, not sure if I should laugh, cry, or throw up before bending down and loading myself up with bags. This time, he doesn't give me a choice as he grabs everything he can.

"Come on, Baby Doll. Let's get this stuff inside," he says before heading toward the door. I walk behind him, a smile blooming on my face that he thankfully doesn't see. Even if it was only because I was wiggling my ass on him, his dick was hard. *For me.*

I make my way into the kitchen and lift my bags onto the counter. Blaze has busied himself with the items he carried in, putting them away.

"Isn't that my job?" I tease, grabbing at the container of spring mix in his hand. He brings it above his head, out of my reach, making me jump to get a hand on it. Obviously, I'm unsuccessful since he has almost a foot on me.

"No way," he replies. "When you first got here, I was completely against having you run around town doing my errands. You're lucky I agreed to you doing the grocery shopping at all."

I roll my eyes playfully. "Blaze, you work your ass off like, twelve hours a day. I intern for twenty hours a week, then I come back here where you don't let me lift a finger other than cleaning up after myself. I'm living here for free. Let me pull my weight."

"Fine," he relents. "But I can help with this."

Just then, I hear a high-pitched squeal coming from the back yard, followed by a deep laugh. I look out the window to see Dalton chasing a petite brunette before grabbing her around the waist and throwing her into the pool. He jumps in behind her, both of them laughing when they breach the surface. I notice three other women sitting on loungers and my heart sinks a little. They're all beautiful, dressed in skimpy dresses with perfect makeup and hair. They fit in with the guys a lot better than I do in my oversized t-shirt and dingy Converse.

I school my expression, throwing on the best fake smile I can manage. "I didn't know you had company. Seriously, go back to your guests. I've got this."

"Those aren't my guests," he says. "Dalton invited them here. I wasn't even out there to begin with. I'm having the pool closed for the winter this weekend, so he insisted on going in one last time before the cold weather comes."

"Oh." I try not to act shocked that he isn't into these

gorgeous women as I return to the bags I'm emptying. When I pull out the tube I had completely forgotten about, a sly smile blooms across my face as the imaginary light bulb blinks above my head. "Come on," I say, grabbing Blaze by the hand and leading him out the back door.

"Mads, what are you—"

"Hey, Dalton!" I say in a saccharine sweet tone. He smiles, lifting himself from the pool before running over and scooping me up in a hug.

"Hey, Shorty! Have fun at the grocery store?" he asks.

I should throat punch him right now, but I stick to my plan, pulling the brown paper bag out from behind my back and handing it to him with a smile.

He takes it from me, still clueless as he reaches into the bag and pulls out the white tube with a very legit looking prescription sticker on it.

"What's this?"

"Remember? Earlier you asked me to run by the pharmacy for your prescription? I was a little confused when they gave it to me, but it's got your name on it, so I guess it's yours," I say, innocently. "I really hope it helps clear up your rash." I flutter my lashes as realization hits him. His cocky smile fades immediately as he goes completely pale.

"Ew," one of girls says from behind us. They all stand, grabbing their things without a word and heading out the gate.

"Wait! I don't have a—" he shouts, but they're already gone. He stands still for a few seconds before turning to me, the tips of his ears bright red. "Mads, what the *fuck?!*"

Picking an invisible piece of lint from my shirt, I give him my most innocent look. "You are *so cute*. Did you really think you could send me on a wild goose chase through the grocery store looking for dick-shaped foods and not suffer any consequences? This is what we call a *learning moment*, Dalton. You might be good at pranks, but I'll always be better. So, think very carefully before you fuck with me again."

He's gaping like a fish as I wink at him and head back toward the house, passing Blaze who is doubled over, holding his stomach while he laughs hysterically.

Some lessons are meant to be learned the hard way.

FOURTEEN
BLAZE

"AGAIN!" Coach Mills yells, spiking his clipboard to the ground angrily.

We line up as Tanner takes his place under center to go over the pass play for the fiftieth time.

"Beckham, how about not running directly into double coverage this time!" Coach screams. I do my best to block out the negativity so I can focus on the play. As soon as I hear Tanner's cadence followed by the ball being snapped, I take off. My heart pounds in my ears as I run my route. He fires a beauty of a pass at me, and just as I open my hands to make the grab, I'm blindsided by a hard hit from my right. The ball hits my hand, but I'm unable to secure it before it bounces off, landing into the stretched fingers of our cornerback, Jalen Morgan.

Fuck.

Whistles blow as the defense celebrates, but all I can do is lay back on the grass wondering why the hell I am having such an off day. I close my eyes, but I can feel the loss of light and heat from the sun as a tall body looms over me.

"You seem a little distracted today, Becks." I peel one eye open to see Tanner standing above me, helmet shoved up to his forehead. He chews on his mouthguard while he waits for a reply.

Sitting up, I wince because whoever the fuck hit me must've temporarily forgot we're on the same team. I'm going to need to sit in an ice bath immediately. Pulling my helmet from my head, I toss it aside as I look up at him. "I guess I am."

He outstretches his hand, helping me to my feet before we head toward the sidelines. I guess coach felt like he's seen enough because he's nowhere to be found. His clipboard still lays on the ground where he spiked it. Tanner sits on the bench, motioning for me to join him. We sit there in silence for a moment, watching the rest of the team gather their belongings before heading down the tunnel toward the locker room. He's a great captain and teammate, so I feel like talking this out with him might be a good thing.

"My assistant just moved in with me."

He looks at me, confusion taking over his features. "And that's distracting you?"

"Yes. No. Yes," I reply, running my hands down my face. "I don't know."

Tanner chuckles quietly next to me. "So, you're attracted to her."

Of course, I'm attracted to her. I have been since the moment she busted through my door hoping to find Maury Povich. But having her in my space all day, every day? That shit is a lot harder than I thought it would be. And the fact that I don't know if she's feeling it too is making me crazy. I know she was jealous at the boutique. I felt it radiating from her when I followed her into the alley. And I thought I saw it briefly pass over her expression again when she saw those women out by my pool the day she went grocery shopping.

"She's gorgeous and fucking amazing," I begin. "I know I shouldn't be thinking about her as anything more than an employee, but it's hard when she walks around in next to nothing all the time. Or passing by the bathroom, knowing she's naked in the shower with only a door separating us. I have a constant case of blue balls and there's nothing I can do about it. I know she's focused on trying to land a job at Tailgate Media, so maybe she's oblivious to the way I look at her. Or maybe she's purposely ignoring it because she doesn't want me like that. Whatever it is, its fucking with me."

He blows out a breath, thinking before he replies. "That sounds complicated, man. The way I see it, you have two choices. You can either let her know how you feel and hope she doesn't react by packing her shit,"

I look up at him, hoping whatever's behind door number two is better than confessing to Mads that I'm dying to put my hands and mouth all over her. "Or?" I say, hopefully.

"Or you keep things strictly business and move on. This city is full of women who would gladly take a ride on the Beckham Express. Why don't you go fuck someone else and get your head back on straight?"

Abso-fucking-lutely not.

Even if I wanted to go find a random girl to hook up with, my dick isn't on board. The only way I can even get hard anymore is to thoughts of Mads. Then I stroke myself, imagining her hand instead of my own, each orgasm more powerful than the last as I come, grunting her name every time. It's all so fucking complicated. I should've never asked her to move in with me. But when she said she'd have to leave Boston, I panicked and said the first thing that popped into my head.

I got myself into this mess and I'm the only one who can get myself out.

"Yeah, maybe you're right." I lie. "Maybe I will go find someone else to get my mind off it."

"Alright," Tanner replies, although I have a feeling he knows I'm full of shit. Standing, he reaches out and I give him a quick five before we make our way toward the tunnel.

When we hit the locker room, I immediately cringe as the thought of an ice bath makes my ballbag shrivel up on instinct.

Deciding I've put myself though enough torture already, I hang a right, heading for the hot tubs. I take off my gear, lowering myself into the bubbling water. I feel my stress melt away as my muscles begin to loosen. All my problems will definitely be waiting for me when I'm done here, but maybe some time alone will give me a little clarity on how to unfuck my life.

FIFTEEN
MADS

"OKAY, EVERYBODY," Janine says, walking up to the cluster of desks that belong to Tailgate's interns. "Those social media posts are due tomorrow, so I hope you have everything you need."

Before I can show her what I've got so far, Chance stands and struts in her direction. "I scored some exclusive photos of the Blizzard's long snapper. I'm going to use them on Instagram with some of his stats from college." He looks back at me with a smug grin, like this company would even approve such a ridiculous post on their social media. Dawson Mays has been in the league for ten years and is all but irrelevant. I want to scream that nobody cares about him, but I don't want to sound like a bitch. Nor do I want to stoop to his level of putting other interns down in an attempt to look better.

Janine nods before moving along to Jason, who is working on an article for the Tailgate Media app. Another pointless topic that people will scroll right by. But, again, I'm taking the high road. She scans his screen before turning back to us. "Okay. Great start, everyone." She turns back to Chance and Jason. "I'd like you to meet some people in our web development department. Follow me." She turns to Ella and me. I will bring you two down there tomorrow. For now, you can keep working on your posts." She pats my shoulder before walking away, Tweedle Dee and Tweedle Douche hot on her heels.

"Wow. That looks amazing," a meek voice says from over my shoulder. I was so engrossed in creating a TikTok video with footage from my interview with the Beavers' goalie, Alexei Bertrand, that I didn't even notice Ella behind me. "What? Sorry," I smile sheepishly. "Guess I spaced out."

She laughs, twisting the bottom of her flower-print dress in her fingers. "I was just admiring your video. You seem so calm in your interviews. How do you do that? I get so nervous every time, I have to do breathing exercises to stop from throwing up."

This poor girl. I'd never say it out loud, but there's no way she'll hack it in this industry. She's really great at creating content, but she's so awkward and unnatural when she has to speak to anyone. To be honest, I have absolutely no idea how she got here. Chance and Jason seem to have found their footing and I think we are all kind of neck and neck in the race to become a permanent employee here at Tailgate Media, even though it seems like they're doing everything they can to make me look like I don't have what it takes. Thankfully, I think Janine has seen through their attempts to interrupt or speak over me. But I'm not like them. We're all here to learn and I want to use some of my strengths to help Ella build on her weaknesses.

I motion for her to pull up a chair, which she does. I turn slightly to face her so I can look into her eyes when I talk to her. "Ella, I know from the outside, all of these athletes look like gods. But you have to remember that they're regular people, just like us. They put their pants on one leg at a time. You don't have to be afraid to speak to them."

She sighs, defeat marring her features. "I can't. I try so hard to put myself on their level, but I get so intimidated. It's easier to say they are real people than it is to actually think of them in some of the same day-to-day circumstances as us."

I have an overwhelming need to help her get over this fear, so I do something that I told myself I definitely wouldn't. "I want to show you something, but you have to promise me that you will not tell anyone."

Her eyes go wide before she nods her head rapidly, like I hold all the answers to her problems. "I promise."

I look around to make sure we're alone before grabbing my phone and typing in my password. I go to the photos app and click the videos album. I scroll for a second, pulling one up and turning the device so she can see. She squints, trying to make sense of what she's looking at, gasping when she realizes who is on the screen.

Blaze stands in the backyard wearing a pair of basketball shorts and a t-shirt with the sleeves cut off. He uses his forearm to wipe the sweat from his brows before bending over. A string of obscenities leaves his mouth as he yanks on the pull cord of the lawn mower. It locks, causing the string to break and come off in his hand. "Piece of fucking shit lawn-mower!" he yells, throwing the broken piece into the swim-ming pool. He kicks the machine before flipping it off. The person behind the camera, *which is me, but she doesn't need to know that*, starts laughing, drawing Blaze's attention. "Oh, you think that's funny, Baby Doll?" he says as he starts running toward the camera, his angered expression now turned mischievous and playful. The phone drops to the ground before a loud shriek fills the air and the screen goes black.

I remember that day vividly. Blaze refused to let me help him mow the lawn, leaving me to sit on the steps while he struggled with the mower. He finally lost his shit when it broke, but only for a moment until he saw me filming him while laughing at his expense. He immediately switched back to his flirty self, chasing me through the yard, tackling me to the ground, and tickling me until I couldn't breathe.

"See. Even Blaze Beckham struggles with his lawn mower sometimes. They're just like us."

She smiles at me, relief covering her face. I'm thankful that she doesn't ask where I got the video from because I think I would have trouble lying to her. She stands from her chair, putting her shoulders back as if I've given her a little more confidence to get through her day. "Thanks for that, Mads."

"You're welcome." I wink at her; truly glad I could help.

She starts to walk away but turns back to me. "Whoever you got that video from is the luckiest girl on the planet. I wish Blaze Beckham looked at me like that."

Dumbfounded, I swallow thickly before nodding my head as she turns back toward her desk. I release a slow breath, putting my head in my hands because as fun as it's been living with Blaze, my promise to remain professional is getting harder and harder to keep. But with everything to lose, I have to find a way to stop myself from falling for a man I can never have.

"Blaze! I'm home!" I say from the entryway, kicking off my pumps and placing them in the closet. I know he's home because, first, I literally create his daily schedule, and second, his truck was in the garage when I walked through. The house is dark and quiet. Eerie, almost.

"Blaze?" I say again, heading toward the kitchen. When I don't get a reply, panic sets in. I walk back toward the closet, opening the door to see the shoes he had on this morning. His duffel bag is on the bench next to his keys. He's definitely here.

"Blaze?" I yell, more frantically this time. I quickly go from room to room, throwing on the lights to find them empty. I head upstairs, pushing his bedroom door open roughly, hoping to find him in there. But like all the others, this room is dark and vacant. Rushing back down toward the kitchen, I'm almost knocked on my ass when I run into a hard wall of muscle. Before I can fly backwards, a strong set of hands grips onto my forearms.

"What's wrong?" Blaze says, panic taking over his face at the sight of me. "Mads, are you alright?"

"I couldn't find you," I say on an exhale, leaning my head forward onto his bare chest in relief.

He wraps his arms around me, making me melt into him immediately. "I'm right here, baby," he whispers into my hair, so quietly I can barely make out the words.

Not Baby Doll. Just *baby*.

I'm sure that was just a mistake, but I allow myself to believe, just for a moment, that it wasn't. That I'm his and he's mine. But before I can get too comfortable in my fantasy, I pull away. He drops his arms at his sides, concern still etching his features.

"I came in and it was dark and quiet. I was worried," I say, trying to regulate my heartbeat. I still feel like it could burst in my chest.

"Worried about me?" he questions. His warm smile makes my heart slow to its normal rate instantly. "I was in the theatre room, about to start a movie. The walls are sound-proof, otherwise I would've heard you come in. I'm sorry I scared you."

"You didn't scare me, I just—" I stop myself because honestly, yes, he did. I was terrified thinking something might've happened to him. I realize the chances of that are so slim, but I guess my anxiety went into overdrive when he wasn't where I thought I'd find him.

Blaze must understand because he nods once and leaves it at that. *Thank fuck.* "If you aren't busy, want to come down and watch a movie? Your choice."

"I'd love that," I say with a smile. "Just let me change and I'll meet you down there."

I go to my room, still feeling a little confused by my reaction downstairs. Shoving it aside, maybe to unpack later, I focus on changing into my pajamas. I throw my hair into a messy bun, remove my makeup, and slide my feet into my fluffy pink slippers. Grabbing my comfy plush blanket, I head downstairs to find Blaze in the kitchen, shaking a bag of freshly popped popcorn. I take a second to appreciate his shirtless back, watching his muscles ripple as he moves. He's so hot, it should be illegal.

He turns, finding me in the doorway behind him and a cocky grin blooms across his face when he notices me staring. I roll my eyes because I know I'm busted. Thankfully, he doesn't say anything about the eyeful I just got.

"Ready, Baby Doll?" he says, winking as he holds up a large bowl of popcorn in one hand and two boxes of Sour Patch Kids in the other.

"Yeah," I say coyly, grabbing both boxes from him. "But you should definitely bring some candy for yourself." I turn toward the stairs as he chases me, yelling about what a *little shit* I am before we both plop down on the custom couch that may as well be considered a giant bed. It's soft and covered in pillows. It could easily fit fifteen adults comfortably, but we huddle together with our snacks as I flip through our movie choices.

I decide not to go full-chick flick on him and choose the new Jennifer Lawrence comedy. I make it about twenty minutes before my eyelids get heavy and I lose the battle, falling asleep peacefully next to Blaze's warm body.

SIXTEEN
MADS

"FUCK. *Yes, Blaze. Right there. Don't stop,*" I moan as he angles *his hips upward, the head of his cock brushing my g-spot.*

"*You feel so fucking good, Baby Doll. So tight. This pussy was made for me.*"

I feel like I'm floating, my back arching from the bed, trying to get more—something. More everything. *He begins thrusting harder as I feel my walls start to flutter around him. He reaches between us, rubbing teasing circles on my clit with two fingers.* God, he knows my body so well.

"*That's it, Mads. Fucking come for me. Soak my cock,*" *he grits out as he continues his delicious assault on my body.*

I'm there. The orgasm that's been evading me for months feels like it's ready to tear through me. I could almost cry at the anticipation. I thought I was broken. That the only way I'd ever come again was if I was tied up and dominated. But maybe that's not the case, because feeling Blaze inside me, hearing him grunt as he gets closer to his release, that's giving me everything I need to get there.

"*Oh my god, I'm gonna come!*" *I cry out.* "*I'm—I'm…*"

I wake with a start, the ache between my legs very apparent as I try to piece together what just happened. It all begins to come back to me as the fog from my deep sleep dissipates. The movie, the candy, falling asleep next to Blaze. That *dream.*

I go to sit up, but I'm being held in place by a thick, muscular arm. Turning my head slightly, a feel a soft breath fan over my neck. Blaze is fast asleep behind me, holding me tightly to his hard, warm body. I steal yet another moment that doesn't belong to me as I push myself further into him. Still asleep, he tightens his arm around me and buries his nose into the back of my neck. I sigh, so content with the way he feels against me.

Just then, his hips give a slight rock and I feel something long and hard between my ass cheeks. My previously cozy state turns to immediate panic as I realize his morning wood is poking my backside. Knowing I need to get out of here to save myself a world of embarrassment, I slowly pull my body from his.

"Come back. Just five more minutes," he mumbles and I'm pretty sure he's still asleep as I roll my way off the couch, grabbing my blanket and slippers. He rolls onto his back and his breathing evens back out before I creep my way over to the door and head back upstairs. Once I'm sure I'm out scot-free and he's not following me, I take a moment to collect myself, resting my head on my crossed arms against the kitchen counter.

"Holy fuck," I say under my breath, still reeling from the events of the last twelve hours. I try to relax, taking some deep breaths. I finally manage to calm my racing heart before I open my eyes and stand straight.

"Sleep good?" a gravelly voice says from behind me, making me jump.

I quickly reach for the coffee maker, lifting the carafe to make myself look busy. "Uh, yeah. You?" I can feel the blood rushing to my ears while I wait for him to mention how I just shamelessly rubbed myself against him while he pretended to sleep.

"Like a baby, actually," he replies, sparing me the embarrassment of having to talk my way out of whatever the fuck got into me down there.

I make a noncommittal hum as I fill the decanter with water before pouring it into the top of the coffee maker. I'm feeling suffocated by this whole situation. I'm starting to feel things for Blaze that I definitely shouldn't be feeling. It doesn't help my delusions that he's always so flirty. I know that's his personality and that he's like that with everyone, but I'm starting to have trouble not blurring the lines in my own mind. I swear, sometimes it feels like he actually wants me.

I busy myself wiping down the already clean counters in an attempt to avoid looking at Blaze, but he catches me off guard as he cages me in with his arms on the edges of the counter before pushing his body against mine.

"Sorry," he murmurs into my ear. "Just need to grab a mug." Goosebumps cover the entirety of my body at his proximity. He reaches to the cupboard above me, removing a coffee cup and backing up. I miss the heat of his body instantly.

"Any plans for the weekend?" he says, pouring his coffee. He looks up, his piercing brown eyes full of curiosity.

"I—" I pause, trying to come up with something. I can't think clearly around him anymore.

"We're playing Dallas at home on Sunday, and I thought maybe you'd want to sit in the WAGs suite with the wives and girlfriends. You met a couple of them at the pop-up and I figured—"

"I have to go home," I say at a much higher volume than necessary. "To Chicago."

His eyes fill with something…maybe *panic*, as I continue. "My parents actually asked me to come for a visit. And since you don't have anything going on other than the game, I thought this weekend would be a good time."

"Oh," his face relaxes. "Yeah. Cool. Maybe you can catch the next one."

I feel bad leaving if he wanted me at his game, but I need some time to think. I need to get my head back on straight before I derail my entire life. This morning could've been really bad if he knew what I was dreaming about or if he had been awake for my moment of weakness after I woke up in his arms. I'm not sure he realizes how what he thinks is flirty, harmless behavior is fucking with my mind. Maybe a trip home and putting some distance between Blaze and I will help me remember why I'm here so I can focus on creating a solid future for myself.

At the very least, it'll give me a moment to breathe.

SEVENTEEN
MADS

"MY BABY'S HOME!" Dia yells like a maniac as I fling open my car door and make a beeline for her. I jump into her arms, wrapping my legs around her as we fall to the ground in my parents' driveway.

God, I missed her.

We laugh hysterically before I finally unwrap myself from her. We sit up, both crying like I've just returned from war and not just a couple months in Boston. We dust ourselves off, holding hands as we walk toward the front porch, where my parents wait with their arms around one another.

"Car give you any trouble?" My dad grunts.

I roll my eyes, smiling because that's his way of saying he missed me. He's a man of few words, but when he cares, he shows it.

"Nope," I lie. "The old girl did me proud." I leave out the part where I had to stop at a drive-through to have the oil topped off halfway here. I also don't mention the two new blinking lights adorning my dash. "Hi, Dad." I grin before sinking into his embrace. It's warm and familiar, just like I remembered.

"Give me my girl, Tom," my mother says, playfully

shoving him away before wrapping me in her tiny arms. She pulls back slightly, taking me in. "You're even more beautiful than you were when you left."

I laugh because she's totally lying. At least I don't *feel* more beautiful. I feel confused. I've lost so much sleep this past week trying to figure out how to stop myself from falling further for Blaze than I already have. I know I'm reading more into his flirty behavior than I should, and I just wish I could find a way to not be so affected by him every time he touches me. I'd definitely say our relationship has gone beyond the boss/employee dynamic. I'm sure he sees me as a friend and that's why he acts so playful when we're together. Friends hug. Friends fall asleep watching movies. It's totally normal.

So, why won't my mind stop trying to make it into more?

I don't even realize that my family has ushered me and my luggage inside until Dia's voice breaks me from my thoughts. "I can hear those wheels turning. What's going on?" she says from beside me on the couch.

"So much. *So. Fucking. Much,*" I tell her, peeking into the kitchen where my parents are preparing dinner. "But let's wait until we're alone."

Her eyes go wide. "Please tell me you fucked your boss."

I gasp, looking back into the kitchen to make sure my parents didn't catch that. "Jesus, Dia! No, I did not *fuck my boss.*" I whisper. "And if you don't shut your whore mouth right now, I'm not going to tell you anything."

"Okay, well *that* was uncalled for," she says, sinking back into the couch. "You can make it up to me by describing his dick, *in detail*. I don't care if you haven't seen it yet. You have the entirety of dinner to make something up or I'm telling Tom that you've been taking rides on Football Boy's bologna pony."

I raise a brow at her. "Fine. I may have seen the outline a time or two. But if you even breathe wrong before my parents are asleep, I'll leave you to imagine it in that little pea brain of yours. And I can promise you, the reality is even better than what your slutty mind will come up with."

That does the trick because she leans forward, grabbing her wine glass and taking a sip. "Deal."

"Girls!" my mom yells from the kitchen. "Dinner's ready!"

I look at my best friend, using two fingers to point at my eyes before turning them on her. "*I'm watching you,*" I mouth as she smiles sweetly like she isn't considering throwing my ass under the bus.

It's good to be home.

Two hours later, my mom wakes my dad from his pre-bedtime nap in the living room recliner. "Come on, Big Man. Let's go to bed so the girls can gossip without us hearing." He grunts as she lifts him to his feet. They give us both our customary forehead kisses before heading upstairs. As soon as their door clicks shut, Dia whips her head in my direction.

"About that dick," she says, wiggling her eyebrows.

I huff a breath, knowing she won't shut up until I give her something to keep her warm at night. "Okay, *fine,*" I relent. "It's huge."

She squints before taking a large sip of what has to be her fourth glass of wine. "How big are we talking?"

I may as well lean into this because I really am going to need her advice if I want to get my mind straight before I head back to Boston. "You remember that pool party in ninth grade where Julian Carmichael's older brother showed up wasted and his wang fell out of the leg hole of his trunks?"

She sits up straight, riveted. "Yeah."

"Bigger than that."

She gasps. "Stop it right now. Bigger than 'Big Dick Nick Carmichael'?"

I take my time swallowing my wine. "Yup."

She sits back, speechless before slamming the remaining wine in her glass. "Thank you very much for that Girl Dinner. I will be eating well this evening."

Now that she's satisfied, I turn the conversation into a more serious direction. "I need some advice."

Just like that, she flips a switch and listens intently when I tell her everything. From Sarah getting engaged to Blaze asking me to move in with him. I've only given her bits and pieces during our phone calls, so she listens carefully, collecting each puzzle piece I give her. Hopefully the picture they make is clearer for her than it is for me.

"So," she begins, "I know you don't think he could possibly see you in a romantic way, but I honestly believe that you're wrong. You're fucking gorgeous, have an incredible body, and you're the kindest person I know. Any guy, no matter how rich or famous, would be lucky to have you, Mads. So, let's just jot that down, 'kay? I don't want to hear any more talk about him being able to do better. Got me?"

"Yeah," I sigh. "But even so. Let's just say we're living in a universe where Blaze Beckham wants me. He's my boss. I don't make enough at my internship to pay my student loans, car insurance, phone bill, and all the other things I'm responsible for every month. I can't screw up this job with Blaze or there's no way I'd be able to continue going for the job with Tailgate. He pays me well and now he's letting me live in his home, rent-free. Blurring the lines between us could ruin everything I've worked for my whole life." I look at her with pleading eyes. "What do I do?"

Dia takes a moment to think before she replies. "I hear you. And I know how important your career is to you. You're just going to have to keep your eye on the prize. There's no reason you can't have a friendship with Blaze. You're both adults who can be playful with each other and not have it turn into anything more. That's a pretty normal thing for two roommates. Go back there, act totally natural, and remember the boundaries you've set for yourself. Keep your head on straight and your heart out of it. It's only a little while longer, then you can move out and stand on your own two feet. Things will be a lot clearer for you then."

I smile at her, feeling a million pounds lighter knowing she's always on my side. How she turned out to be so wise and loyal when her parents were anything but is something I'll never understand. I hope that one day, a man will come along and give Dia all the love she should've had her whole life.

"I don't deserve you," I tell her for the hundredth time since I've known her.

"I know," she laughs, bringing me into a hug. "Now that we've figured that out, tell me more about this monster cock."

EIGHTEEN
BLAZE

THERE'S nothing worse as a professional athlete than an off game. I had five dropped passes today. I haven't had five dropped passes in my entire professional career before this game. How we pulled out a win against the Dallas Sharp-shooters is a mystery to me when I played the way I did. Yet, for some reason, Tanner kept giving me chances. He targeted me consistently all game long, even when I had given him every reason to back off and start utilizing the other receivers. The game winning touchdown I scored on a quick slant is the only reason I'm not currently in a fetal position under my locker bench, crying like a little bitch.

But still, it sucks balls. Big ones. And it has me in a funk.

As I pull up the driveway, I notice that Mads' car is in the driveway. The thing is a literal shit box. I wish she'd let me buy her a new one, but I know better than to even offer. She would never accept such an extravagant gift. The fact that she drove it from Boston to Chicago and back to visit her parents this weekend has me ready to *accidentally* spill some sugar directly into her gas tank, so she has no choice but to never drive it again.

Seriously, though. *"Hey, Siri. Add sugar to my shopping list."*

I pull past her car and into the attached garage, breathing a sigh of relief that she's home safe and under the same roof as me again. I have increasingly become a simp for this girl the more time we've spent together. She's everything I want. If I brought Mads to meet my parents, I bet you my mom would have my Nana's engagement ring shoved into my pocket to propose with before I even got both of Mads' feet into her house.

I allow myself to daydream about what it would be like to slide a rock on her hand and ask her to let me love her forever. To fuck her and hold her every morning. To watch her waddle through the house, belly swollen with my baby.

Fuck. That escalated quickly.

I shake my head, the impossible future fading away as quickly as it came as I make my way into the door connecting the garage to the laundry room. Setting my bag down, I hear the telltale sign of Mads being on a cleaning rampage. Justin Bieber's Confident blares through the kitchen speaker as I round the corner, the most domestic scene coming into view and making me forget about my dropped passes and shitty game.

Mads stands in front of the refrigerator, digging through the crisper. The cupboard containing the trash compactor is wide open. Her back is to me, which I'm thankful for because there's nowhere else in this world I want to be other than right here watching my crazy, adorable assistant go ham on the rotten vegetables in my fridge. Grabbing a head of lettuce, she yells "Kobe!" before sending it in a perfect arc toward the trash can. I laugh quietly as she raises her arms and shakes her cute little ass along to the beat when she drains the shot.

She returns to the drawer for more bad vegetables, twerking as she leans forward. My dick twitches in my pants as her t-shirt rides up, revealing her extremely short might-as-well-be-underwear spandex shorts. What I wouldn't give to reach out and take a handful of her tight ass.

I watch her for several more minutes and the music fades into her favorite song. You're Perfect, I Hate It by Mickey Valen fills the room and she slows her movements to match the tempo. Holy fuck, I'm hard. Like, fully hard watching her dance, the lyrics resonating in my head as my feet move me toward her. The faster part of the song hits just as I reach out for her elbow, spinning her around and into my arms. Once the initial shock wears off, a big smile covers her face as she wraps her arms around my neck and moves with me.

Laughing, I grab her hand and spin her. This gives me an opportunity to pull her back in, this time wrapping my arm around her waist even tighter than before. We're both laughing into the next song, neither of us stopping or loosening our grips on one another as her upbeat playlist goes on. We dance and laugh for the next few minutes, all the stress and worry about the game leaving me like a popsicle melting in the sunlight of her smile.

Just as the music fades into a much slower, sexier song, I slow my movements and drop my head to the crook of her neck, inhaling the scent of her sweet skin. Her mouth drops open slightly as I slide my hands down, resting my pinky fingers dangerously close to the top of her ass. The hitch in her breath doesn't go unnoticed. Instead of pulling back like I should, I stand straight before lowering my forehead to hers, my smile not faltering as I breathe her in before speaking.

"I missed you," I say quietly, closing my eyes.

She's still grinning as she pulls away just enough to look at me, rolling her eyes. "I'm sure you had plenty of fun without me this weekend. I had to stop looking at the backyard security footage after I got a notification and saw Dalton with a leggy blonde bent over the table. Can't unsee that," she says, giggling.

I have a sudden urge to clear the air with her. "I didn't have any women here, I swear," I rush out, the defensive tone I'm using painfully evident. She raises a suspicious eyebrow at me, pulling her arms from around my neck and leaning on the counter behind her. I miss her warmth as soon as she backs away.

"Blaze, this is your house. Whether I'm here or not, you're allowed to bang whoever you want. Wherever you want. Just let me know and I'll make myself scarce." She shrugs, avoiding eye contact. But other than that, her reply sounds so unbothered and nonchalant. Why does that make me so upset? What was I expecting? Her to pee on my leg to mark me for all other women? Kinky, but that's not Mads. She doesn't want me like that. But I still don't want her worrying that I'd ever bring someone back here while she was home. *Or at all.*

"I wouldn't, Mads." I reach out, lifting her chin with my finger as our eyes connect. "I respect you. This is *our home.*" The phrase comes out so easily and I realize that I never want there to be a day where I wake up and she's not standing at the coffee maker in an oversized Blizzard t-shirt and messy bun, eyebrows furrowed because she hasn't been caffeinated yet. I want her to be comfortable enough to stay here with me. Forever.

I continue holding her chin lightly as my body slowly leans in, my eyes locking on her mouth just as she wets her lips. I hesitate, waiting for her silent consent before I make the leap and kiss her. But apparently, I take too long because she snaps back to reality, stumbling away from me and turning back to the refrigerator.

"I'm thinking turkey burgers for dinner tonight. Is that okay?" she says on a shaky breath.

"Mads," I say softly. When she doesn't reply, I close some of the space between us. "Madison." I speak louder this time. "Look at me."

She whips herself around, glossy eyes and a fake smile plastered on her face. "Don't say it, Blaze. It was a moment.

We can keep things professional going forward. I really need this job."

I nod my head before lifting the corner of mouth slightly in agreement, although I can do nothing to mask the look of disappointment in my eyes. And when I walk away, I try to figure out how I'm going to continue living with her like this when all I want is make her mine.

NINETEEN
MADS

"MORNING, BABY DOLL," Blaze says, entering the kitchen. I turn to find him in his usual bedtime attire of low-riding sweatpants and nothing else. *Fuck you very much, Blaze, for unknowingly preying on my weaknesses.* How I haven't spontaneously orgasmed during our morning briefings yet is honestly a mystery to me.

It's been a few days since our almost kiss in the kitchen. Blaze is back to his normal, flirty self, while I've spent my nights laying awake trying to sort out the things I'm feeling.

God, I wanted to feel his lips on mine. More than anything. But the voice in my head kept warning me that I need to stop myself from crossing that line with him, even though that line is getting blurrier every day I'm here.

I'm learning things about Blaze that make it so hard not to imagine what it would be like if I actually gave in to what I want. Still, the fact remains that I need this job. So, I'll have to settle for the scraps. The little moments we share, that while masked as friendship, I can't help but pretend are more.

"Good morning," I reply, turning back toward the bowl in front of me. I grab the whisk and mix the batter, careful not to make a mess. I feel him step up behind me and while it should make me tense up, it does the exact opposite. All my muscles relax when his scent wafts over my shoulder.

"Mmmmm," he says. "Pancakes. Wish I could—"

I cut off his sentence by grabbing the box of mix and holding it up in front of his face. I catch his expression out of the corner of my eye and give him a satisfied grin as he reads.

"Pumpkin Power Cakes?" he says, excitedly. "These are my favorite! How did you know?" I can't decipher the look in his eyes, but if I had to guess, people don't really pay attention to the small details with Blaze. The thought makes me sad because he's one of the most giving people I've ever met, and he deserves to be cared for like this.

"I saw an interview from when you were entering the draft. They asked you a bunch of stupid questions, one being what your favorite non-football part of fall was. You said it was all the pumpkin flavored foods and drinks. I figured it would be a good alternative to your morning protein shake. It's just one small cheat," I say, peeking around him before lowering my voice to an exaggerated whisper. "I won't tell anyone."

He raises a brow. "Madison Rodgers, did you Google me? Did you spend hours falling down the Blaze Beckham rabbit hole, watching every interview I've ever done?"

I scoff. "You wish. I just wanted to know what I got myself into here."

"Yeah, right," he teases. "I bet you dug deep into the archives. You spend some quiet time with those underwear ads, Baby Doll?"

I freeze for a moment before I feel his fingers dig into my sides, tickling me. "No! Blaze!" I wheeze. "Stop! I'm ticklish!"

I wiggle, trying desperately to escape his grip, but he's too strong. Turning to face him, I shove at his chest, unable to budge him even an inch. Instead, he drops his head into the crook of my neck, tickling my sensitive skin with his nose. I squeal in response as he laughs, his warm breath puffing below my ear.

When he digs his fingers further into my sides, I reach behind myself, dipping my fingers into the bowl of mixed pancake batter. I swipe a thick line of it from his ear to his mouth, halting his assault on me. His jaw drops in disbelief.

"Oh, you're in trouble now," Blaze says, mischief dripping from his tone. As he reaches into the bowl, gripping the handle of the whisk, I take off. I make it to the other side of the island, laughing hysterically as I try to think of my next move. I've essentially trapped myself, the only exit to the room behind him. Deciding there's only one option, I juke left, faking him out for a split second before running around the right side of the island. But I'm no match for him and he catches me from behind, one muscular arm wrapping tightly around my waist.

I scream loudly as I feel the whisk drag from my cheek down to my neck, leaving a trail of sticky batter in its wake. I somehow manage to drag us both back over to the counter, returning my hand to the bowl and throwing a clump of goo over my shoulder, making a direct hit to his face and hair. I turn to see my handiwork and start laughing even harder when I see that he's completely covered in batter. He huffs an angry breath, but I know he's not really mad.

In an attempt to lessen his retaliation, I bite my lip innocently. "Oops, sorry," I say.

"You're sorry?" he replies, jutting out his bottom lip in a fake pout. "I bet you're *sooooo sowwy*." He's trying to imitate my girly voice, which just makes me laugh harder.

"That's it."

That's the last thing I hear before he runs up on me, tossing me over his shoulder like I weigh nothing. I giggle uncontrollably, beating my small fists against his back which earns me a firm smack to my ass. It takes everything I have not to moan at the contact, but I don't have long to think about it as I hear him twist the handle to the shower.

"Blaze! No!" I scream in a panic, knowing exactly what he's about to do. Even though I'm kicking my legs with all my might, his grip remains tight as he laughs.

"What kind of roommate would I be if I didn't clean up my messes?" he coos before stepping into the shower, both of us fully clothed. My screams bounce of the walls as my tank top and shorts soak, sticking to my skin.

He finally loosens his iron grip, sliding my body down his to stand in front of him. My nipples harden on instinct and although I should be panicking and running out of here, I don't. I just stand there, comfortable in my own skin as he brushes my wet hair away from my face.

We stare at each other wordlessly as he fills his hand with shampoo. He rubs it between his hands before moving them to massage my scalp. It feels heavenly. I let loose a small moan when he flexes his fingers, tightening them around my wet locks. He uses his grip to tilt my head back into the stream of water, suds rinsing out and down the drain.

When he's satisfied, Blaze follows the shampoo with a generous amount of conditioner. I exhale contentedly as he finger combs my hair, massaging firmly as he does. Rinsing it out all over again, he smiles down at me before reaching behind me to turn off the water.

"Wait," I rush out, making him drop his arm back to his side. I grab the body wash, squeezing a generous amount into my hand before warming it between my palms. I reach out, rubbing the suds over his chest and abs. This is probably close to crossing a line, but I can't tear my hands from his body. He's as still as a statue, allowing me to explore him for a moment.

To avoid doing something I can't take back, I rinse his body before shampooing the clumps of pancake batter from his hair. I'm waiting for the awkwardness to set in, but it never does. Even though we're standing wordlessly, fully clothed, washing each other, I couldn't be more comfortable. My heart squeezes in my chest because for the first time since I left Chicago, I'm not missing home.

We stand under the warm water for a few minutes longer before Blaze shuts it off. Stepping out first, he grabs two towels from the warmer he must've turned on while I was over his shoulder and wraps one around my back. My shorts and tank top continue to drip onto the floor, and I notice that his sweats are heavy and hanging dangerously low on his hips.

Looking at him with a soft smile, I tighten the towel around me. "I'm going to go change out of these wet clothes, then I'll clean up the kitchen."

"No way," he argues. "I'll clean the kitchen. You make the pancakes."

"Deal." I wink at him before turning and leaving him alone.

As I reach my room and strip out of my wet clothes, I wait for feelings of regret to settle in my stomach, but all I feel are butterflies. It's confusing, but I don't overthink it. Blaze and I can be friends. We can enjoy some flirty moments without it turning romantic and ruining everything. People do it all the time, right?

I finish changing, then head down to the kitchen to see the damage we caused with our little food fight. Blaze is already hard at work, wiping the now dried batter from where it landed on the counters and floor.

I make quick work of mixing up a new bowl of batter before pouring it onto the griddle. Using the spatula, I flip the pancakes to see that they're perfectly cooked. Blaze sidles up beside me, two plates in hand as I fill them both for us. We work seamlessly, serving our breakfast and sitting at the island to eat.

It all just feels so normal. The whole morning has, actually.

In another world, I could see myself falling hard for Blaze. He's sexy, kind, smart, caring...everything I've hoped for in the man I chose to spend my life with.

For now, I'll enjoy every moment we share, even if I know that in the end, I'll never get to experience what it really feels like to be his.

TWENTY
BLAZE

I'M SITTING on the pool deck watching last week's game film on my tablet when Mads walks out the door and heads toward me. I do a quick double take because the dress she's wearing should be illegal in every state, but I school my expression before she notices. We've been spending a lot of time together lately. There's no way she doesn't see the way I react to her every time she's near me, but I'm still trying to honor her wishes that we don't cross any lines with our relationship.

But that shit she's wearing right now? It's testing my goddamn self-control.

Seriously, I thought her summer dresses were hot. But her fall wardrobe? *Fuuuuuuck me*. Everything she owns is low cut and tight around her tits. It isn't indecent at all, but that doesn't stop my cock from swelling at the sight of her. It's like she's moving in slow motion, the autumn leaves falling around her as she approaches me.

"Hey," she says, a hint of frustration in her voice. "Can I use your truck to drive over to Connor Paul's house? My car is making a clunking noise when it idles. Jacob just called and said they're having some type of equipment emergency and they're supposed to start recording a podcast episode in a half hour. The sponsor is already there, and we don't want to lose the advertising revenue."

I'm about to toss her my keys when I replay her words. "Connor Paul? The nineteen-year-old social media star who has *three* sex tapes?"

She rolls her eyes. "That's the one. He's good at railing his mom's friends on video, but it seems as though wiring podcast microphones isn't on his list of talents."

"I'll take you," I say, standing up abruptly. Because one thing I'm not letting her do is go to a house full of horny teenage boys wearing that dress.

Fuck. That. Shit.

She raises a defiant brow. "Blaze. You're busy and I can take care of myself."

"I'm the highest paid receiver in the league for a reason, Baby Doll," I say, walking past her. "That won't change if I miss an hour of watching tape."

I head through the house and thankfully, she follows me to my truck. I know she doesn't want to let Jacob down. We'll run by Connor's, she can abracadabra the equipment, and I can get her the fuck out of there.

Twenty minutes later, we pull up to a house almost as big as mine. This guy makes bank for being an absolute douchebag. Mads hops out of the truck and tosses her backpack over her shoulder, walking toward the front door like I'm not even here.

Hold on, woman. Give your puppy dog a minute to catch up.

Before she gets a chance to knock, the door swings open and Fuckboy McDickwad answers wearing nothing but a pair of swim trunks that look like they came from Baby Gap. Everything's fucking bulging out of everywhere.

"Well, hi there," he says, eyes absolutely glued to Mads' tits. "Jacob didn't say he was sending my birthday present early this year."

She smiles, but I know she's annoyed. Or maybe that's me. I'm annoyed. My wheels are already turning, coming up with a believable story to tell Jacob when he asks why I beat the shit out of his employee.

I slipped and punched his teeth down his throat. My bad.

He tells Mads what's going on with his equipment as we walk down a set of stairs that leads to a giant game room. In the corner sits a u-shaped table with four microphones and a large sound board. Two young guys sit there, and I recognize them from some of Tailgate Media's viral videos. A third man who looks to be closer to my age stands with his back to us. The sponsor, I would guess. His clothes look like they were bought at a store for adults.

When he turns around to face us, his eyes go wide.

"Madison?" he says, choking on a gasp.

"Oh my God, Brady! What are you doing here?" She walks over and gives him a hug. It looks awkward and I hate it.

"I own Hustle Supplements. We're the new sponsor of the podcast, so I'm here to talk about my products. I didn't know you were in Boston." His arms linger around her waist.

Did I mention I hate it?

Mads pulls out of his grip and flashes him a comfortable smile. I'll be honest. I liked it better when she was awkward, but my girl is a professional. So, no matter what, she'll be polite and do what she came here to do.

"I'm interning with Tailgate," she tells him. I'm relieved when she doesn't go any further into detail. Even though they seem familiar, she isn't divulging any more information to him than she would anyone else.

I clear my throat because I'm a selfish fucker and want to know who this guy is to her.

"Oh!" Mads says, remembering I exist on this planet. "Brady Jones, this is Blaze Beckham. I'm sure you know who he is. I also work for him as his assistant."

"She lives with me," I say, for no good fucking reason. Nobody asked. Brady smiles and extends his hand. I take it firmly, shaking it. "How do you know Mads?" *Right to the chase.*

"We went to high school together," she rushes out.

Brady furrows his eyebrows slightly before speaking. "Wow. That's it?" He smiles and turns to me. "Madison and I dated for most of our junior year."

Mads turns away and heads toward the podcast table while I stare at Brady. I can see why she would go for him. He's handsome and well-built. His biceps are nowhere near as big as mine, but I can see he takes care of himself. He's well-dressed, has straight white teeth, and doesn't seem super full of himself, at least from what I can see. He just seems…*normal.*

But Mads is exceptional.

I turn toward her and watch as she follows the cables coming from the back of each microphone. She looks quizzically at the sound board and reaches out to make sure everything is plugged in all the way.

Digging through her backpack, she pulls out a small flashlight and puts it between her lips before bending over to look under the table.

Every eye in the room goes big. The dress she's wearing isn't the shortest one in her closet, but I'd be willing to bet the two young guys behind her have a pretty good idea what she's hiding under there.

I do my best not to act like a fucking caveman and rip her out of there, throw her on the table, and fuck her in front of every one of these assholes. I can't do that. She's not mine… yet. But she's not theirs either, so I walk up behind her and ask if she needs help. What I'm really doing is blocking her from their view.

"I'm good," she says, her words muffled from the flashlight in her mouth. *That's probably not the only battery powered thing that's living my dream these days.*

Mads wiggles around slightly before coming out and turning off the flashlight. Leaning forward, she adjusts a slider on the board. From the right angle, it could probably look like my cock is touching her ass, so I send a message to the room by putting my hand on the small of her back. The action seems innocent to her because she's in her zone, but it's possessive to everyone else watching.

Mine.

She straightens and grabs a pair of headphone, putting them on and talking into the microphone.

"Check. Check."

Satisfied, she moves to the side and away from my touch.

"Somebody must've kicked the main line down there. The connector was bent, so it wasn't powering the board. You're good now." She smiles, handing the headset to Connor. "Anything else I can help you with?"

He laughs. "Yeah. How about you tell Brady here how to save his joke of a fantasy football team." He's being sarcastic because he doesn't know her knowledge of every player in the league.

Brady rolls his eyes. "You're just mad because I drafted the head coach from the Sharks."

Mads scoffs. *Get 'em, baby.*

I don't have a fantasy team because, well, I *am* the fantasy team. But I know exactly what she's thinking.

"What? He's the best coach in the league," he says, defensively.

She goes to stop herself, but if Mads knows anything, it's football. You couldn't pay me to enter a fantasy league that she was in.

"Well," she says like she's not about to embarrass him. "In a standard PPR league, a win gets a coach two points. Say the Sharks win every single game. That's a total of thirty-four points. On the season. Carson Dash, the sleeper from San Diego is projected to put up an average of seventeen points per game. So, congrats. You just wasted a roster spot when you could've left the coach position empty, put Dash in your flex when he starts to ball out, and gotten that back in two weeks."

"Marry me," Connor says, looking at her with hearts in his eyes.

"Got him!" one of the younger guys in the corner shouts, face in his phone, no doubt securing Carson Dash and dropping a head coach from his team.

Brady is speechless as he watches Mads zip up her backpack. She smiles sheepishly at him before waving goodbye. "Nice to see you." She turns to Connor next. "Watch your feet."

We turn to walk up the stairs before Brady runs after us and yells "Madison! Wait."

He closes the distance before speaking to her.

"Do you want to meet up Sunday night? We can grab a drink and catch up."

We play the L.A. Stars away in the early game that day and I have a feeling he's asking her because he knows that I won't be around.

"Ummm, sure. Yeah," she replies. She seems uncertain but she's way too nice to decline. Or maybe she actually wants to go out with him.

Fuck that.

"Great. I'll get your number from Jacob and we'll figure out the details later this week." He kisses her cheek before walking away.

TWENTY-ONE
MADS

MADS: Good game today! You got me 40 fantasy points.

BLAZE: I was thinking of slacking off today, but then I remembered that Cleats n Cleavage was counting on me. So, I decided to give it 100%. Just for you, Baby Doll.

MADS: Thank you for your service.

BLAZE: What's your plan tonight? Bathing in the tears of your opponents?

MADS: I'm meeting Brady at Donatello's for drinks.

BLAZE: Isn't Donatello's a little intimate for catching up with an old friend?

MADS: Is it? I've never been there. Brady suggested it.

BLAZE: Of course, he did.

. . .

I PULL off my Beckham Blizzard jersey and walk into my closet. I'm meeting Brady at some restaurant tonight and have absolutely no idea what to wear. Blaze said it's fancy, but I don't want to dress up and have Brady think it's an actual date. It is very much *not* a date. Been there, done that, and as our Lord and Savior Ariana Grande once said, *Thank you, next.*

He's a nice enough guy. Kind of spoiled, but he was raised that way, so it's not entirely his fault. We were the cutest little cliche couple in eleventh grade. The star basketball player and the captain of the cheerleading team. From the outside, it looked perfect. But I always felt trapped. I felt like I couldn't completely be myself with him. I had to give him the same watered-down version of me that I give to a lot of the men I date now. That's not what I want for my future. That's why I don't want anything more than friendship with Brady Jones.

Flipping through the hangers, I settle on a short-sleeved black t-shirt dress and denim jacket. I go with a 'no-makeup' makeup look and twist my hair up into a neat bun before tying my new white Converse. Taking a look in the mirror, I see a hint of sadness in my eyes. I get like this every time Blaze has a road game. If he were here, I'd be in one of his Blizzard hoodies and my pink fluffy slippers that he calls 'the ugliest things ever', popping popcorn for the Sunday night game.

I miss him.

I'm sure he and Dalton will have a night out in L.A. before the team plane brings them home tomorrow. The women there might as well be from another world. If they aren't actual models, they could be. Tall, tan, and drop-dead gorgeous. Those are the kind of women Blaze dates.

I grab my new Gucci bag, because Blaze Beckham makes up holidays just so he can give gifts. This was my "Happy

First Day of Fall" present, after he saw me eyeing it in an online ad. I guess those are the perks of working for a guy who makes thirty million dollars every year. Fifteen hundred dollars is a drop in the bucket for him. Checking my phone one last time to make sure Brady didn't cancel, I grab my keys and head toward Donatello's.

Twenty minutes later, I park my car in the lot where it sticks out like a sore thumb. A quick glance around at the Range Rovers, BMWs, and *is that a fucking Maybach,* gives me an idea of how out of place I am about to be here. The outside of the building is covered in ivy and fairy lights. A green awning hangs over the entrance.

I step out of my car and adjust my dress. Taking a deep breath, I shut the door and turn to see Brady walking toward me with a bright, white smile stretching across his handsome face.

"Madison," he reaches his hand out and I take it, although I probably shouldn't. I really don't want him to get the wrong idea. But friends can hold hands, right? Blaze and I do it all the time. "You look beautiful. Although you might be a touch underdressed," he says, taking in my denim jacket. "It's fine, though."

I feel like a child who just got reprimanded as he leads me through the door and to the front desk. As if I wasn't feeling uncomfortable enough, the girl standing behind it scoffs, *loudly,* at me before looking at Brady. I already want to go home.

"Reservation for Brady Jones," he says, completely ignoring her underhanded disrespect toward me.

"Right this way," she replies with a toothy grin, leading us to the far back corner of the restaurant. I'm expecting her to sit us at a table for two, and I'm slightly horrified when she ushers us directly to a small, *dimly lit* booth.

For fuck's sake. He thinks it's a date.

"We'll take a bottle of Cabernet Sauvignon," Brady tells the server.

"I think the fuck not," I inwardly scream, because give me a shot of whatever you have that's strong enough to conjure up the nerve to let this guy down gently. I need to keep his ego intact. The last thing I need is for him to pull his sponsorship from Connor's podcast because he associates it with me. If I remember correctly, Brady is petty as hell, so I have to tread carefully.

As the server retreats to the bar, I make a point to stay on the opposite end of the booth, so my not-date doesn't get any ideas. But he scoots over to my side, turning his body toward me.

"You look amazing, Madison," he says, running the backs of his knuckles over my arm.

Words? What are those? I'm fresh out.

I offer him a nervous laugh and try to inch even closer to the edge of the booth but stop in my tracks when my butt cheek tells me that if I move another inch, I'll be on the floor in front of all these people.

Get your shit together, Mads. This is Brady Jones. He used to eat his own boogers in Kindergarten.

"Look, Brady," I start. "I don't want you to —"

"Your wine, sir," the server speaks over me, showing the bottle to him. He nods in approval as she uncorks it and fills both of our glasses a third of the way.

I look up at her and smile. "Can you like, fill it all the way?" They both stare at me blankly. "Or is that not a thing?" My cheeks heat from embarrassment, but I have a feeling I'm going to need to be at least a little bit fucked up to get through this.

Why did I agree to this?

The server smiles awkwardly as she fills my glass to the brim. "Are we ready to order?"

I go to speak, but Brady cuts me off.

"I'll have the Chicken Marsala. And my date will take the Caesar Salad, no croutons." He flashes a smile, handing her both of our menus before she walks away, leaving me looking like Billy the Bass with my goddamn mouth hanging wide open. The audacity of this man to not only order my food, but to deny me the goodness of *carbs*? So what if that was my order in high school? I've changed a lot since then, starting with not trying to fit into whatever body image society tells me I should be. It's cool to order salad if you *like salad*. But this girl? She wants a big, juicy burger.

I'm reminded of last week when Blaze and I had a contest to see who could fit the most fries in their mouth at once after a midnight run to Mister Burgers. I almost choked from laughing so hard while he used his finger to carefully load his mouth up like he was playing a serious game of potato Tetris. Of course, his strategy paid off when he beat me by several fries.

I *really* miss him. Especially right now when I'm feeling ridiculously out of place. The funny thing is, Blaze has millions of dollars more than Brady, but you'd never know it. He'd fit in perfectly at a place like this just like he would at a hole-in-the-wall burger joint. And he'd make me feel comfortable at both.

That realization jolts me back to the present. I look at Brady, still sitting much closer to me than an old friend just wanting to catch up, and I know what I have to do.

"I really appreciate you bringing me here, but I think maybe we aren't on the same page," I say as he furrows his brows in confusion. "I'm not really looking to date right now. And if I was, I think we've already proven that we live completely different lifestyles. I can offer you friendship, Brady. But I can't give you anything else."

His whole demeanor changes in an instant and I find myself worried about what he'll do or say next. He slides away from me, scoffing.

"Lifestyles?" he says, thankfully keeping his voice low enough so nobody around us hears. "You mean you haven't grown out of whatever fucked up shit you enjoy in bed, and you know I'm not into that." I know he's hurt and deflecting, but this is exactly why I don't show myself to people. If I had known Brady would use it against me years later when I asked him to bind my wrists together with his tie on prom night, I certainly would've never done it. "Is that why you live with Blaze Beckham? Does he do...all of that to you?" His words are spit at me like venom and I don't know what emotion I'm feeling more. Embarrassment? Anger? Shock?

All of the above.

He continues. "I'm not even surprised. He doesn't exactly hide the fact that he fucks anything that walks."

"Don't talk about him!" I say, pointing my finger in Brady's face as I stand from the booth. "Blaze is an amazing guy. He's been good to me and if you think I'm going to let you sit here in last year's Prada shoes, wearing entirely too much cologne, and insult him, you're dead wrong." I look him up and down. "You'll never change. You're still the same spoiled douche bag you always were," I say, my words full of indignation, before walking away. I stop halfway to the door before turning to the room full of people, all of which are staring at me.

"He used to eat his boogers. Probably still does," I quip, turning and flipping him off over my shoulder, leaving him in my past for good, right where he belongs.

TWENTY-TWO
BLAZE

I PULL open the sliding glass door and walk out onto the balcony of my bedroom. I was supposed to be living it up in LA tonight. I planned on taking one or two cleat chasers back to my hotel room and letting them do whatever they wanted to me. Anything to get my mind off the fact that Mads was back here in Boston, on a date with Brady.

But I *couldn't*. As I watched the two women walk hand-in-hand toward my hotel room, all I could see was my little brunette spitfire in the arms of that charming, safe, handsome motherfucker. I just had to get home, so I booked a ticket and hopped on the first plane out of there.

To do what? Fuck if I know.

When I entered the kitchen, I breathed a sigh of relief seeing her purse on the table. She's home, which means she isn't in his bed. The house was quiet and pitch black, so I made my way to my bedroom, padding quietly down the hall in case she was asleep. Last thing I need is to be face-to-face with Mads while I'm sorting through all the fucked up thoughts I'm having about her. I don't even know where to begin. Do I want her? Of course, I do. I can't even watch her grumpy ass pour a cup of coffee in the morning without getting hard. But she's made it very clear that she needs this job and she won't do anything to complicate our relationship. I've done my best to act like I'm okay with just being her friend, but it's getting to a point where I can feel myself starting to snap. My feelings for her have spiraled into something I can no longer control. I either have to find a way to get her out of my head, or I have to show her that exploring something with me is worth the risk.

So here I am. Sitting on my balcony with a glass of whiskey, racking my brain to figure out how to make all these feelings disappear. Getting drunk seems like a killer start.

A steady gust of wind blows and I notice the curtain from Mads' balcony flowing. She must have the door open because the weather has been surprisingly warm for it being the middle of fall. I'll be sure to address that in the morning. This is a gated community with the most high-tech security, but I don't want to spend my nights away hoping she hasn't unknowingly put herself in danger.

Just as I try to shake away the intrusive thoughts, I hear a small, breathy moan coming from the direction of her room. My first thought is that Brady is here. That has me ready to heave myself off this balcony, scale the house Spider-Man style, and rip him off of her. But as I listen closer, I hear a soft, steady buzz.

Fuck. Me. She's masturbating.

I can't tear myself away, even though I know I should. This moment isn't for me to hear. In fact, I'm sure the only reason she's even allowing those sweet little noises to escape her body is because she thinks I'm not home.

I shouldn't be listening. And I *definitely* shouldn't be going back inside, out my bedroom door, and walking toward hers. The voice in my head is trying to reason with me. *What are you planning on doing? Putting a glass up to the door to hear her better?* But I don't just want to hear her. I want to *see* her.

I'm having an internal war with myself, but the urge is too

strong. It's like my hand has a mind of its own as it reaches out and slowly turns the doorknob. I only have to crack it a few inches before she's in full view. Her head is angled away, thankfully. She has the blanket kicked down, wearing nothing but a long t-shirt, pulled up to her navel. Her legs are spread wide as she holds the vibrator against herself, heavy breaths and soft moans escaping her open lips.

I palm my growing erection, squeezing once before dropping my hand. *Not tonight, little buddy. Sorry.* My other is still holding the doorknob so tightly that I'm surprised it doesn't turn to dust. She's fucking beautiful. Even in the low light of the moon, I can make out every dip of her skin. The flair of her hips as they rotate slightly. The deep rise and fall of her chest as she chases her release.

She stops abruptly, sitting up, and I'm sure I've been busted. I'm standing outside her door, completely unmoving, trying to come up with a story for why that isn't *"I heard you moaning and wanted to watch you come."* But she doesn't see me. I quietly exhale, thanking the God of hallway creepers. I should go to my room and forget what I saw. And that's exactly my plan until she speaks.

"Fuck this," she whines as she sets the vibrator on her bedside table and throws her head back on the pillow. It takes me a moment to realize that she never came. She had to have been holding that toy to her pussy for at least the last fifteen minutes before she gave up.

I watch as she rubs her thighs together, her discomfort obvious before pulling her covers up with a frustrated huff. That spurs me into action. Even though I know this is wrong and I should be doing everything I can to escape this situation unnoticed, my hand pushes the door open and I step into her room.

She turns her head abruptly toward the door and sits up, stiffening.

"It's just me," I say as I move toward her.

"Blaze? I thought you were in L.A. until tomorrow?" she replies, her body relaxing.

I don't say anything as I grab the vibrator from the table and lightly push her shoulder until she's laying back on the pillow. Her eyes are wide, mouth agape, but she doesn't resist. I feel like I'm having an out-of-body experience. I've been with plenty of women, but the goal with them has always been the same. Get them off so I can get off. There's something different about this moment with Mads. My cock is like granite behind my zipper, but I don't give a fuck. All I care about is the ache between her legs and making it go away.

I pull the blanket down, exposing her completely. Pushing a shaky hand between her thighs, I coax her to open. As soon as she does, I flick the vibrator on and gently lower it to her clit. I can feel it slide along her opening with how wet she is. She never takes her eyes off me as I lower my mouth to her ear, careful not to touch any part of her skin with mine. I'm afraid of what will happen to my tightly wound self-control if I do. This isn't for me. It's for her.

"Is this what you needed, baby? A little help getting yourself off?" I say as her pants and moans start back up, much louder than before. "This greedy little pussy of yours is aching, isn't it? You're such a bad girl, touching yourself with the door open where anybody could see the way you're dripping."

"Fuck," she whimpers quietly, hips beginning to move on their own accord. I want to reach out and touch her, but I know I can't. So, I continue talking as if I could use my voice to stroke her body.

"Play with your tits, Mads. Pretend it's me doing it."

Without hesitation, she reaches up her shirt, hands immediately going to her nipples. I know the moment she's followed my instruction because her back bows off the bed.

"That's my good girl," I praise as I increase the speed on

the toy still pressed between her legs. I watch in awe as she writhes on the bed under me. I'm still not touching her, but I can feel her hands brush my shirt as she moves them over her tits. I can't even feel my cock at this point with how hard it is. It could've fallen off and I wouldn't even know it.

Her moans are so loud as her body begins to tense. *She's close.*

"Almost there, baby. I know this little cunt of yours wants to soak the sheets. Give it to me, pretty girl. And don't take those eyes off mine. I need you to see who's doing this to you." I'm almost taken aback by the possessive growl that comes out of me with that last sentence. I shouldn't be, considering the number of times I've cut good ole' Brady's brake lines in my head. I don't want anyone else to see her like this...make her *feel* like this.

Mads' legs begin to shake as her ass lifts off the bed. She fists the sheets tightly beside her.

"Blaze!" she screams as her orgasm hits and if I wasn't already hard enough to come in my pants, my name on her lips would get me there. She fights to obey, keeping her eyes on mine until she can't anymore and they slam shut while she continues convulsing for what seems like hours. I decrease the pressure of the vibrator on her sensitive clit and slowly run it along her very soaked entrance as she lowers herself back down and begins to relax.

As she reopens her eyes, focusing back on me, I turn off the toy before bringing it to my mouth and running my tongue up the length of it. "So fucking sweet, just like I knew you would be."

She's still staring at me with a look between satisfaction and awe as I pull up the blanket, set the vibrator on the table, and walk out of the room, closing the door behind me.

MADS

I wake up feeling light as a feather. Until I remember why. I know it wasn't a dream that Blaze came into my room last night, no doubt after hearing me struggle, and handled my body better than I ever have. I don't think I've ever had an orgasm that intense.

And now, the gravity of the situation is hitting me like a Mack truck. We *live together*. It's not a matter of *if* I'll have to face him again. It's a matter of *when.* And unfortunately for my uncaffeinated soul, when is in about ten minutes.

But first, pants. Long ones. And a thick sweatshirt. Maybe a winter coat, zipped up to my neck. Because if I know my traitorous bitch of a body, she's about to have a Pavlovian response to being in his presence. The very last thing I need right now is for Blaze to see my hard nipples through my t-shirt when I pass him on my way to get my coffee.

"Why did you let that happen, you dumb bitch?" I mutter to myself as I pad over to my dresser, grabbing a pair of sweatpants. I think twice before putting them back in the drawer and reaching for my regular morning attire of booty shorts. If I want him to think things are fine, I need to act natural. Just go down there, pour my coffee, and go through his agenda for the day, just like we do every morning.

Thankfully, he has to watch film this morning, followed by practice, then he's hosting a barbecue for the offense. So, by the time he gets back here, I'll be so busy getting the house ready for guests that we won't have much time for awkward silences. Or worse, an awkward talk where he tells me he was just helping a friend who was struggling and that he doesn't want me like that.

I pull on my shorts and tie a knot in the bottom of my oversized t-shirt before looking in the mirror. As I'm pulling my hair up into a messy bun, I'm stopped in my tracks at my reflection. My skin is plump and glowing. I look different.

Beautiful, even. Maybe that's why all the women Blaze dates are so gorgeous. They spend so much time with his hands on them that it affects the way they look.

Sadness and jealously overtakes me at the thought. Because he didn't put his hands on me. He didn't kiss me. He could've, but he didn't.

It's better this way. I told him in the kitchen the day I got back from Chicago that I'd keep things professional. I've been keeping my feelings for him at bay. Last night was a minor hiccup…one that I didn't initiate. He gave me a hand, I appreciate it, and now I need to move forward and play it cool.

Good luck with that, Nipples McGee.

I take one last look in the mirror before turning on my heels. Pushing my shoulders back, I head out of the room and down the stairs. Blaze is standing at the coffee maker with a mug the size of a small cereal bowl and my favorite creamer out on the counter as he waits for it to finish brewing. I stand there quietly because honestly, I don't know what to say.

"Hey, friend. Thanks for the big O you gave me last night. Good lookin' out. Also, was I seeing things or did you lick my cum off of my vibrator?"

No. Fucking awkward.

Blaze pours the creamer into the mug and lifts the carafe, filling it to the brim. My mouth is watering already. Obviously from the coffee, and definitely not because he's wearing thin cotton pajama pants and nothing else.

Acting as natural as possible, I move toward him. He turns with the mug in his hand and hits me with a smile that has my knees ready to buckle underneath me. And yep, my nipples react just like I knew they would. This is exactly why we can't have nice things.

"What's the plan today, boss?" he says, handing the mug to me. I tell myself that he made my coffee to speed the morning along, not because last night changed anything between us. I have to keep my eyes on the prize here. And that prize is keeping my job so I can focus on my internship without having to worry about how I'll pay my bills.

I hold up my hand, silencing him while I take a sip of the hot liquid because orgasm or not, he knows better than to expect me to function before my cup is at least half empty. Walking over to the counter, I pull out a bar stool and sit.

"Sorry," he chuckles before walking over and catching me off guard with a kiss to the side of my head. "I'm going to go jump in the shower while you wake up. Then you can tell me where I'm supposed to be today so I don't get lost."

He turns and walks out of the room like everything is fine while I stare into my mug like it has all the answers to how the fuck I'm supposed to be near him without wanting more.

TWENTY-THREE
MADS

THE BACK YARD is full of football players as I move around the kitchen, pretending to busy myself in an attempt to keep some distance between Blaze and I. After last night, then him acting like everything was normal this morning, I need some time to sort things out. The more I think about it, the more confused I get about what I even want anymore. Whether I want them to or not, I can feel my priorities starting to shift.

When I went outside to check the fuel level of the outdoor heaters fifteen minutes ago, Blaze was standing at the grill with Dalton, preparing the main course. This is the last cookout of the year for the group of offensive players he likes to host once a month. Even though the colder weather has made its way to New England, we're making it work.

The timer on the stove goes off and I drain the tri-colored pasta, transferring it to a bowl before I start adding the ingredients for my mom's famous pasta salad. My arms burn from the weight of the food as I mix it together, but when you're feeding twenty professional football players, you have to make enough for an army.

Just as I throw the final touches on the pasta salad, I hear the sliding door open and close behind me, followed by approaching footsteps.

"Need any help?" Blaze asks.

Avoiding eye contact because, well, I don't know why, I nod. "The baked beans can come out of the oven."

He goes over and removes the bubbling dish, setting it down on the stovetop before tossing the foil into the trash. "What next?"

That's a great fucking question.

"Umm," I say, awkwardly. "That's—I think that's it. Thanks."

He leans on the counter next to me, folding his arms over his chest. "If you want to talk about last night, we can. But if you want me to apologize for it, I won't. I can't."

I chance a glance in his direction, finding myself unable to look away once our eyes meet. His expression is completely unbothered. I stay quiet, but he continues.

"It can be whatever you want it to be. If you want to stay *friends*," he says the word like he doesn't believe for one second that's what I truly want, "we can. If you want to be more, that's okay, too. But don't shut down on me." He pauses, waiting to see if I'm ready to speak, but I don't say anything.

He huffs an annoyed breath. "You know what? We don't have to make a big deal out of it," he goes on. "You sounded like you needed help, so I helped." He shrugs. "If that's what you need to hear to stop yourself from overthinking, fine. I'll give you that. But I won't act like it meant nothing to me."

He doesn't give me a chance to reply before he grabs both dishes and leaves the house. I exhale, leaning forward onto the counter. My whole body shakes as I try to make sense of the last words he said, and the ones that still sit unsaid on the tip of my tongue.

BLAZE

I sit on the edge of my bed, going through the events of the last twenty-four hours. After last night, towering over Mads as she came for me, I thought the safest move would be to pretend everything was fine. But now I realize that was probably not the best way to handle things.

All through the cookout, I could tell she was battling with herself. And part of that is my fault. One minute, I tell her I am on board with just being friends. Next thing I know, I'm doing everything I can to make her see how I feel about her. The real truth is that I'm fucking falling for her. Maybe I already have. But me ping-ponging back and forth isn't fair to her.

She was clear with me. She told me her internship and securing the job at Tailgate is her number one priority. I respect the fuck out of her for that. If anyone knows what it's like to give everything you have to succeed at the highest level, it's me. So, why does it sting so badly when she's afraid to risk it by taking a chance on us?

What I told Mads earlier, about not needing to make a big deal out of what we shared last night; felt like vinegar in my mouth as I said it. But I knew it was the right thing to do. If she is warring with herself over this, the least I can do is give her an out.

I need to leave the ball in her court from here on out. At least for now, I'll let her figure things out on her own, without the pressure of me trying to turn us into something more. It might make me crazy watching her explore dating with other guys if she decides to do that, but I'll wait. I'd wait a lifetime for her.

I just hope that when she's ready to share her future with someone else, she lets me back in. In the meantime, all I can do is focus on keeping a tight grip on my emotions *and* my restraint.

TWENTY-FOUR
MADS

MY PHONE VIBRATES from somewhere in my room. I've finally decided to unpack the rest of my suitcases and make this space my own. It's mostly just the winter clothes I haven't needed yet, but I figured I might as well get them ready to be worn soon. In the process, I've made a huge mess.

It's been nearly two weeks since that night in my room. Thankfully, all the awkwardness between us has subsided. We're back to hanging out as much as we can, doing 'friend stuff' like watching movies and playing video games. He's still his same flirty self, but he's definitely backed away from the subtle touching I used to love. I miss it, but this is what I wanted, right?

Is it, though?

I rush around the bed, turning my head slightly as if that will help me locate the buzzing sound faster. My efforts pay off when I put my hand down on a particularly thick clump of sheets and feel a vibration. Grabbing a chunk of fabric, I whip it, sending my phone flying through the air.

Please don't be broken. I'm still kinda poor.

Thankfully, when I pick it up, I find that the screen is still intact and that I have a missed call from Dia. I dial her back and, of course, she picks up after one ring.

"Heyyyyyyyy bitch! I thought you were busy boning your hot boss, so I left you a voicemail."

"Oh my God, Diamond. Would you please take it easy on the crack? It's making you hallucinate," I say, rolling my eyes..

She continues. "Oh, okay. You've been living with the literal hottest human being on the planet and you haven't taken him for a spin but *I'm* the one on drugs?"

I never told her about the night in my bed where Blaze gave me the best orgasm of my life without even laying an actual finger on me. She's my best friend and I love her more than anything, but I'm not dumb enough to give her that kind of ammunition. Even though she knows I'm struggling with my feelings for Blaze, she still texts me several times a day asking if I know what his dick tastes like yet. Dia has the dirtiest mind of anyone I've ever met. I know for a fact that she could even make Dalton blush with some of the shit that comes out of her mouth. I silently laugh in my head at the thought of everyone's favorite douchebag being brought down by one-hundred and twenty pounds of Italian feistiness.

"Never gonna happen. Now move on," I say sternly as I round the bed, putting the phone on speaker before throwing it onto the pillow.

"Whatever," she replies. "How about dates? I know you went on a few. How'd they go?"

Ugh. The *dates*. Every last one of them felt like I should've been paid for babysitting. Unfortunately, I like a certain kind of man. And not to stereotype, but the ones with the bodies that I want generally come with...less in the brains department. These guys were all very cute, but I just couldn't see myself going anywhere with them. The conversation was lacking, and they were just missing something. A lot of somethings, actually. It's not that I need to hear wedding bells to connect with a guy. I just need to get that vibe that he can give me what I need.

"They were okay. I don't know," I shrug. "You know how I am. I need someone to take control. None of the guys I've met here seem like they had it in them to throw me on the bed, cuff me, and dominate me until I beg them to stop," I say. I'm trying to keep things light, but Dia knows me well enough to understand why I'm so frustrated.

"Babe, are you upfront with these guys before you meet? Do you tell them you're a sub?" she says, her tone completely serious.

I know she knows it isn't easy for me to just throw that on someone when I first meet them. I've had reactions from every end of the spectrum and it's impossible to know what each person will think when I tell them what turns me on. Some guys love it and if they don't already have experience being a dom, they're ready to learn. Others think it's slutty or they're intimidated by it. So, I try to water myself down at first. If there's chemistry, I'll do the whole vanilla sex thing until I feel comfortable enough easing them in. Maybe I'll start by mentioning handcuffs or some other cliche bondage item so they don't suspect that I'd prefer to be blindfolded and flogged while being told what a good girl I am.

I sigh, abandoning the clothes I should be folding. "I try, but I can kind of tell when someone isn't ready to hear it. They haven't been. And to be honest, I don't know if any of the dudes in Boston are."

"Keep looking," she says, reassuring me. "Maybe you should give one of those BDSM apps a shot. They vet every member and it's generally very safe and positive. At least then you'll find someone who knows exactly what you need and can give it to you. You deserve that."

She really is an angel.

"Thanks, D. You're the best friend in the whole world," I

say, my eyes burning with unshed tears of gratitude and a new sense of determination.

"Right?" she replies, snickering. "Okay babe, gotta run. I'm meeting your dad for drinks." I know she's trying to wind me up to lighten the mood. She never goes long without reminding me that my dad is a total DILF. I know she's just messing with me, though. She sees Tom Rodgers as her dad just as much as he's mine.

"Oh my God, bye!" I say, hanging up on her before she goes any further. I'm sure my parents invited her to dinner because missing me is a common interest for them these days. I'm glad she has them. Dia's parents are shit bags who definitely don't deserve her acknowledgement.

"Okay," I say to myself while signing into the BDSM app I've had downloaded on my phone for weeks. "Come find me."

BLAZE

I walk into the locker room at the practice facility with about thirty minutes to spare before the rest of the guys start strolling in. I get into a full-fledged wrestling match with my duffel bag, trying to shove it into my locker. My hair is completely disheveled from being finger fucked by my hands for the entire ride here. I feel so out of control.

When I unintentionally overheard Mads on the phone talking about her…bedroom preferences earlier today, I was equal parts turned on and scared shitless. But when she fired up the BDSM app that her friend recommended, I went downright feral. Like hell I'm going to let another man tie her up and touch her. Not when I already know the chemistry between us is explosive. I made her come just by fucking existing. Okay, maybe the vibrator in my hand helped a little.

But it certainly didn't help when it was in her hand, did it?

"The fuck crawled up your ass, Becks? Your period show up a few days early?" Dalton says, setting his bag down and sitting on the bench next to me. The one day I need some time to myself, this fuck stick shows up early. Just my luck.

I debate telling him any of this because I haven't seen him take a serious situation like an adult in the three years I've known him. But I need to talk this out or I'm going to have a goddamn heart attack on the field. Plus, he's my best friend. It's not like he's going to laugh at me when I'm clearly fucked up over the whole situation.

"Fuck it," I mutter quietly before launching into the full story. I tell him about the phone call and even include some of the non-descriptive details from the night I found Mads wet and needy in her bed. Ten minutes later, I wrap up the story and wait for him to hit me with at least some semblance of a supportive reaction that will move me in a positive direction. Maybe he'll even surprise me and give me some solid advice.

But this is Dalton fucking Davis we're talking about. And I *should've known.*

"So," he says between wheezes. The motherfucker is in hysterics, complete with actual knee slapping. He attempts to rein it in, but fails miserably, continuing to laugh while I look at him slack-jawed. "What you're saying is…you don't know how to spank your assistant, so she's going to bring some other dude in to do it for her?" He laughs for another thirty seconds before he looks at me, realizing he's laughing *alone* and finally gets his shit together. His expression drops back to a serious one, but the dickhead's eyes are goddamn twinkling right now.

"That's tough, man," he replies, cleaning his throat.

"That's what you have for me? 'That's tough'?" I say, even more frustrated than I was before. "What the fuck am I going to do? You're right. I don't know how to *spank her.* But I can't let anyone else do it, either."

Just the thought of Mads even talking about what turns her on with another man makes me want to put my fist through a wall. I don't have a bad temper. I'm pretty good at saving my aggression for the field, but there's just something about her that makes me feel so protective. Ever since that night in her room, I've known I could make her feel things no other person on this Earth ever could.

Dalton gets up from his chair and picks up his bag. Before walking away, he slaps my shoulder. "Better figure something out, dude. You're too pretty for prison. They'd eat you alive in there."

"Thanks for absolutely nothing, dick bag," I say, turning to my locker before I see Tanner out of the corner of my eye.

"Don't you know the captain is supposed to be the first one here? You're making me look bad, Becks," he says jokingly before lowering his voice.

"You busy tonight?"

"No. Why, what's up?" I reply.

He nods his head, grinning. "I'll pick you up at nine. I want to show you something. It'll help your situation."

As he walks away, I furrow my brows before wondering to myself exactly how much of that conversation he heard. Then I realize that I don't give a fuck if whatever he wants to show me stops Mads from ending up in anyone's bed but mine. I know I said I'd back off and let her figure things out. But now? All bets are off.

TWENTY-FIVE
BLAZE

IT'S nine o clock on the dot when Tanner pulls up the driveway. I managed to get myself dressed and sneak out without running into Mads. I just don't know how I'll react if I see her right now. I'm not mad *at her*. She didn't do anything wrong. But I'm definitely mad that I have no idea how to be the man she needs. And the thought of her finding someone else makes me absolutely sick to my stomach.

"How's it going, bro?" he says as I climb into the front seat of his Tesla.

I run my hands down my face. "I don't know how much you heard in the locker room earlier, but I've got a lot going on right now and it's got me pretty fucked up."

"I heard enough," he replies cryptically, putting on his blinker as he leaves my complex and turns onto the main road. I still have no idea where we're going, but I don't even have the energy to ask for details. Tanner is a cool guy, solid teammate, and someone I trust. It's not like he's going to take me to a field and murder me. Plus, he said he could help me with my situation.

He's also apparently not into small talk because we barely speak two words for the entirety of the twenty-minute ride.

I'm shocked as shit as he pulls into the parking lot of a place called Bliss. I've heard of it, but I've never been here. All I know is that its a luxury sex club with a hefty monthly membership fee.

And fuck me running. It seems that our pretty boy quarterback actually frequents this establishment.

Tanner pulls toward the gate, scans a card, and enters the back of the lot as it swings open. I might be having a stroke or something because I can't come up with anything to say. Do I have five million questions? Fuck yeah, I do. Who wouldn't? This unproblematic, private, mostly quiet regular guy gets kinky at a sex club in his free time. But instead of making an ass out of myself trying to put my thoughts into words, I follow Tanner silently as he gets out of the car and heads toward the entrance.

We walk to the desk, where a beautiful woman in a black dress waits, holding a tablet.

"Hello, Mr. Lake," she says with stars in her eyes. That's not a surprise. Tanner was voted Sexiest Man Alive last year and had a six-page spread in ESPN's Body Issue.

"Hey, Cameron. This is Mr. Beckham. He's my guest this evening. He's just here to watch."

Uhhh, come again? Watch what now?

She turns to me. I'm still standing silently, eyes wide like a kid who just got caught with his dad's titty magazines. "It's nice to meet you, Mr. Beckham. I'll just need to see some identification. Since you won't be participating this evening, we won't need proof of a clean STI screening, but if you decide you'd like to go into a room, we'd need that first. We have a bar that you're free to use, but there is a very strict two drink maximum. No exceptions." She taps on her tablet as I reach into my pocket for my wallet. She grabs my driver's license when I hand it to her and begins typing before turning the device to me.

"This is a non-disclosure agreement. Please read it and sign at the bottom."

I take it and pretend to read through all the legal mumbo-jumbo. I get it. Rule number one of Sex Club and all that. I use my finger to scribble my name at the bottom and Cameron hands me a black key card.

"Enjoy your evening, gentlemen. Mr. Lake, you'll be in Room 211. It's ready for you now."

Tanner nods his head and thanks her before turning toward a long hallway. I follow him because what else am I going to do? He takes a few steps before speaking.

"Bet you weren't expecting this when I asked you to come out with me tonight, huh?" he says. I continue following him into a large room with tables scattered around. A stage is lit in the front of the room, where a man in a mask carefully winds a black rope around the torso of a woman kneeling in front of him. I try to act at least somewhat unaffected as we make our way to the bar, but in the back of my head, I wonder if Mads has ever been tied up that way.

Would she let me do that to her? *Could I* do it?

"No, man. Can't say that I had you down as a kink club kind of guy," I reply. "Why did you bring me here, Tan?"

He orders two whiskeys from the bartender and waits for them to be set down in front of us before he considers my question. Taking a long sip of his drink, he hesitates for a moment. Tanner is normally a pretty happy guy. But something about seeing him in this setting has me thinking there's a lot more to him than that. He almost looks like he's trying to figure out which parts of himself he's willing to share with me right now. And fuck if I'm not curious.

"When I heard you talking about your assistant earlier, I knew I could help. It's obvious you care about her and want to be able to provide what she needs. I can show you how."

I have to admit, I'm still a little lost here. I get that he brought me to a club where I'm assuming people practice

BDSM. But how can Tanner show me how to take care of Mads? *Unless…*

It all clicks into place.

"Ohh," I say, finally understanding why he brought me here. "You're a dom?"

He exhales on a laugh, downing the rest of his drink. "Yeah. Come on."

He gets up and heads toward a staircase covered in soft red carpet. I follow him, but my nerves are definitely on high alert. I can actually hear my pulse.

"Dude, I really appreciate this, but I'm not completely sure I want to watch you fuck someone here."

He stops abruptly, looking at me before continuing up the stairs. "I won't be fucking anybody."

Okay, *now* I'm really confused.

"Just trust me, Becks. I can help you with what you need. And I promise you will never see my dick." He smirks. "Well, I don't know what you get up to in the locker room, but you won't see it here."

I decide that I do trust him. Whatever happens from here on out, I'm just going to try my best to remember why I'm here. Madison Rodgers will be in my bed soon. And I'll do everything I can to satisfy every part of her sweet little body in all the ways she craves. Just the thought has my cock thickening behind my zipper. How would she take being tied to my bed and edged until she was begging to come?

Fuck. Focus.

We turn down a hallway that's separated from the main part of the floor by a velvet curtain. A security guard scans both of our cards then silently steps aside, pulling the heavy fabric away for us to pass through. We stop in front of a door marked 'Room 211' and Tanner uses his key to open it. Stepping inside, I notice what looks like a very small waiting room. There is a luxurious deep blue velvet sofa with two tables on the ends facing a window. When I look through it, I see an attached room with a round bed, several high tables and other pieces of furniture that I'm unfamiliar with. There are various restraints, ropes, whips, and other items hanging on hooks along the wall. Then, I see her.

On the floor next to the bed, a blonde woman kneels with her back to us. She's completely naked except for a thin metal collar around her neck. Her head is down, and her hands are on her knees.

Tanner motions for me to sit down and nods once before entering the room, shutting the door, and walking over to the girl. I take a seat on the couch and hear his footsteps through a small speaker in the corner before he stops in front of her. I can see the rise and fall of her body as he reaches down and caresses the top of her hair. He does that for a moment before speaking to her.

"I brought a friend to watch tonight, kitten. Is that okay with you?"

She doesn't look up at him when he speaks. Instead, she continues staring at her hands in front of her as she replies softly.

"Yes, sir."

"Good girl."

He removes his gold cufflinks and sets them on a table before rolling the sleeves of his white dress shirt up his fore-arms. Walking over to the wall, he grabs a crop and a flogger before returning to her.

"On the bed, sweetheart."

Without hesitation, she stands and lays on the bed, moving herself to the perfect spot. Tanner reaches over to another table where he picks up a blindfold and two sets of soft black cuffs. First, he puts the blindfold over her eyes before taking each wrist and securing them to the posts above her head.

I shift in my seat, glad I'm alone. I don't think I could watch this with strangers sitting next to me. I'd be lying if I said this whole thing didn't turn me on a little. And the thought of doing these things to Mads while she writhes beneath me, under my control? I picture her defying me at first until I'd have to force her to her knees like the dirty little brat she is. I'd stroke myself inches from her face while she whined with the need to take me into her warm mouth.

Okay, so I'm a lot turned on. Sue me.

At some point during my daydream, Tanner attached what looks like a metal bar to the woman's ankles with two cuffs at the ends. He grabs it by the middle, pulling outward, forcing her legs further apart before locking it in place. He seems hesitant to touch her body, which is a little strange to me, but I'm certainly no expert. I watch, barely blinking as he reaches for the leather flogger.

"What's your safe word?" He asks her, running the falls of the flogger over her torso and breasts.

"Turtle," she replies on a shaky exhale.

"Such a good girl for me," he praises as he continues teasing her with the thin leather fringes. "Here's what you're going to do for me, kitten," Tanner says, towering over her. "You're going to show my friend here how beautifully this pussy weeps for me. But don't you dare come without my permission. I'd hate to have to punish you in front of company."

I can see the woman shaking with anticipation as he finally brings the flogger down on her skin, *hard*. At first, I am expecting a reaction of pain, but I'm surprised when she lets out a low moan.

"What do you say?" Tanner says, firmly.

"Thank you."

Jesus. Fucking. Christ.

He continues flogging her on various parts of her body. Her stomach. Her thighs. Her tits. She thanks him after every one and I can see that she's very clearly turned on. Her nipples are so hard it almost looks painful. And her pussy is so wet, I can see it leaking out of her from here.

Tanner turns around to switch the flogger for another item and I see the woman attempt to bring her knees together, no doubt to give herself a little relief. He catches her in the act, and I watch with rapt attention to see what he'll do.

"Aww," he coos, releasing her wrists from the headboard and walking to the end of the bed with a leather crop loosely hanging from his fingers. "Is that spreader bar in your way, sweetheart? Can't quite get those thighs pressed together, can you?" He chuckles darkly before grabbing the bar in the middle and twisting swiftly, forcing her to flip to her stomach. "I told you not to even think about coming without my permission, didn't I?" he says, rearing the crop back and landing it with a loud smack on her ass cheek. A red welt raises on her pale skin instantly.

"Yes, sir," she replies, her voice shaking.

"Looked to me like that's exactly what you were trying to do. Face down, ass up, sweetheart."

The woman obeys instantly, pushing back on her knees with her face pressed into the sheets.

"Good girl," he praises. "You wanted to come so badly, didn't you?" His voice is dark and condescending as he drags the crop from her shoulder blades to her dripping slit. She sucks in a quick breath at the sensation. Just as she relaxes, he slaps her directly on her clit with it. She lets out a loud whimper before she begins rocking her hips slightly. Tanner allows the action, continuing to bring the crop down on her slick pussy.

I can see she needs to come. I almost feel bad for her at this point. Could I really do this to Mads and let her suffer this way? Or would I give in and eat her until she had an earth-shattering orgasm?

I'm expecting Tanner to use his hand or mouth to end this torture for the poor girl, but he doesn't. Instead, he reaches his free hand around and closes it on her throat. I swear I see her lean into him, increasing the amount of pressure he's choking her with. Leaning over her back, he finally gives her what she's been waiting for.

"Come for me."

One last slap of the crop against her core sends her into a violent orgasm. She shakes uncontrollably as her hips continue to thrust forward. When she finally relaxes, Tanner frees her ankles, rubbing at the marks from the restraints.

As if a switch was flipped, he gently helps the woman onto her back, soothing her by rubbing her hair. Walking over to a small refrigerator, he grabs a bottle of water and hands it to her while sitting down on the bed. She cuddles into him as she drinks half of it in one go.

After a minute, he asks her if she's alright. She nods her head yes and he gives her a gentle kiss on the forehead before walking through another door off the room. I watch her as I sit and wait for him to come out. She snuggles into the covers, and her breathing slowly evens out as she falls asleep.

Thankfully, the erection I was sporting a few minutes ago has gone down by the time Tanner emerges from what looks to be a bathroom. He gives the girl one more kiss on her forehead before stepping into the room I've been watching from. Sitting on the couch next to me, he leans forward with his elbows on his knees.

"I know you probably have questions, but there's a lot about me that I'm not ready to discuss. I brought you here because I wanted to show you how pleasurable it can be for a woman when she's able to submit to someone she trusts. It's freeing for them. It can be freeing for you, too, if you know how to do it right."

He sighs, a hint of sadness, taking over his features, before continuing. "I've made a lot of mistakes in my lifetime. And I wish I knew back then what I know now about this lifestyle. I wish I had somebody to show me how to do it right. That's why you're here. I'm not saying this magically makes you an expert, but hopefully you have a little bit better idea of how to take care of your girl."

We both stand, and I pull him into a bro hug because for some reason, I feel like what he just showed me might have completely changed my life.

He chuckles before turning to the door. "Let's get you home now that you know how to *spank your assistant.*"

TWENTY-SIX
MADS

"SO, I TOLD HIM," my date says, barely pausing to take a breath, "'If you think I'm selling for less than five K a share, you're fucking nuts.' I'll hold those stocks until I die if I have to, you know?"

"Yeah," I reply even though I most certainly do not know.

He takes a sip of his craft beer, the slurping sound making me inwardly cringe. We've been here for an hour, and I'm already planning my escape. The twenty-minute run through on how he just became the proud owner of a new Rolex Submariner would've been enough on its own to bore me to tears, but he's been telling me about his stock-bro adventures since the waitress dropped off our drinks and I'm genuinely starting to think a root canal would've been more exciting than this date.

I wonder what Blaze is doing right now. I know he was home earlier, but he was really quiet. I didn't even realize he had left until I opened my bedroom door to an empty house. I would much rather be at home, curled up on the couch with him watching game tape, but I promised Dia I would keep putting myself out there when it comes to dating. So, here I am.

"Another drink?" he asks, noticing that I've finally finished my first one of the evening.

"No, thanks," I reply awkwardly. I'd love to be able to fill the silence that follows, but we couldn't be more different. I know nothing about watches or stocks and he hasn't even attempted to ask me anything about myself beyond what I told him while we chatted on the dating app.

Thankfully, I'm saved from more awkward conversation when my phone rings. *Right on time.* I give a fake confused look as I answer. "Hello?"

"Hey, you dirty slut," Dia greets me. "I'm calling to save you from another bad date if you need it. How's it going?"

I knit my eyebrows together, channeling my inner sub-par actress. "Wait. What? Where are you?" I say, frantically.

"At Disneyland. Just sucked Prince Eric off on the teacup ride," she says.

"Oh my God!" I yell, putting my hand over my mouth for a little extra razzle-dazzle. "Stay where you are. I'll be right there!"

"Ok, cool. Byeeeeeeee," she says before the line goes dead.

And that, right there, is why Dia will always be my best friend.

I look up at my date to see him waiting for my explanation. Shit. I didn't really think up a good story.

"Everything alright?" he questions, concern evident in his features.

"That was my grandma. She dropped her teacup," I rush out.

Confused, he waits for me to continue.

"Uhhh, yeah, she dropped her tea and burnt herself. I have to take her to the hospital, right away. I'm so sorry to cut our date short," I hurry out, grabbing my coat and handbag. "It was nice meeting you, Troy."

"It's Tony," he says, disappointed. "Can I see you ag—"

But I'm already out the door before I'm forced to tell him

that there's no way we'll be repeating this snoozefest. I shoot Dia a quick text thanking her for her service before pocketing my phone and heading toward home.

BLAZE

Tanner pulls his car up my driveway, putting it into park as I undo my seatbelt. My mind is going a million miles a minute, still trying to process everything that's happened today. I'm still not completely sure how I'm going to move forward, but being at the club with Tanner definitely gave me some insight on what to do next. Like he said, I'm nowhere near being an expert on any of this. I'll have to do more research to find the best and safest ways to take care of Mads. I need to make sure that every experience she has with me is good for her.

I only realize I haven't moved and I'm still sitting in his car when Tanner breaks the silence. "Do you have any other questions for me?"

I know he's talking about the BDSM lifestyle, but it takes everything in me not to ask how his life turned out the way it did. I know the woman at the club tonight is not his girlfriend. Matter of fact, I've never seen or heard of him being in a relationship with anyone. He shared something very personal with me tonight and I want him to know that he doesn't have to go through anything alone from here on out.

I think carefully before speaking. "Thank you for tonight. I can't say I'm not terrified to take the next step with Mads, but everything you showed me and the things we talked about will hopefully give me the courage to be what she needs. The thought of her with someone else makes me want to set this entire world on fire."

He continues facing forward, looking out the windshield like he can see every part of his past. There's still a sadness lingering over his face, but I let it go. When he wants to tell me more, he will. As if he's snapping back to reality, he shakes his head before turning to me.

"Take good care of her, Becks. And don't let her go. Take it from me. Losing her will be the biggest regret of your life."

"Thanks, man," I say, before giving him a look of gratitude. I get out of his car and watch him drive away before turning and walking through the door.

As soon as I enter, I can tell the house is empty. Every light is off, and the only sound is coming from the running refrigerator in the kitchen. I head toward the island and immediately notice a piece of paper. Holding it in my hand, I read it silently.

Blaze,

I'm out for the evening. I might be back late, so don't wait up. I'll be quiet when I get back since I'm sure practice tired you out. There are protein cookies in the tin on the counter if you're craving something sweet. See you in the morning.

xoxo,

Mads

ANOTHER FUCKING DATE. I have no idea if the guys she's been out with are from a regular dating app or the BDSM app she signed up for. The thought of the latter has me mindlessly shoving my hand into the liquor cabinet, looking for something strong. I find a bottle of Macallan single malt scotch and pour myself a generous glass. Letting the alcohol burn my throat, I swallow before walking down the hall to the office. I don't bother turning on the light before sitting at my desk and opening my laptop.

Clicking in the search bar, I take a moment to decide what I'm even looking for. I don't think it is a good move to jump into the deep end of the BDSM pool right off the bat, but there has to be something I can do to show Mads that I have what it takes to give her what she needs.

An hour later, I feel like I have a good idea of where to start. I've spent time reading the numerous lists of dos and don'ts and I feel confident that what I have in mind will bring mind-blowing pleasure to my girl. Every time doubt tries to creep into my head, I push it away. There's no room here for me to be nervous about this. If I can't go through with it, I'll be forced to watch Mads get it from somebody else.

The truth is, the thought of dominating her is making me harder than I've ever been. I want this. I just hope she'll trust me to care for her in this way. Because as hot as it is thinking about the things I want to do to her, I can't do any of them without her consent. She has to submit to me. And once she does, I'll show her that she'll never need another man. It'll be me until the day I die.

Closing my laptop, I glance at the clock that sits on my desk. It's almost two in the morning. The bars close soon and she'll be home. Unless her date goes well, that is. The thought has me finishing what's left in my glass before returning to the kitchen for a refill.

I keep the lights off as I sit, waiting, trying not to lose my fucking mind at the thought of my girl ending up in bed tonight next to some sorry son of a bitch that isn't me.

TWENTY-SEVEN
MADS

I QUIETLY OPEN THE DOOR, tiptoeing inside the dark house. Deciding to walk all the way home from the bar in this cold weather wasn't my best idea, but it seemed fitting that my awful date would end with me punishing myself for swiping right on yet another fuckboy. All that walk did was freeze my limbs and intensify the ache that's been residing between my legs since the night Blaze got me off.

I could go up to my room, get in the shower with one of my toys, and try to chase my own release, but I still haven't been able to orgasm on my own. I'm reminded of how quickly Blaze had me coming undone without even having to put his hands on me. That was weeks ago. *No wonder I've been such a mess.*

I signed up for the kink app Dia suggested, but everyone I've met on there just feels wrong. Maybe it's because I haven't been in a dom/sub relationship for a while, or maybe Brady bringing up our past at dinner rattled me. Either way, I know these things can't be forced, so I've been sticking to regular dating apps for now. Nothing has come of any of it, which has made getting my mind off Blaze even more difficult. I don't even think I care anymore that fucking him could put my whole future in jeopardy. Even though I told him we couldn't, I don't think I'd have the strength to tell him no if he made a move. He's probably balls deep inside some super-model as we speak anyway, so I shouldn't even be thinking about him.

I'm startled from my sad revelation when a shadow in the corner of the kitchen catches my eye. My survival instincts kick in as I chuck my bag toward what I can only assume is a masked murderer, sending the contents sailing in all directions. As my eyes adjust to the darkness of the room, I realize the familiar face staring blankly at me.

"Jesus Christ, Blaze! You scared the shit out of me! You're lucky I didn't have a shank in my pocket!" I take off my jacket, setting it on the back of one of the kitchen chairs. He continues staring as I reach for my phone that's lying face down on the hardwood. "If I turn this over and the screen is cracked, you're paying for an upgrade. And I'm going all out. You'll spare no expense." I look up again and see that his stare has turned into something darker. He still doesn't speak as he drains what's left of the dark amber liquid in his glass. Finally cutting into the silence, his eyes bore into mine.

"Another date? Let me guess. He couldn't get the job done."

I am pretty sure he's at least a little less than sober because I'm not understanding where this conversation is headed. "The job?" I ask, raising an eyebrow.

"Yeah. I've been watching you go out with these losers every night, but you always come home with that same look on your face." He stands and stalks toward me, lowering his voice. Chills run through me as I feel moisture start to gather between my legs at the sound. "Do you want to know why? Because you're unsatisfied. It's going to take more than some *little boy* to scratch that itch you have. You need a real man. Someone who will worship every inch of your body like the queen you are."

At first, I'm stunned silent. I try to breathe, but the air between us is thick. He's so close, he could lean onto the balls of his feet and kiss me. For a moment, I think he might. But if he wanted to, he could've done it while I was beneath him in my bed. From the way he's put himself back into friend territory, it's clear that he's moved on from whatever it was he was feeling that night.

I need to get out of here, and fast before I do something stupid like give in to my urge to taste his lips. When I finally break free from the invisible hold he has on me, I turn to walk toward the stairs. I get two steps before I feel his hand dig into my scalp, tightening around my curls. I gasp as his free hand grips my waist and he walks us forward, my back to his front, until I'm trapped between him and the wall.

My breathing is shallow and ragged as he leans his mouth to my ear. The scent of his cologne with a hint of whiskey overtakes me as his low growl tells me that he's finally snapped.

Thank. Fuck.

"I'm done watching you come home like this, baby. I know you ache, right here." He lowers the hand on my waist down to the apex of my legs, brushing my clit over the thin lace of my panties. I jump as the light contact sends a jolt through me. "I bet you're dripping. I can smell it from here. And I'd bet every dime I have that nobody's even come close to getting you as hot as I did."

I remember that night, vividly. And he's right. I've been on a handful of dates. I haven't been able to get past the kissing stage with any of them. I've been chasing that feeling Blaze had given me without even touching me, but it's been impossible to replicate.

"Please, Blaze. I need you." I let out a strangled breath in relief as I feel myself submitting to him.

That's all he needs before he spins me to face him and grabs under my ass, lifting me. He crashes his lips to mine in a bruising kiss that steals what little breath I have left in my lungs. Electricity flows through my body, crackling from the tips of my fingers and toes before gathering in my core. He tastes amazing. I instinctively wrap my legs around his waist as he brings me to the closest bed and lowers us down, his tongue still invading my mouth. I'm pretty sure we're in one of the guest rooms, but I could be wrong. My brain has checked out until further notice.

Pulling his mouth from mine, he stands over me. The moonlight filtering through the window gives me just enough visibility to see that he's shirtless, his chiseled abs on display. Gray sweatpants hang low on his hips, the evidence of his arousal tenting the material. He's fucking breathtaking. And he's about to be mine...even if it's just for tonight.

Blaze wastes no time lifting my dress over my head, leaving me in my black lace bra and panties. He stares down, seeing the darkened spot between my legs before letting out a feral groan and ripping them down my legs. "You're fucking soaked, baby. And I'm starving."

I'm panting as he grabs me around my waist and drags me up the bed. Laying my head on the pillow, he kneels between my legs, leaning in for another kiss that quickly turns frantic. His hand finds my nipple through my bra as the other reaches behind my body to free me of the tight lace. Backing away slightly, he takes me in. "You are fucking stunning, Mads. Do you even realize that?" he says as he lowers his mouth to my other breast, nipping at the tight bud before soothing it with his tongue. I moan loudly, still unable and unwilling to even try to form an intelligent sentence.

All I can manage is a breathy *"Blaze. Fuck."*

He chuckles as he continues his descent down my body, dipping his tongue into my belly button before making a wet trail past where I need him most. He drops firm open-mouthed kisses to my inner thighs, making the throb in my pussy even more excruciating as I feel a drop of my arousal slide down my lips and through the crack of my ass.

Just as I'm ready to start begging again, Blaze stops his torture and flattens his tongue over my slit. He drags it upward, quickly flicking it over my clit before he stops to look at me. "Listen carefully, Mads. I'm going to eat this beautiful cunt of yours until you come on my face. And I'm not going to stop. You can scream, beg, and cry. I won't be removing my tongue from between these legs until I decide you're done. And when I do, I'll replace it with my cock and fuck you full of my cum. Are you sure you want to do this?" I try to clamp my legs shut for some friction, but he wrenches them back apart, waiting for my answer. "Use your words baby."

I did not have 'Blaze Beckham Being Dominant in Bed' on my Bingo card for this year.

Breathing as though I just ran a marathon, I reply. "Y-yes."

"Such a good girl for me," he praises. "What's your safe word?"

It takes me a minute to register because I've never had a guy ask for a safe word then give me vanilla sex. But I suppose I already know he plans to be a little rough with me. Does he know the depraved way I want to be treated? He couldn't possibly.

"Kiwi," I answer.

He repeats the word, committing it to memory before he leans forward to feast. There's nothing gentle about the way he works his mouth and it's everything I need. He alternates from using his tongue to fuck my pussy, to flicking it with just the right amount of pressure. It feels like only seconds before my legs begin to shake. This is it. The orgasm that I've been unsuccessfully trying to replicate is building so fast I can barely breathe. Blaze continues his skilled assault, replacing his tongue with his thumb, rubbing my clit from side to side. "Come on. Give it to me," he practically growls. "This orgasm is mine. I've fucked my hand so many times thinking about what you sounded like when you came for me." His mouth returns to my swollen, aching clit as I detonate, my orgasm violently ripping through my body. My legs spasm uncontrollably as I ascend into another dimension.

After what seems like seconds and hours all at once, I begin to float back down to Earth, my clit becoming sensitive. Staying true to his word, Blaze continues to lick and suck at me. The muscles in my stomach contract and I can't help slamming my thighs to his ears.

"Blaze! Please! I need a s-second," I whine. The words come out choked as I beg him to let my body fully recover before he continues. But I may as well be talking to a wall because he doesn't even hear me. Blaze continues licking my overstimulated clit as he pushes a thick finger inside me. He lightens the pressure of his tongue as he adds another finger to my pussy, pumping them in and out to the beat of my thudding heart, which I wouldn't be surprised if he could actually hear. I try to squirm away, but he holds my hips in place.

Seconds later, I'm surprised as another orgasm hits me out of nowhere. I lose control of my body, screaming into the dark room and convulsing wildly as Blaze continues to finger fuck me through my release. I can hear my wetness as his fingers quickly move in and out of my body. I see literal stars, and black starts to overtake my vision. As I come down, I realize I'm crying. I've lost control of myself physically and emotionally. Part of it is the overstimulation, but part of it is also relief. He can't possibly know how he's just set free a part of me that I try so hard to hide.

"It's okay, baby. I've got you," Blaze coos as he slows his fingers, but doesn't stop completely.

"Wh-what are you doing? Please. I just need a second," I beg shamelessly. It hurts, but not enough for me to want him to stop.

He finally relents, moving his body up mine before kissing me gently. I barely get a taste of myself from his tongue before he pulls away and looks down at me. "I've been waiting to put my mouth on you for what seems like a lifetime. And baby, it was worth every single second of agony I felt." He leans back in, kissing me so passionately that I can almost feel my heart busting out from the wall I've placed it behind. I should be worried about how this will change things for us, but I can't bring myself to care when being under Blaze feels like the only thing that matters. Having his arms around me and his mouth on me feels like home.

It's then that I realize he's still wearing pants and is probably painfully hard. Gathering what little strength I have left in my still shaking body, I reach down and pull his sweats and boxer briefs down enough for his thick cock to spring free. I look down to see that he's leaking pre-cum. The sight gives me a second wind as I shove him away, rolling on top of him.

I smile down at this beautiful man, my mouth watering as I grab on to his hard shaft. "I need to taste you," I say, licking the wetness from the tip before taking him into my mouth.

TWENTY-EIGHT
BLAZE

OH, fuck. Mads is sucking my cock. The girl of my dreams is on top of me, sucking my cock and it feels so fucking good.

Wait. No.

I'm supposed to be in control. That's what she needs and that's what I'm here to give her. I wasn't anticipating her flipping the script on me. Because right now, I'm anything but in charge. I'm at her fucking mercy as she runs her hot, wet tongue up my shaft from base to tip. She moans, bringing me to the back of her throat before gagging on my length. I allow myself just a few more seconds of what is already the best blow job of my life before I regroup and try to figure out how to get the control back, internally panicking because how the fuck am I supposed to stop her right now?

Think, Beckham. Think.

WWTD. What Would Tanner Do?

Gathering all the strength I have, I dig my hand into Mads' hair, gripping and pulling her face to mine.

"I'm sorry, baby. Did you think you were in charge here?" I chide. Her lips are glistening, and her eyes are wide as she stares at me. "Only good girls who ask nicely get to suck my cock. And you have been very, very bad." I tighten my grip on her hair, making her wince slightly, followed by a low groan.

She fucking loves it.

Spurred by the sight of how aroused she is, I flip us over so Mads is under me. I reach down and shuck my sweats and boxer briefs that she only managed to get down to my knees.

"Open for me," I say.

She opens her fucking *mouth.*

"I meant your legs, baby." I smirk. "But since you've decided to be good for me all of a sudden, I think you deserve a reward."

I'm taking a big fucking risk here. And I'm out of my comfort zone, but something is telling me that what I'm about to do is exactly the kind of thing my dirty girl gets off on.

I use my thumb and forefinger under her chin to open her mouth wider before spitting into it.

"Swallow," I tell her, firmly.

She moans and closes her mouth, following my command.

I can't help but rock my hips, rubbing my hard-as-steel cock against her. She meets her hips with mine, thrust for thrust. "Good fucking girl, Mads," I say, slowing my movements before I blow without even being inside her. "I'm going to fuck you now, baby."

She lets out a whine. I know she's still sensitive from her orgasms and I want this to be good for her. How much pain is too much? Should I give her body some time or should I push in and pound her into the mattress?

Maybe I can't be this guy for her.

"Blaze," she whispers, pulling me from my thoughts. I look into her eyes and see a hint of trepidation. "I...can I tell you something?"

"Anything," I reply, still rubbing my cock slowly against her dripping heat because I can't stop myself.

"I like pain. During sex. I want you to hurt me." She looks nervous, but hopeful. And the thought of her trusting me enough to ask for this flips a switch inside me, reminding me that I am giving her exactly what she wants.

I kiss her again before I reach up and put my hand around her throat, slowly adding pressure. It's not enough to cut off her air supply, but I know she's fuzzy-headed as I finally sink myself into her, completely bare. I've never, ever fucked without a condom. I probably should've asked, but I can't imagine putting anything between us. I know she's on birth control because I've seen her take it before her morning coffee. "My dirty little slut wants to be fucked hard, doesn't she?" I coo before leaning down to press my lips to her cheek.

"Yes, Daddy."

Don't come. Don't come. Don't come.

Mads' pussy is tighter than I could've ever imagined. I rut into her like a man possessed. My hand is still on her throat, but I've taken away the pressure. I want her completely in her right mind for this. I want her to remember how I made her feel the next time she thinks she has to find someone else to give her what she needs.

"You take Daddy's cock so well, baby. This pussy was made to be used by me," I grit out as I continue slamming into her. I pull back onto my knees, gripping her hips and lifting them off the bed. There's not a chance in hell she won't have ten perfect finger-shaped bruises on them tomorrow, but I don't give a single fuck. She wants me to hurt her. And I think I like it, too.

Trusting that she'll use her safe word if she needs to, I pull out and flip her over. Yanking her hips into the air, I set her on her knees before pushing her head down to the pillow. "Arch that back for me," I say as I slap her ass, hard. "Look at that beautiful handprint. It's like art next to your swollen pussy and tight little asshole," I say as I begin fucking into her again. She moans so loudly, I'm sure everyone in Boston can hear. And fuck if I'm not proud.

When I look down, I see the prettiest fucking sight. Next

to her head, she fists the sheets. Her ass bounces with every thrust of my hips. I look down at where we're joined to see my cock glistening with her arousal every time I pull back. This is fucking heaven. Better than any touchdown or trophy I've ever gotten.

"Tell me," I say, grabbing her by the hair and pulling her up so my mouth is right at her ear while I continue thrusting into her. "Any of those little boys you've been out with fuck you like this? Did they give this wet little cunt the punishment it craves?"

"No," she whimpers.

"That's because it belongs to me, baby," I growl into her ear. "It always fucking has."

Her walls start to tighten around me, and I realize that my possessiveness is turning her on even more. Maybe I'm a selfish son-of-a-bitch, but I use that power for my own benefit.

"Whose pussy is this, Mads?" I ask. She doesn't reply at first. I can tell her orgasm is about to hit and I know I'll follow her as soon as she clamps down on me, so I don't have much time left and I *need* to hear her say it.

Releasing her hair, I shove her between the shoulder blades, pressing her face back down to the bed before slapping her ass again. "Answer me," I demand. "Who owns this fucking pussy?"

"You do! I'm yours, Blaze!" she yells as she comes hard. She's not just wet anymore. She's actually running down the back of her thighs and the front of mine. The sounds we're making are nothing less than obscene. Her legs are shaking, and she has me in a vice grip as I pound into her one more time before I fill her, grunting through the most intense orgasm of my life.

I lay down, rolling onto my side before pulling her back to my front. She's still shaking a little as I run my hand over her hair, smoothing it away from her face. Mads sighs contently as her breathing becomes less erratic. My heart squeezes and I realize that I'm fully fucking gone for her now. I don't even want to attempt fighting it anymore.

"You did such a good job, pretty girl," I praise before kissing the back of her head. "I'll be right back."

I remember my research, and aftercare is the most important part of all of this. I have to make sure she's okay after that. I quickly run to the bathroom, clean myself up, grab a warm washcloth, and fill a glass with water before returning to find Mads out cold in the bed. I chuckle quietly and set the glass on the nightstand before gently wiping between her legs with the cloth. She doesn't move at all other than her slow, shallow breathing and soft snores as I climb back into bed and wrap my arms around her.

"Good night, baby. I love you," I whisper into the quiet room before dozing off peacefully within seconds.

TWENTY-NINE
MADS

I SLOWLY DRIFT AWAKE, memories from last night filling my head as I come to. I open my eyes to see that I'm completely naked, alone in Blaze's bed. I know I didn't fall asleep in here. Was I that out of it after my life-changing orgasms that I don't remember walking upstairs?

How did I get here? Did I sleep alone? Where is Blaze? He had to have carried me up here after we had sex. I was so sated and exhausted that I was dead to the world before he even returned from the bathroom.

Before I allow myself to overthink the fact that I woke up by myself, I sit up and get out of bed. I cross the hallway to my own room, making a beeline for the bathroom so I can clean up and brush my teeth. I can't help but look over my reflection in the mirror. My hair is a knotted mess. My nipples are peaked from the cold air in the room. There is a smattering of small bruises decorating my hips, no doubt from Blaze's fingers as he fucked me from behind.

I turn to find several red handprints covering my backside. I feel a rush of arousal between my legs at the sight of them. Last night was everything I've been needing. I would've never expected Blaze to be the type to take control, but it was like he'd been doing it all his life. I can't believe I've been living with him this long, fighting my attraction, just to have him prove to me that he's perfect for me in every possible way. As exciting as it all is, I can't shake the intrusive feelings in the back of my mind that are telling me we just complicated our relationship by sleeping together. But I owe it to the both of us not to panic or freak out. At least not until we talk about what all this means for us.

I return to my room, throwing on my silk robe. I definitely need to shower and figure out what to do with this mess of hair, but first, *coffee*.

As soon as I reach the bottom of the stairs, I'm stopped in my tracks by the sight in front of me. Blaze stands at the stove in nothing but a pair of black boxer briefs, flipping sausage links on the griddle. Holy fuck, he's even hotter now that I'm allowing myself to openly gawk at him. The muscles in his back and shoulders ripple under his taut skin. His ass looks so good, it takes all my self-control not to walk over and take a bite out of it. I don't realize my heavy breathing until he turns around.

"See something you can't live without, Baby Doll?" he winks.

I can only smile at him because, yes, I do. But I can't find the right words to tell him that before he turns back to his breakfast. Making my way over to the coffee maker, I'm relieved to see he's already brewed a fresh pot. I fill a mug and head to the refrigerator to grab the creamer, but I'm halted when a strong arm snakes around my waist from behind.

"You smell so fucking good," Blaze says, burying his face in my neck. "I can't get enough of you." I sigh as his warm lips ghost over my skin before he darts his tongue out for a taste. He continues leisurely licking and sucking at my neck and earlobes while I moan under his touch. It feels like heaven. I loved the dominant side he showed me last night, but this part of him that's slow and exploratory is a welcome contrast. I want them both. I want all of him.

"Mmmm," he mumbles into my neck. "Do you know how good it feels to finally be able to touch you without worrying that you'll punch me in the junk?"

I laugh. "I still might if you don't let me go long enough to drink my coffee."

Blaze kisses me once before releasing me. He turns back to the stove and plates breakfast while I caffeinate.

"So," he says between bites of egg. "We should talk about last night."

"Do we have to?" I groan.

"Last time, I thought it would be best to ignore everything and act normal, but in hindsight, we should've talked the next morning. Shit ended up awkward and I thought I was going to lose you. I just want an open line of communication. We have to be honest with each other if this is going to work."

I want to ask him what *this* is, but I stop myself. I'm falling hard for Blaze and the last thing I want to hear is that he isn't there yet. Or that he never will be. So I let him lead the conversation, hoping he'll give me some indication that he feels the same way I do.

"I don't regret a single thing we did last night. And I meant everything I said. I've been waiting a long time to get you into my bed, and I know I don't want to spend another night sleeping without you. Unless I'm on the road. But I still want you there when I'm not. We wasted too much time fighting this. I don't want to do that anymore."

Okay, well that provided zero clarity.

I think about my next words before I say them out loud. "I don't want to do that either. Why don't we just take things one day at a time? We can have fun and see where it takes us."

He smiles softly before rounding the island and pulling me into his arms. Weaving his fingers into my hair, he tips my head up and brings his lips to mine. We kiss passionately for what feels like seconds and hours all at once before he pulls away. "Finish your coffee, dirty girl. I'll go grab your iPad so we can go over my schedule for today."

I roll my eyes playfully as he starts toward the hall. "Blaze?"

He stops in the doorway, turning back to me. "Yeah, baby?"

"How long have you been into, ummm…kink?" I ask, scared of his answer. I don't even want to think about him sharing the kinds of things we did with anyone else.

"Since last night." He winks before walking off, leaving me both confused and surprised.

BLAZE

"Wait. What?" I hear her say from behind me, her bare feet slapping quickly against the hardwood floors.

Fuck.

I just waxed poetic about how we need to be honest with each other, so there's no way I'll lie to her about this. I reach the office with Mads hot on my heels. I know her. She won't let this one go. I turn to face her, deciding that we need to get everything on the table so we can really start exploring with one another.

"First of all, just know that I wasn't eavesdropping on purpose," I say nervously, making her eyes widen immediately. "Yesterday when you were talking to Dia, your door was open, and your speakerphone was pretty loud. I heard her talking about that BDSM app and, I don't know. The thought of you doing those things with somebody else?" I pause, trying to calm myself. "I saw red. I wanted to tear the whole city apart with my bare hands."

She pushes her shoulders back and lifts her chin defiantly. I can tell I'm not going to like whatever she says next, but I'm all in with her. We'll work it out. "You don't *own me*, Blaze."

My initial instinct is to placate her and diffuse the situation. To tell her I know I don't own her. That she's a grown woman who can make her own decisions about what she does and with who. But from the research I did yesterday, I know that a lot of submissives like to give control outside of the bedroom. The strong-willed look in her eyes is telling me she's standing her ground, but the rough swallow and visible pulse in her neck is telling me something completely different. I decide to test the waters, taking two confident steps in her direction. The hitch in her breath spurs me into action as I close the rest of the distance between us.

I reach out, closing my hand around her throat as I bring my mouth to her ear. "That's where you're wrong, Baby Doll. I *do* fucking own you. From now on, the only tongue that will be tasting your cunt is mine. The only cock you'll be coming on," I grind my hard length into her clit, earning me a soft moan, "is mine." I pull back, looking into her eyes while I continue adding pressure to her throat. Her eyes flutter as her face begins to turn a beautiful shade of pink. *Holy fuck, I'm so goddamn hard right now.* "Do you understand?" Loosening my grip, I wait for her answer.

"Yes," she breathes.

"Good girl," I say, kissing her lips gently. I hear her contented exhale as I turn to the desk and thank God that didn't all just blow up in my face. I grab her iPad and hand it to her. "We doing this in here or are you too far away from your emotional support coffee mug to concentrate?"

She scoffs, sitting in her fluffy chair before opening her calendar app. "Not sure there's enough caffeine for today," she huffs a breath. "You have an offensive team meeting at nine. Practice with a full walkthrough for tomorrow's game will go from ten-thirty to three. After that, I assume you'll watch game tape for a while, so I left you an open slot of time for that. I need you to stop by the tailors on your way back to get your tux for the Children's Hospital fundraiser fitted. I sent your measurements, but they need you to try it on. Then, you have a video interview with Bruce Meyers from BSN at six. I'll have everything set up for you here in the office when you get back. I told them they could only have you for fifteen minutes because you'll need to rest this evening. You play the Hurricanes tomorrow afternoon and you'll be dragging ass on the field if you aren't in bed by eight-thirty."

"Hopefully, I'll be in *you* by eight-thirty," I say with a wink.

She rolls her eyes playfully, setting the iPad down on her desk. "Yeah, I'm definitely going to need more coffee."

God, I fucking love her already. I decide not to take my chances this morning by repeating the words I know she probably isn't ready to hear. Instead, I give her a tender kiss on the forehead before tackling what promises to be the longest day of my week.

THIRTY
MADS

I'M in the living room, scrolling through my phone for last night's hockey highlights. As much as I love football, it takes some effort for me to really get into other sports. I like them, but for some reason, the stats and facts just don't stick in my head the same. In order to make sure I'm prepared for the workday ahead, I spend at least an hour every morning checking scores and watching highlight reels from each game. Even though I'm off today, the grind never stops. I'll need to know what went on over the weekend for my Monday assignments.

I'm in the middle of a video showing Lars Kanken's hat trick when I hear my name being called from down the hall.

"Mads?" Blaze yells. "Baby, can you come here for a minute?"

I hop up, because I'd rob a bank for him if he called me baby first, and pad toward the office. I've never been one to enjoy cute pet names in the past. But coming from him, I swear I melt into a puddle every time. When I arrive at the office, I find him sitting at his desk, shirtless. My mouth waters instantly and I imagine myself kneeling next to his desk as I wait for him to tell me what to do. Maybe he'd tell me to get under and suck his cock while he did a video inter-view. He'd caress my hair and use all of his self-control not to groan when I took him to the back of my throat.

I snap out of my fantasy to see Blaze staring at me, one brow raised.

"I don't even want to know what you were just thinking about, dirty girl." He pauses. "On second thought, yes I do."

I roll my eyes, trying to tamp down my arousal as I walk over to him. When his laptop screen comes into view, I see a black page with a bunch of multiple-choice questions. "What is this?" I ask him.

He reaches for me, pulling me into his lap before he buries his face into my neck. I sigh, relaxing into his touch like it's my lifeline. Like he wasn't just inside me eight hours ago. "It's a kink quiz," he mumbles, hot breath fanning against my skin.

Trying to keep my composure, I look forward. "I've taken one before," I moan when he coasts his lips down the side of my neck. "That's how I— how I found out what I like." I can feel the wetness already pooling between my legs as he continues. "Did you take it?"

He pulls away, knowing I'm fighting for my life trying to stay focused, and turns my body so I can see him better. "I haven't yet. I was hoping we could take it together, so we can see if we're sexually compatible."

I scoff. "Blaze, I saw *God* the other night. I'm pretty sure we're compatible. Unless it wasn't good for you." Concern hits me like a truck. I was so wiped out; I didn't even ask how it was for him.

He grabs my chin, pulling my gaze to his. "Baby, I have never felt anything like that in my life. I'm sure this is the last thing you want to hear, but I haven't exactly been an angel. I've been with a good number of women, and it's never *ever* been like that before. The fact that you trusted me with your needs was so fucking hot. I still can't stop thinking about it."

Just then, he thrusts his hips up, showing me exactly what the memories from that night are doing to him.

I giggle, turning back to the computer. "Okay, but don't look. I want the results to be accurate, so I need some privacy. Actually," I say, hopping off his lap, "you take yours here. I'll do it on my phone."

"Sounds good, Baby Doll. Then we can compare our results and talk about everything. We should probably discuss soft and hard limits at some point, too."

I stop in my tracks, a warm feeling taking over my body. I know Blaze wasn't into kink before he overheard that phone call. The fact that he's put time into researching everything, *for me*, has me feeling all sorts of things. I'm equal parts turned on, giddy, and scared shitless, but I'm not going to let my emotions drive this ship. I really like Blaze. I might even be falling in love with him. And as much as I know how badly all of this could complicate my future, I'm having a hard time rationalizing that anymore. Especially after the other night. The way he took care of me. The way he gave me everything I needed like he had a direct line to my brain and body. As confused as I should be about it all...I'm just *not*. It's all crystal clear in my head. I want Blaze. I want to keep doing this with him.

I lean forward, capturing his lips with mine before turning away and heading toward the living room. I grab my phone off the couch and return to see Blaze hard at work on his quiz. I do the same, pulling up my browser and finding the same one he's taking. The questions are all pretty standard as far as I'm concerned. And when I'm done, I'm not surprised in the least by my results. But I'll admit, I'm really curious to see his.

Since he's new at this, he's going to find out things he probably never knew about himself. I can't say it wasn't a shock to me the first time I took a kink quiz and it told me I was ninety-nine percent submissive. I'm also ninety-three percent rope bunny and eighty-seven percent masochist. To nobody's surprise, all of my quizzes have also highlighted my brat tendencies. Something about being punished for misbehaving makes me want to do it that much more.

Once I'm finished, I wait patiently for Blaze. I watch him repeatedly click his mouse, his brows furrowing, then shooting up toward his hairline. He makes a few audible noises as though he's surprised by the audacity of the questions before dramatically hitting the return button on his keyboard and sitting back in his chair.

I can't help the laugh that comes out of me.

"Something funny?" he asks.

"I'm just trying to figure out which questions had your eyebrows ready to yeet themselves into outer space," I reply.

He raises a brow. "Nobody says 'yeet' anymore."

"Oh really?" I reply, looking around the room. "Are the Yeet Police going to come and arrest me? Let me live, Blaze." I return to the matter at hand as he huffs a breath, feigning annoyance.

Tapping my bottom lip, I pretend to think. "Anyway, I'm thinking maybe it was the question about pet play." I wiggle my brows at him. "Or maybe it was the one about letting your partner pee on you," I joke.

His face twists dramatically as he scoffs in disgust. "I'm not trying to kink shame, but I'm never letting you pee on me."

"Peeing is a hard limit. Noted," I say, chuckling. "Anyway, I'm dying for your results."

He looks at me nervously. "You first."

I turn my phone to him. He takes it from me, spending some time reading down the line of kinks. I wasn't surprised by any of it, and by the looks of it, neither is he. "Rope bunny, huh?" he says, a sly grin blooming on his lips. "Looks like we are a good match. I'm ninety-one percent rigger." I can't help the throb between my thighs at the thought of him tying me up and using me for his pleasure. "Fuck, I can't wait to try that out," he says, as if his mind is exactly where mine is.

I stand behind him, looking over his shoulder at the results of his quiz. I knew we'd be compatible, but I had no idea that we would complement each other so well. Where I am submissive, he is dominant. Where I am a brat, he is a tamer. He even has my degradation kink covered.

"Looks like we're a perfect match," I say, looking down at him. The words, as simple as they are in this situation, hold so much meaning. When I first met Blaze, I did feel an instant physical attraction between the two of us. But after pushing it down for so long, when I finally allowed myself to face the way I felt about him, I was shocked that the initial attraction had grown into something much deeper. There have been so many nights where we've just talked about life, or sometimes nothing at all. The silences are never awkward, but I also feel like we could talk all day and never run out of things to say to each other. I don't think I've ever met another person besides Dia that understands me the way Blaze does. He's the calm in the crazy storm of my life right now. It could all come crashing down and I know I'd be safe with him.

Holy shit. *I love him.*

I wait for the feelings of panic to set in. That lump in my throat that comes whenever I make a decision that I'll immediately regret. But there's *nothing*. Only peace. That, in and of itself, should scare me. And in a way, it does. But not in the way I expect. I'm no longer afraid to give Blaze my heart. If I'm being honest with myself, it's been his since the moment he saved me from having to leave my internship by opening his home to me. Maybe even before then.

Everything that used to worry me about being with Blaze has changed. I think my main fear now is that I won't be enough for him. He's dated actresses, supermodels, and some of the most beautiful women in the world. He's rich, famous, and successful. I'm just out of college, desperately trying to get hired at Tailgate so I can start my career in a field where women are disrespected and told they don't belong. I may never make it. I could end up back in Chicago, working at the local newspaper, not even making a livable wage. Then what? I make Blaze Beckham the laughingstock of the NFL as his loser girlfriend? Getting upset every time I scroll through Instagram comments calling me a "gold digger" and telling him he can do better? How long could we endure that before he'd start to believe it? *That's* my fear.

I'm brought back to reality when Blaze stands, his hands cradling my face. "Where'd you go?"

I shake my head, bringing my focus back to the here and now. "Nowhere. Just thinking," I say, hoping he'll let it go. Thankfully, he does by pulling my face to his and kissing me slowly.

He pulls away, leaving me breathless. "Whatever you're thinking, quit it. We said we'd take it one day at a time and have fun exploring with each other. Wherever it goes, we let it. Right?" he reassures me. And it really does make me feel better.

"Right," I whisper.

"That's my girl," he replies. "Let's go shower so I can get you dirty all over again."

THIRTY-ONE
MADS

"HOLY SHIT," I say in amazement as I descend the steps leading to the first row. Blaze talked me into taking a little vacation this weekend since the Blizzard are playing in Tampa Bay. It wasn't like he had to do too much convincing. We haven't seen the first snowfall in Boston just yet, but the air has been so chilly. It wouldn't be football season without thick hoodies and beanies, but a getaway to a warm location was definitely a much-needed break for me.

I don't know how he managed to score these tickets, but I guess when you're playing in the game and you have a boatload of money to offer, you can buy anything you want. I am on the fifty-yard line, right behind the Blizzard's bench. The home team is still in the locker room, but our guys are on the field doing warmups. I watch Blaze as he leisurely stretches his quads before doing a few sprints up the sideline. I've been to a few home games to watch him, but it's always been in a suite. I've never been this close to him while he played. And fuck, he looks good.

I watch him as he continues warming up, lining up next to Tanner to go through plays. I'll never get over how they play like they share a brain. As soon as Tanner rolls back, Blaze is off the line, ready with open hands for the throw. They're effortless.

I'm pulled back to reality when a woman in a white blouse tucked into a burgundy skirt walks in front of me. She stops near the bench, getting herself settled in front of a cameraman who has obviously been awaiting her arrival. It takes me a moment, but when I realize who she is, my jaw hits the ground in front of me.

Molly McMahon.

The journalist I saw at that very first game with my dad. The woman I aspired to be when I was eight years old. My hero.

I'm shocked as she turns, motioning toward Blaze to come over. He tosses the ball in his hands back to Tanner before jogging her way with a dimpled smile. He gives her a quick side-hug and they fall into a friendly conversation. I'd like to say I'm jealous of her, getting to be so close to him right now. But honestly, I'm more jealous of him. He has no idea he's doing an interview with the woman who made me want to be a sports reporter all those years ago. Blaze doesn't know who she is to me, but I'll definitely be filling him in on that fun fact later when I grill him for information on what she's like in real life.

I watch intently as they put on their game faces and turn to the camera for the interview. Unfortunately, I can't hear them, but I can see how comfortable they are talking about the game.

They finish up and go back to their friendly conversation. I watch with rapt attention as Blaze turns and points to me, saying something to her while she nods her head in approval. Next thing I know, Blaze has taken off toward the tunnel while Molly heads my way, smiling.

On instinct, I look around, making sure she's actually coming over here for me, but the seats around me are still empty. I turn back to see her standing right in front of me. I try desperately to look normal, like I'm not having a full-on fangirl moment on the inside, when she extends her hand toward me.

"Hello, Madison," she says. "I'm Molly. Blaze mentioned you were on your way to becoming a reporter and I wanted to come introduce myself."

I lean over the railing, stretching my arm to shake her hand. "Ms. McMahon," I say, swallowing the lump in my throat. "You've been my idol since I was a little girl. I saw you interview Jonathan Walters when I was eight years old and decided I wanted to be you when I grew up."

She throws her head back in a laugh. "Wow! I'm so flattered. Things weren't always easy for me back then, being a woman in this industry. I'm so glad to hear I inspired you."

I give her a warm smile. I know how it is for us today. I can't even imagine the pushback she got over a decade ago. Although we've come a long way, there's still so many changes that need to be made. In sports journalism, not only do women have to worry about wage gaps, discrimination, and sexual harassment, but we also have to fight that much harder to be taken seriously. Molly paved the way for girls like me to have a chance at doing what we love.

She interrupts my thoughts by speaking again. "If Blaze Beckham is endorsing your talent, I look forward to seeing you on the sidelines soon."

I hardly know what to say. But I do know that meeting her has given me even more of a drive to succeed. So that, maybe one day, I can inspire other little girls to follow their dreams the way I did mine. "Thank you, Molly. It was so nice meeting you."

"If you ever need anything, Blaze knows how to contact me. I'd love to chat more when I don't have a bunch of giant man-babies to wrangle for interviews," she says with an exaggerated eye roll.

I laugh before reaching down to shake her hand again.

"I'd love that." And then she's on her way to the other side of the field. *Holy fuck. Did that just happen?* I just met my hero and now I have a new fire burning inside of me to finish my internship and show Jacob Shane that I belong at Tailgate Media permanently.

BLAZE

"Let's fucking go, boys!" I yell through my mouthguard as we line up for the next play. We're down by a touchdown with less than a minute on the clock. It's fourth down, and unless we convert here, we'll be turning the ball back over to the Copperheads. Their defense has been on Tanner all day, blitzing every chance they get. Our offensive linemen have been working their asses off trying to protect him, but Tampa has the best rushers in the league, and they came to play.

Tan must see the blitz coming because he calls an audible. "Kill! Kill! Kill!" he yells, using both hands to point at his helmet. The crowd is doing their best to drown him out, so I listen carefully for the new play, although I already have an idea.

"Black twenty-two!" he yells before stepping forward and readying his hands for the snap. It's a hot route, and if I can execute it perfectly, I should be able to get to the ball. Tanner signals for the snap and I take off like a rocket. Thankfully, the defense hasn't had time to react to our changed play, so I'm able to beat my defender. I run down-field about twenty yards before slanting toward the middle, looking for the pass that I already know is coming my way. The cornerback is making a beeline for me as the ball hits my hands, but I manage to juke him as he lunges for me. Realizing I've broken free, I run as fast as I can, knowing it's just me and their safety. He's fast, but I'm faster as I spin out of his grasp and run the final ten yards into the end zone.

The stadium erupts in a chorus of cheers and boos from our respective fans, but I'm on autopilot as I dodge my teammates who have come to celebrate, and head toward my girl in the stands. As she comes into view, I see that she's losing her damn mind. She's got both arms up, high-fiving the random stranger wearing a Blizzard jersey next to her. She turns away from him, jumping up and down before noticing that I'm headed her way. That stops her in her tracks, and I'm rewarded with a huge smile as I reach out, handing her the ball that's still clutched in my hands.

As she leans down, I notice what she's wearing. When I first saw her, I figured the jersey she had on was her own. But now that I'm closer, I can see that it's mine. "Nice outfit, Baby Doll," I say as she takes the ball from me, hugging it in her arms. "Love it when you wear my clothes."

She looks around, no doubt worried that people can hear us, but other than a couple people next to her, everyone has already shifted their focus to our kicker, who is lining up for the extra point. Tampa missed one earlier in the game, so all Ramirez has to do is send it through the uprights and the win is ours. But I'm not worried about that as I admire Mads in my jersey.

"Like it?" she says, pulling on the hem. She isn't wearing pants, but has on a pair of thigh-high sequined boots that match the ice blue in the jersey. *Aaaaand my dick is hard.* "I figured you wouldn't mind me borrowing it. It was in your closet. Is that okay?" she asks, like I wouldn't give her any fucking thing she wanted.

"First of all," I say, "you are welcome to anything in *our* closet. Secondly, that looks way better on you than it did on me." She gives me a soft smile. *Fuck, I love her.*

"Beckham!" Coach yells. "Get the fuck over here."

"Gotta go," I say, rolling my eyes. "Wait for me after the game."

I reluctantly leave her, returning to my team just as the ball sails straight down the pipe. The win feels amazing, as always. But knowing that pretty girl is about to be naked in my hotel room soon feels even better.

THIRTY-TWO
BLAZE

AS SOON AS the hotel elevator doors close, I'm on Mads. I shove her against the mirrored wall, my lips on hers as fast as I can get them there. She reaches up and tangles her hands in my hair, making me groan. I've seen her in Blizzard gear at home games. And I've seen my jersey on her at home. But something about looking into the stands and seeing her with my name and number across her back, going wild after I scored the winning touchdown, made me want to beat on my chest with my fists.

Grabbing the thick material, I fist the hem, lifting it just slightly. It's a long jersey, the one that I was wearing in the game where I broke the season record for receiving yards. If I thought it had meaning before, it's definitely being framed after seeing Mads in it cheering for me. I expect to see that she's wearing short shorts underneath, but when I slowly push my hands up her thighs, I only feel the thin fabric of her panties.

"Madison," I groan. My cock is steel behind my dress pants. I want to spank her for walking around all day with nothing under my jersey.

"What?" She says, biting her lip.

"You're in so much fucking trouble, Baby Doll," I say just as the elevator doors open. The little brat gives me a coy wink before slipping out of my arms and walking toward my room. It takes every ounce of control in me not to grab her by the hair and force her to her knees right in this hallway where anyone could see.

Finally making it to the door, I dig in my pocket for my key card and unlock it in record time, forcefully pushing Mads' lower back to get her in the room. I'm feeling frantic, the feral beast inside me charging at the bars of his enclosure, begging to be released. I don't bother turning on the lights. The glow from the city below is the only thing illuminating the space. But I can see plenty.

Turning, I see Mads waiting, like the good girl she is, for me to tell her what to do next. And as much as my next words pain me to say, I need her naked for what I have planned. "Take the jersey off."

She obeys, reaching for the hem and pulling the heavy material over her head. She's fucking breathtaking in just an ice blue thong. It almost has me giving in and dropping to my knees for her. But then it all clicks in my head. Not only did she wear my jersey with that poor excuse for underwear, but she has no bra on. Her nipples are puckered and beautifully pink. Fucking mouthwatering. But I'm too infuriated to admire them for long.

In two long strides, I'm invading her space. I don't miss the visible shiver that makes its way through her body. Bringing my mouth to her ear, I lower my voice darkly. "I played an entire game, oblivious to the fact that you were practically naked under my jersey. You sat there in the stands knowing the only thing between everyone in the stadium and *my cunt* was this tiny scrap of fabric?" I say, reaching out to fist the front of her thong. She sucks in a sharp breath when I yank it upward, wedging the fabric between her puffy pussy lips. "You don't think that deserves a punishment?"

She stands there silently, broken breaths escaping her as she tries to gather her thoughts. After a minute of her not answering, I tighten my fist and pull, ripping the flimsy material right from her body. She yelps in response. "Answer me," I demand. "Do you think you deserve to be punished?"

"Y-yes," she chokes out.

"Get on your knees."

She obeys, sinking down in front of me. I slowly undo the buttons of my dress shirt. "You'll use your safe word if it gets to be too much. Understand?"

"Yes," she says on a breathy moan.

I take a moment to look her in the eyes. I've been wanting to experiment more with her since we took the kink quiz, but I need to see for myself that she's ready for this. Her eyes hold so many emotions, but heat and anticipation are at the forefront. Leaning down slightly, I grab her chin with my thumb and pointer finger, tilting her head up toward me. "Do you trust me?"

She swallows thickly, her thighs rubbing together at the discomfort I know she's already feeling. I know, because I'm aching for her, too.

"I trust you, Blaze. Punish me."

My cock is so fucking hard. And I can feel it leaking inside my boxer briefs. "You're such a little slut, Mads," I coo. "But you're my good girl, aren't you? Accepting your punishment." Removing my belt in one fluid motion, I hold it out in front of her. Her eyes widen for just a moment before a mask of arousal slips back over her face. "If at any point you need me to stop and are unable to speak, reach up with your right hand and squeeze twice. Do you understand?"

"Yes," she replies.

"Show me," I demand. She reaches her hand up, balling her fingers into a fist then repeating the motion. I want to make sure she knows how to stop this if she can't handle it. The last thing I need is for us to try something new, her to become uncomfortable, and me not to know it. But by her eagerness to comply, I know she wants this as much as I do.

"Good girl, baby. Now," I begin, the beast inside me foaming at the mouth to be set free, "get on all fours for me."

Mads lowers down to her hands, looking up at me for direction. I say nothing as I bring my belt around her neck, putting the tail through the loop of the buckle and pulling until it's taut to her throat. Taking a step backwards, I stop when my arm is fully extended, the belt in my hand like a leash. "I've been your little puppy for far too long, Baby Doll. It's time for you to be mine," I say, smirking down at her. "Now, crawl to me."

Just then, I pull tighter on the tail of the belt, putting more pressure on her throat as she begins crawling on her hands and knees toward me. She looks like a dream, naked except for her thigh-high boots. When she thinks she's made it to me, I begin to walk backward. I lead her through the room, heading straight for the bed. She crawls behind me, until the back of my knees hit the mattress, causing me to stop. I can see a sheen of moisture in her eyes from the tightness of the belt, so I take a moment to check in. "Is this okay?" I ask.

"Yes," she replies, her voice quiet in the empty room.

"Good girl," I praise. "Take off your boots and sit back on your heels while I stroke my cock."

Mads obeys immediately, removing her boots before sitting back on her haunches, hands resting in her lap. I slowly remove my shirt, followed by my dress pants and boxer briefs. I leave some slack on the belt, but never let it drop from my hands as I switch them to undress. Once I'm completely naked, I grab ahold of my aching dick. Pulling tighter on the leather in my hand, I bring her face close enough that her lips graze my tip on every upstroke. *God, this feels good.*

She lets out a whimper and I can see that she's uncomfortable. When she begins to rub her thighs together, I jerk on the belt, stilling her as she gives me her undivided attention. "This is a punishment. That throbbing clit of yours will stay that way until I decide whether or not you get to come tonight. Don't you even think about trying to create friction between those thighs until you have my permission to do so. Am I clear?" I ask.

"Yes, Daddy."

Fuck, I love it when she calls me that.

"Good. Now, stick that tongue out for me, puppy."

She whines, loudly, before opening her mouth and sticking her tongue out. I stroke myself onto the tip a couple times before pulling on the leather in my fist, filling her mouth with my cock. She reaches up, her nails biting into my thighs as I use the belt for leverage while I fuck her face. I keep my eyes trained on her, making sure she isn't giving me any indications that she needs to stop. Her face is turning a beautiful shade of red as she takes me as far down her throat as my belt will allow. When I hear her gag, I pull out of her mouth long enough to let her take some deep breaths. Thick strings of saliva hang from the tip of my cock to her lips, and I've never seen anything more stunning in my entire fucking life.

When I can no longer take the distance, I pull her back to me and stifle a groan when she immediately resumes devouring my length. My self-control has hit its breaking point. I need to be inside her. Without a word, I pull myself from her mouth, reaching down to undo the belt from her neck. "Get on the bed. Face down, ass up," I order. She's a little slow and unsteady getting to her feet, more than likely from the fact that I was cutting off some of the blood to her brain, so I don't rush her as she follows my command. "Do you want to keep going?" I ask.

"Please," she begs. She sounds as desperate as I feel.

As soon as she's on the bed, her holes presented to me, I snap. I can't look at her like this and not make her mine in every way. I drag my index finger around the rim of her entrance before entering her just an inch. I don't need to go any further to know that she's ready for my cock. She's a soaking, needy mess in front of me. "This is still a punishment, Mads. Don't think for one second that I've forgotten that you chose to wear next to nothing under my jersey. You sat there and watched me play, probably growing wetter with every catch I made, soaking that pathetic excuse for a thong," I growl.

I can barely see straight as I thrust my hard cock into her tight pussy. She cries out, pushing back to take me further. I rear my hand back, spanking her hard. A red handprint raises on her creamy skin before my eyes, and it makes me think of all the dirty, depraved things I want to do to her. The fact that I know she'd love them is almost enough to have me busting early. "You're not in charge, baby. I'll fuck you how *I want to*. If I want to move at a slow and agonizing pace, keeping you on the edge but never letting you come, I will. Don't you fucking move," I grit through clenched teeth.

She lets out a whimper and I take mercy on her, fucking into her faster. My balls are soaked as they slap against her wet clit. I'm so close already, but I'll be damned if I blow before I make her really regret being a naughty girl tonight. I feel her starting to clench around me, her release barreling toward her. When I know she's there, I pull out, leaving her empty and aching.

"Blaze!" she cries, desperately. "P-please."

I grab her ass cheeks, using my thumbs to pull them apart as her holes come back into view. Looking down, I spit on her puckered bud, rubbing it in with my fingers as the muscle clenches under my touch. "Fuck, baby. I want to claim your ass soon. Will you let me?"

"You can do whatever you want to me, Blaze. Please. I just need to come," she whines. She's close to breaking for me, but she's not quite there yet. So, I thrust back in slowly, keeping a steady tempo as I bring her back toward her release.

After what seems like only seconds, she's clenching again, her pussy getting tighter and wetter with every thrust. Right when I hear the telltale moan that says she's about to orgasm, I pull back out. I watch as she slumps down further into the mattress, her body trembling with need. "You come when *I* say so. I might not even let you tonight," I chide. "I might just make you go to bed covered in my cum without your release. Every time you wake up throbbing throughout the night, you'll remember what a bad girl you were."

"N-no," she says, her shoulders beginning to shake. *She's crying.* I'm proud of myself for getting to this point. When Tanner first brought me to Bliss, I wasn't sure if I'd ever be able to give Mads the things she craved. I thought I'd cave at the first sign of her tears. But right now? They're the fuel that's driving me to keep going.

Leaning over her back, I bring my mouth to her ear as she continues sobbing under me. "You break so beautifully for me. Look at you. Crying for my cock like a desperate little slut." She whimpers, the sound making my balls draw up tight.

Deciding she's had enough, I enter her again, this time picking up my pace to get her to her peak. When she tightens again, she cries out. I thrust harder and faster while reaching around her front. "Come on, baby. You can come now," I say as I pinch her clit, making her detonate. I see stars as her cunt clamps down on me so tightly, I can't even think straight. In an instant, I'm emptying myself completely inside her.

Careful not to squish her, I roll off to the side, pulling her spent body to me. "Are you okay?" I ask, softly.

"Mmhmm," is all she can get out as she turns, snuggling into my arms.

"You did so good, baby. I'm so fucking proud of you," I praise. "I'll be right back." As hard as it is to leave the warmth of her body, that was a pretty intense scene, and she needs to hydrate. I grab a bottle of water and bring it to her, making her drink as I pad over to the bathroom. I clean myself up then hold another cloth under the warm tap. Returning to the foot of the bed, I gently grab her ankle, pulling her legs apart so I can clean her.

"Blaze, I can—"

"I know you can. But let me take care of you," I interrupt with a soft smile. Fuck, I want to open the balcony door and scream that I love her loud enough for the whole world to hear. It's getting harder and harder to stop myself with every moment we spend together, but I'm afraid she still isn't ready to hear it. I was stupid that first night for saying it out loud, even if she was fast asleep. But I *do* love her. So much that it scares me. But if she's not there yet, I don't want her to pull away. So, I'll keep it to myself as long as I can.

I help her to the bathroom on shaking legs so she can pee before I lead her back to the bed. As we snuggle under the blankets, our bodies melted together so closely that I don't know where I end and she begins, I realize just how perfect Mads is for me. She's my whole fucking world and I'll do whatever it takes to give her everything she deserves.

THIRTY-THREE
MADS

> Dia: I saw you on tv. You looked like a girl who was definitely about to get railed within an inch of her life. I want details.

WE GOT HOME from Tampa yesterday morning. I made it to Tailgate with only minutes to spare before I had to clock in. The day flew by, as it always does on Monday with all the games we didn't cover over the weekend. By the time I got home last night, I was dead on my feet as I poured myself into bed next to Blaze.

I woke up early today, finding a message from Janine that a pipe burst in our building and to do my assignments from home for the next couple of days. I got so much done, cuddled up next to Blaze on the couch with my laptop while he watched game tape on the TV.

It's officially the Blizzard's bye week, so Blaze, Dalton, and I are having a movie marathon tonight. None of us have to be up early tomorrow, which is really rare. They're on a snack run right now and I'm finally taking the time to reply to Dia's text message from yesterday.

I told her, very briefly, that Blaze and I had sex the

morning after she saved me from my bad date. Ever since then, she's been hounding me for details. Apparently, the television cameras broadcast me making googly eyes at Blaze after his touchdown the other night for the entire country to see. Luckily, I'm able to operate under the rouse that I'm his assistant and nothing else. I'm sure it'll get back to someone at Tailgate, but I'm not breaking any rules, so I'm not worried about it.

Dia, however, won't leave me alone.

Mads: Don't be ridiculous. It was like, TWO inches. He went easy on me.

Dia: I hate you. I'm so jealous that you get to fuck that God of a man whenever you want. Is he meeting all your needs, my delicate little flower?

Mads: If this is your way of asking if his kinks match up with mine, then yes.

Dia: *raises hands to the heavens* HALLELUJAH!

Mads: As much as I'd love to give you the play-by-play of Football Boy taking me to pound town, I'm afraid I have a date. With two hot guys. At once.

Dia: Excuse me. WHAT?

Mads: Ok, love you. Byeeeeeeeeeee.

I get out of bed and wiggle my feet into my slippers just as I hear the garage door opening. I can't help but feel a little sad that I'm not sharing these moments with my best friend. Back in Chicago, we did movie nights every weekend. We'd do full makeovers and gossip like teenagers, even after we'd grown up.

I miss her so much. We knew it would be hard being separated like this, but it's nights like this, where I'm about to curl up and watch a movie, that I feel a missing Dia-shaped puzzle piece in my life.

I head downstairs to see the guys unloading several bags of junk food. I guess they abandon all their normal habits during bye week. Otherwise, Blaze would never put stuff like that in his body. Well, other than the occasional large fry from Mister Burgers.

"Hey, Shorty," Dalton says as I enter the kitchen, taking a seat on one of the barstools at the island they're currently covering in snacks.

"Hey," I say, quietly, resting my chin in my palm.

"What's wrong, baby?" Blaze asks, concern in his eyes. "You look sad."

I huff a defeated breath. "I'll be okay. I'm just missing Dia a little bit. We always used to have movie nights where we'd eat junk and do makeovers. I just feel kind of…incomplete." As tears begin to gather in my eyes, Blaze rounds the island, wrapping me in a tight hug. The gesture makes me break, tears running down my cheeks as I softly sob into his chest. "I'm sorry. I don't know why I'm crying."

He pulls back just enough to look at me, using his thumbs to wipe away my tears. "You're crying because you packed up your entire life to come here by yourself, leaving behind the one person who has always been your safe space. It's okay to be sad about that." He kisses my forehead and pulls me back into a tight embrace.

As hard as this move has been, I couldn't have done it without Blaze. He's kind, gentle, protective, and I'm falling more in love with him every day. It's scary because we really haven't talked about labeling whatever we are, but I'm still taking things one day at a time with him. Maybe he'll break my heart in the end. But, right now? I'm grateful for these moments.

I'm broken from my thoughts when Dalton speaks. Honestly, I forgot he was here for a second. That's no easy feat since he's usually the loudest, most obnoxious person in every room.

"Use me."

Blaze and I both turn our heads to him, confused. "What?" we both say, in unison. My voice sounds genuinely perplexed, while Blaze sounds like he might jump over this island and strangle him. Dalton must read his friend's tone, because he puts both hands up in surrender.

"Not like *that*," he says to Blaze before turning toward me. "Make me over. I'll be Dia tonight."

"Dude, no," Blaze says at the same time I shout "Yes!"

Before he can say anything else, I jump out of Blaze's arms and fly up the stairs toward the bedroom. I go straight to the ensuite bathroom and fling open the drawer that holds all of my skin care products. Filling both arms to the brim, I head back downstairs, blowing past the guys and into the theatre room. I hear them come in behind me just as I dump everything onto the couch.

"Sit," I say to Dalton, motioning for him to take a seat.

"Fine," he says, raising a brow. "But not because you told me to. Because I *want to*."

"Jesus Christ," Blaze says, shaking his head as he sits on the other side of me before grabbing the remote. "I'm going to let you two girls do…whatever it is that you do, while I find a movie. Any requests, Baby Doll?"

I don't even look at him as I tear open the foil package containing a pink sheet mask. "Doesn't matter. It just has to have cute boys in it." I look back at him. "It's tradition."

He huffs a frustrated breath. "Alright."

"Whoa," Dalton says as I approach him with the mask. "What the fuck is that?"

"You've never used a sheet mask on your face before?" I ask. "Please tell me you're not one of those guys who uses a three-in-one shampoo to wash their face a few times a week and still has skin like *that*."

"Of course not," he scoffs. "I use bar soap."

It's unfair, honestly, how guys can get away with doing stuff like that and still be so pretty. Meanwhile, we have to get a special soap for every single part of our body, otherwise we'll break out and look like we rubbed a greasy pizza all over our skin.

"I'm going to pretend that doesn't make me want to put my fist through this wall," I say, putting my hand under his chin to tilt his head up before laying the mask over his face.

Once the mask is in place and Blaze has queued up the new Ryan Reynolds movie, *good choice by the way*, I sit between the two guys.

"What now?" Dalton asks.

Blaze looks over me, eyes landing on his best friend. "Now you shut the fuck up so I can watch this movie."

"Nope," I say, turning toward Dalton. "Now, we eat snacks and gossip."

Dalton grabs a bag of chips and pulls it open, popping one in his mouth, careful not to jostle the mask. "Soooooo," he looks at me. "You and Blaze, huh?" He uses the thumb and pointer finger on his left hand to make a circle, moving the pointer finger of his right hand in and out of it in a lewd gesture that has me throwing my head back in a loud laugh.

"What the fuck," Blaze groans from behind me, making me laugh even harder.

Turns out being in Boston isn't so bad after all.

|ₗₗₗᵢₗ|₁|0 2|0 3|0 4|0 5|0 4|0 3|0 2|0 1|0ₗₗₗₗ

An hour later, Dalton snores next to us as I move to cuddle

up in Blaze's lap. He kisses me softly for a moment before he pulls back and rests his forehead against mine.

"So, your birthday is this weekend. What do you want to do?"

Ugh. I was trying to be stealthy about that. I hate birthdays. I don't really even know why. My parents would always plan a special dinner where I'd unsuspectingly eat my meal before the entire restaurant staff sang Happy Birthday to me in front of all the other patrons. Is birthday anxiety a real thing? Because if it is, I have it and that's probably why.

"I don't know," I sigh. "We don't have to do anything. It's not even a big deal."

He pulls his head away, raising a brow. "It's a very big deal. And we're definitely going to do something special. I'll figure it all out, Baby Doll. Don't you worry."

I roll my eyes. "Fine, but nothing big. You don't need to be spending all sorts of time or money on me. This is supposed to be your week off."

We turn back to our second movie of the night, but I don't last very long until I'm asleep in his arms.

THIRTY-FOUR
MADS

NO MATTER how much I keep saying today is just another day, I've been reminded *repeatedly* that it's my birthday. The surprises haven't stopped coming since I opened my eyes this morning.

First, I woke up to Dia in our kitchen, making my traditional birthday breakfast of Mickey Mouse pancakes. I thought I was hallucinating until she squealed and tackled me to the ground, smothering my cheeks with kisses as Blaze laughed next to us. When he suggested we go to lunch on him while he hit the gym at the practice facility with Dalton, I was a little upset that he was leaving me on my birthday. But the fact that he arranged for Dia to be here with me after my little meltdown earlier this week made my heart skip a beat.

"Oh my God, these are so cute," I say, looking at the reflection of the gorgeous studded red-bottom shoes Dia insisted I try on after she pulled me into a high-end department store neither of us can afford. I poke out my lip, not taking my eyes off the mirror. "Shame you can't come home with me, babies. I would treat you so well."

"Actually," Dia says, her suspicious tone making me pinch my brows together while I wait for her to finish. She turns to the sales associate. "We'll take them. Thank you for your help."

I laugh at my best friend because, last I checked, neither of us has an extra fourteen hundred dollars just laying around. I walk over to the chair, take the shoes off, and hand them to the girl. "My friend is kidding. I wish I could buy them, but I can't today." I smile and slip my feet back into my red Converse.

Dia turns to her again. "These shoes as well as the black dress. It'll go on the bill that was set up when Mr. Beckham called earlier." She nods once and heads to the register as I sit there, slack jawed and sputtering. I want to say no. I should stop this, but I'm too shocked by the thought that Blaze must've put into this day.

I still struggle with what the future looks like for us. Doubt creeps into my head from time to time, reminding me that I'm not the kind of girl that's worthy of Blaze Beckham. He may enjoy the sex now, but what happens when some tall, thin, beautiful supermodel comes along and shows him that he could do better? And who knows what my future holds? My internship will be ending soon. What if I don't get the permanent position? I can't *not* use the experience I've gained while being here. If Tailgate Media doesn't want me, I'll probably have to apply for jobs in other cities. Where would that leave me and Blaze? How could we nurture a new relationship from opposite ends of the country for half the year?

We can't.

I'm brought back to the present when the sales associate returns with a garment bag. "Mr. Beckham requested that you change into this before you leave for your next stop. Dressing room one is open for you. I hope you have a wonderful birthday, Miss Rodgers," she says with a smile before walking away.

I raise a brow at my best friend, who is doing too good of a job keeping secrets from me today. She shrugs. "Hey, I'm just doing what I'm told because, to be completely frank, he offered me a grand. And I love you a lot, but I love money even more." She winks before shoving me toward the dressing room. "Now go squeeze that bitable ass into your new dress and let's go."

An hour later, we pull up Blaze's driveway. Everything is eerily quiet, and all the lights are off. Dia pulls into the garage, and we leave the Audi that she insisted he let her drive on our adventure today. As we enter the house, she grabs my hand and leads me through the darkness to the back door, pulling it open. Before I can get a chance to ask her what the fuck is going on, the back yard lights up. I quickly notice the outdoor heaters and beautiful enclosed white tent that shields the yard from the chill in the air.

"Surprise!"

I go completely stiff, save for my eyes that dart around quickly to see every single person that means something to me standing there cheering in celebration. Tears fill my eyes and my hand darts over my mouth as my parents step forward and wrap me up in a family hug.

"Mom? Dad? I thought you were taking a road trip this weekend?" I say through tears. Sarah and Tyler stand beside them, drinks in hand.

"Oh honey," my mom replies, pulling herself back slightly. "We lied to you. We're quite good at it."

"Had you believing that Santa Claus business until you were fourteen," my dad chuckles.

They tell me all about how Blaze called them personally and arranged for them to fly out here. He offered for them to stay here at the house, but my dad has to be back to work tomorrow afternoon, so they're staying at a hotel by the airport. I can't believe he did all of this for me.

"Happy birthday, my beautiful girl," my mom says before taking a sip of her drink. "Go say your hellos. We'll be around."

They step away just as Dalton rushes up and lifts me off the ground. "Happy birthday, Shorty!" he says enthusiastically before returning me to my feet. I giggle as he turns to Dia, who is still standing beside me. "Well, hi there. And who are you?" He seems to have forgotten I exist, and I smile as I get ready for her reply. But before she can say anything, he holds up one finger, shushing her as he pulls his phone out of his pocket and begins typing.

"Rude much?" Dia scoffs.

Dalton returns his phone to his pocket and smiles at her. "Sorry. Just had to shoot my mom a quick text to tell her I found the girl I'm going to marry," he says, winking at her. I expect one of her signature witty comments, but all she does is raise her brows in surprise. She quickly pulls herself together, rolling her eyes.

"You're cute," she finally says. "But I would break you."

"Can't wait, Wifey," he replies with a smirk, putting his hand on the small of her back and leading her toward the bar in the corner of the tent.

I laugh at them, then turn to see the culprit of these shenanigans walking toward me. Blaze looks delicious in a pair of dark jeans and a tight white dress shirt. His sleeves are rolled up to his elbows, showcasing the drool-worthy veins that wrap around his muscled forearms. Even though I want to be upset with him for wasting a night where he could be reviewing tape for next week's prime-time game, his grin is contagious. I can't help but smile back at him as he walks up and wraps his arms tightly around my waist, burying his nose in my hair and inhaling.

"Blaze," I say, softly. "You shouldn't have done all this. It's just a birthday."

He looks up at me, eyes widening as he shakes his head.

"It's not *just* anything, Mads. You do so much for everyone around you. You deserve a party like this every weekend. But since you'd rip my balls off and feed them to me if I did that, I figured I could get away with a small birthday celebration."

Looking around at how not small this whole thing is, I'm overwhelmed with gratefulness for this man. Even though whatever this is, is complicated, Blaze Beckham has become a centering force in my world. He knows the real me and he still wants me around, which I can't say about many of the people who have come in and out of my life.

This is just one more reason I should be doing everything I can to protect both of us by not letting it go any further. We said 'one day at a time', but I'm not sure how much longer we can keep doing that. I've been so careless with my feelings when it comes to Blaze, and now I'm afraid I'm in too deep if he decides he doesn't want to take the next step, whatever that is. I couldn't handle losing him. I wouldn't survive it.

As if he can sense my inner turmoil, he releases me and grabs my hand in his, squeezing. He brings me around from table to table, so I can greet the people who decided to spend their evening celebrating me. Almost all of his teammates are here, including Tanner who smiles as he hands me a large orange box.

"Happy birthday, Mads," he says, hugging me before he drains almost an entire tumbler of whiskey in one go.

"Louis? Tanner, you didn't have to spend this much. Holy shit!" I say in amazement, with absolutely zero intention of giving it back.

He laughs and shrugs his shoulders like giving this extravagant of a gift is just another day for him. Then again, as Blaze has made me wildly aware of today and many days before, it kind of is. "It's the least I can do for the reason my main target is back to his old self."

I laugh, sticking out my hip to support the weight of the box. "I don't think I can take credit for that."

"Oh, I think you can." He winks at me before he gets up, slapping Blaze on the shoulder before walking off.

I turn, furrowing my brows as Blaze takes the box from under my arm and sets it down on the table before grabbing me by the hand and pulling me through the door into the house. He just chuckles as I wonder exactly how much Tanner knows about our situation.

"Come on. It's my turn to give you your gift."

I dig in my heels, stopping. "You already have. This dress? The shoes? This whole *party*? This is my gift, Blaze. I don't need anything else."

We're completely alone in the house as he turns, pushes me up against the wall, and presses his lips to mine. It's not a romantic kiss. He's not trying to apologize for going against my wishes and throwing this huge party when I said I didn't want anything. He's kissing me like he just needed to. Like he couldn't wait another second to taste me.

I couldn't either.

He pulls away entirely too soon, placing another quick kiss to the tip of my nose before taking my hand in his and leading me out the front door where a brand-new Mercedes G-Wagon sits, wrapped in a giant pink bow.

I stand there, dumbfounded for several seconds before I can come up with an outward reaction. Unfortunately, that reaction is to run inside, up the stairs, and into my old room, slamming the door just as I see Blaze hitting the landing in front of me. He bursts into the room and finds me looking out my closed balcony door as the party goes on below.

"Baby," he says, closing the door, shrouding us in darkness, save for the moonlight filtering through the glass. I hear him close the space between us, but I can't bring myself to turn around.

"It's too much," I say, unable to stop the tears from flowing. "All of this. I don't need it. I don't need you to buy me all these crazy gifts, Blaze!" I yell, feeling myself starting to spiral. I'm not really even sure what I'm upset about. Maybe it's because I'm not used to just having things handed to me that I didn't earn. Maybe I don't want him to think he needs to buy me things to make me happy. Or maybe it's because, with every act of kindness he shows me, I fall more and more in love with him.

I expect him to be gentle and try to talk me down. But he knows me better than that. He knows what I need.

"Bend over," he commands. "Hands on the glass."

I freeze, looking back at Blaze with confusion all over my face. If I wasn't staring right at him, I'd assume he had smoke coming from his ears by the anger in his voice. His gaze burns into me, making me squirm from the intensity.

"I swear to God, Madison. If you don't bend the fuck over right now and put your hands on that glass, I'm going to make you regret it. If you'd like to sit down painlessly this weekend, I suggest you obey my orders. *Now*," he says through his teeth.

I submit, leaning forward and placing my hands on the tinted glass door. He smooths his hands up the back of my thighs, bringing the bottom of my dress up over my hips. My crying has turned to panting as he kneels down behind me, pulls my black lace thong to the ground, and places a soft kiss to my exposed pussy. I barely even register the feeling before it's gone.

He stands behind me, using two fingers to trace the outside of my entrance before sinking them inside me. My release is already building slowly as he moves in and out of me. I'm so wet from his dominance already. My body reacts to his touch even when my brain is still reeling.

I hear the quiet purr of his zipper as he lowers it. The sound makes my pussy clench around his fingers as he uses his foot to kick my legs apart. Blaze doesn't waste a single second, thrusting his hard cock inside me, allowing my body no time to adjust before he's fucking into me. It hurts, but I need this. *We* need this.

Wrapping his hand around my throat, he covers my back with his body, continuing to thrust. "Do you know how fucking nervous I get every time you leave the driveway in that piece of shit car of yours?" he grits out. "I sit here just hoping you make it back to me in one piece. I'm fucking sick of feeling that way. So, if I want to buy you a new car for every day of the goddamn week, I fucking will. And you'll drive it. Do. *Thrust.* You. *Thrust.* Understand. *Thrust.*"

"Yes!" I cry out as I begin to tighten around him.

"Good fucking girl, baby," he says through his teeth. "Now, come for me."

He stands straight and slaps my ass hard as I do exactly that, orgasming around him as he grunts out his release at the same time.

My legs are shaking as he pulls out, still supporting me with an arm around my waist before lifting me behind the knees and carrying me to the bed. He lays next to me, pulling me into him and kissing my forehead. With that, I feel a shift between us. I wonder if he feels it too as I decide whether or not I should lay it all out on the line. When he pulls back and looks into my eyes, I can't stop myself.

"I love you, Blaze."

He gently presses his fingers under my chin, lifting it before placing a sweet kiss to my lips.

When he doesn't reply, nerves wash over me. "I know it's crazy and it's really soon. And maybe you don't feel the same way I do," I ramble on, feeling more and more desperate as the seconds tick by. "I've been trying so hard not to fall for you. To keep things professional. Nobody gets me like you do, Blaze. Nobody cares for me the way you do. I'm sorry if I made you uncomfortable by saying it first, and before I was sure you felt the same, but —"

"You didn't," he cuts me off.

"I didn't what?" I reply, confused.

"You didn't say it first."

I stare at him, truly bewildered because I feel like I'd know if he told me he loved me.

He continues, "That first night. After we finished, I went to the bathroom to get you a washcloth and a glass of water. When I looked in the mirror, I saw a man staring back at me that I'd never seen before. He was happy. Complete. He was…he was in love. I couldn't wait to get back in bed to tell you, but you were asleep. So, I said it anyway."

My eyes sting with tears as I bury my face into his chest and sob. This whole night has been so overwhelming, but I know I'm safe here in the arms of the man I am head over heels for.

"Look at me, Baby Doll," he says, lifting my chin again, our eyes meeting. "I love you. So fucking much."

My heart feels so full as he covers my mouth with his one more time before smiling against my lips. "Now get this fine ass up and let's go celebrate the best day of my life."

THIRTY-FIVE
BLAZE

I ADJUST my bow tie for the fiftieth time as I pace the living room. Tonight is the Children's Hospital fundraiser and I somehow managed to talk Mads into being my date. She's still hesitant to go public as a couple because she doesn't want anyone thinking she's using me to secure the position at Tailgate. I understand where she's coming from, but I don't know how much longer I can hide how I feel about her from the world.

Checking my watch, I see that we have about ten minutes before our car arrives. It's a weeknight, so Mads blew through the door about an hour ago, stripping from her work clothes as she hustled up the stairs to shower. She told me to stay my ass downstairs so I didn't distract her while she got ready. That was probably a good idea because there's no way I'd be able to keep my hands off her if I saw her fresh from the shower.

I look out the window, noticing how dark it is already. I'll never understand how setting the clock back an hour robs us of so much daylight, but whatever.

Just as I see the car pulling up the driveway, I hear light

footsteps on the stairs behind me. I turn, all the breath leaving my lungs as Mads comes into view.

Mine.

She's stunning in a long silver gown that's tight on top, but flares out right above her knees. Her gorgeous tits are pushed up high. She wears strappy black heels on her feet. My cock twitches behind my zipper as goosebumps rise all over my skin. "Fuck, baby. You look edible," I say, taking her hand and pulling her into my arms. I take a moment to bury my nose into her slender neck, inhaling her scent. I can't stop myself from gently moving my lips along her skin. She sighs contentedly as my hands skate down her body, wrapping around her and grabbing her ass.

She swats at my shoulder, pulling away. "Stop it! I'm getting wet and I'm not wearing underwear."

I groan. "Baby, if you think saying that is going to make me leave you alone, you're fucking wrong. Now I just want to spread you out right here on this floor and clean up the mess you're making with my tongue." The thought has me considering abandoning the event altogether and mailing them a fat check instead.

She giggles. "Come on, you pervert. It's only a couple hours. Then we can come back here and I'll let you do whatever you want to me."

I pretend to mull over her offer. "Okay. Two hours. Then I'm throwing you over my shoulder like a caveman and bringing you home."

"Deal," she replies. "Is the car here?"

"Yep. Let's get this shit over with," I say on an annoyed exhale. I do want to go. I know events like this are important. And I plan on making a good-sized donation to the hospital. I'm so fortunate to have the means to do so, and it feels good to know I'm making a difference. But still, I'd rather be here worshipping every inch of her body.

I lead Mads from the house, opening the car door so she

can slide in before I follow. We make out like teenagers in the back seat the entire ride to the event center, but when I try to take things further, she stops me. I know she doesn't want me messing up her dress, but you can't blame a guy for trying. I just feel like I can never get enough of her. I've spent every night since the birthday party inside my girl and I always want more. Thankfully, the feeling is mutual because she's just as insatiable as I am.

The drive is short, and before we know it, the car door is being opened for us to step onto the red carpet. I grab Mads' hand before I start to slide out, but she pulls me back toward her. "What's wrong?" I ask.

She looks like a deer in headlights. "I— should we be holding hands? I don't know what to do?"

She's panicking but I'm as calm as can be as I sink back into the seat, closing the car door behind me. The red carpet can wait. I'm not going out there until Mads and I are on the same page. "Baby, I understand your concerns about us going public as a couple. And we don't have to tell them anything. But I want your hand in mine out there. I want to be able to pull you close while we're dancing. I don't want to hide this."

She considers for a moment before blowing out a breath. "I don't either."

"Yeah?" I say, relieved. "If anyone asks, we'll dodge the question. Just until you get hired on at Tailgate. After that, I'm tattooing your name on my forehead so the whole world knows who I belong to."

"Face tattoos are so hot," she jokes.

I lean in and kiss her, pulling away a lot sooner than I'd like, but the red carpet awaits. "I love you."

"I love you, too," she says softly as I grab the door handle and step out with her hand in mine. Cameras flash from every direction as we make our way to the doors. Mads has her game face on, smiling and waving to the crowd as we move past. She's a natural in front of the cameras and I can't help but feel the pride swelling in my chest at the woman I've fallen head over heels for. The fact that she's choosing to love me makes me feel like the luckiest son of a bitch in the world. I will never be good enough for her, but I'll spend the rest of my life showing her how happy she makes me.

We enter the ballroom and head toward our table. We're surrounded by Boston's richest and most influential people, all dressed to the nines and ready to pull out their checkbooks for a good cause. I pull out Mads' chair and hold her hand until she's settled. "I'll go to the bar. What do you want to drink, Baby Doll?"

"I'll just have a glass of champagne," she replies.

I nod before turning away and heading toward the bar. After the bartender takes my order, I turn to scan the crowd. It's pretty much the usual suspects I see at these fundraisers. There are athletes from the various sports teams in the city, politicians, high-profile businessmen and women, and a few select members of the media that have signed non-disclosure agreements. They're allowed to report on the event, but the guests are off limits. That's why I felt comfortable being close to Mads tonight. Not that I care if anyone talks about us being together. But I know she does.

Just before I go to turn back to the bar, a familiar head of dirty blonde hair catches my eye. I squint to get a better look...to make sure I'm seeing who I think I am. And *fuck*. Brady. He blends in well with his black tuxedo and bright white smile. I know he owns a supplement company, but I wasn't aware he made the kind of money needed to score an invite to this type of event. Honestly, good for him. As long as he makes a nice donation and stays away from my girl, I'm glad he's here. The more, the merrier when it's for a good cause.

I grab our drinks and head back to our table. Handing Mads her drink, she gives me a warm smile before taking a small sip of the bubbly liquid. I watch her, wishing I could taste it off her tongue. "Dance with me?" I say, hoping she'll just let go for tonight and be with me.

"Okay," she agrees, placing her glass back on the table and grabbing my outstretched hand. I lead her to the dance floor as the DJ plays Yours by Russell Dickerson. I listen to the lyrics, realizing how they express every feeling I have right now. I used to just float through life. No real purpose outside of football. But then this perfect piece of heaven landed on my doorstep and changed everything. She made my life better.

I pull Mads into me and the whole room fades away. It's just us, holding tightly to one another as we sway to the music. I can't help myself as I bring my lips to her ear, whispering the lyrics. *"Thank God I'm yours."* I pull back to look at her and see that her eyes are filled with tears. "What's wrong, baby?" I say softly, pushing a lose strand of hair from her face.

"I'm just happy," she says, softly. "I love you so much, Blaze."

I lean forward, not giving a single fuck who sees, and press my lips to hers. We get lost in the kiss as we move with one another. Only when we hear the sound of a glass breaking in the distance do we pull apart. It's not uncommon for accidents to happen when people have access to an open bar, so I ignore it and pull her from the dance floor as the song ends.

As we reach our table, I notice Brady leaving the room. Good. All that stuff I said about being happy he was here? I'm a liar. Hopefully, he left his check for the hospital before he took off.

I bring my focus back to Mads, who looks content as she sips on her champagne. I realize then that this could be my future. Dressing up for charity events with the most beautiful girl in the world on my arm. Bringing her home to our bed. Sharing our lives with each other.

I used to think my purpose in this world was playing football. But I was so fucking wrong. Loving Madison Rodgers has always been my reason for living. Even before I met her, I was meant to be hers. There was never another option.

She yawns, smiling at me sheepishly. "Champagne always makes me tired."

"Well," I say, standing up and pulling back her chair. "Let's get you home, pretty girl. You can go to sleep while I kiss you all over your body."

"Mmmm," she replies. "That sounds perfect."

I lead her out of the building and hold her close, trying to keep her warm as we wait for our car. It's freezing and she refused to wear a coat because it *'didn't go with her dress'*. She visibly shivers, prompting me to remove my tux jacket and wrap it around her shoulders. I rub my hands up and down her arms, trying to create enough friction to warm her.

I pull Mads into my arms, finally able to kiss her with the passion I've been feeling all night now that we aren't surrounded by thousands of people. I get lost in her taste until footsteps approaching catch my attention.

"I fucking knew it."

I look up to find Brady standing there. He's very clearly drunk as he stumbles up to us, the smell of alcohol hitting my nose as he comes to a halt in front of where I'm still holding Mads tightly in my arms.

He scoffs. "This is why you wouldn't go out with me? Because of *him*?" he slurs.

Mads tries to pull away, but I tighten my hold on her. No way am I letting her go when he's drunk and pissed. I'll do whatever I have to do to protect her.

"Brady," she sighs. She's as annoyed as I am with him for interrupting our moment. "We talked about this. We didn't work the first time. We were never good for each other."

He moves closer and I let go of her, stepping between them. She moves to the side slightly, but allows me to continue standing in the middle, shielding her from whatever the fuck he thinks he's going to get away with here. "Is it because I wouldn't do the things to you that you wanted? I wouldn't tie you up and fuck you like a slut? I probably should've. Since that's what you've always been."

In the blink of an eye, the collar of his shirt is gripped tightly in my fist as I pull him close. "Don't you ever fucking speak to her like that, you piece of shit." I seethe. "Matter of fact," I say, tightening my hold on him, "if you come anywhere near my girlfriend ever again, I will end you."

I shove him backward, making him fall on his ass before he scrambles to his feet. Thrusting a shaky hand through his hair, he spits on the ground near my shoe. "This isn't over," he says.

"Yes, it is," I grit out. "Get the fuck out of here before I make you swallow your teeth."

Thankfully he turns, his body swaying as he goes back into the building. I turn toward Mads, who is shaking like a leaf. I'm not sure if it's from the cold or because she's scared, but I'm thankful that our driver chooses that moment to pull up beside us. I don't wait for him to get out before I open the door and guide her in. Sliding in next to her, I cup her tear-soaked face in my hands. "Baby, you're okay. It's okay." I soothe her.

"It's my fault," she says. "That night we went to Donatello's, Brady made a pass at me." I ball my hands into fists to stop myself from punching out the window. I'm pissed, but I don't want to scare her. She continues. "He accused me of sleeping with you. Then he insulted you and I lost it on him. I embarrassed him in front of everyone."

I grab her hands, desperate to be connected to her somehow. "None of this is your fault. Do you understand me?" I say, firmly. "He's an entitled piece of shit. If he comes anywhere near you ever again, I'll fucking kill him. He doesn't get to hurt you."

"Thank you, Blaze. For never making me feel bad about

the things I like," she says. "Brady always made me feel like some kind of freak. I only asked him once, but he made sure I knew how he felt about it. He told me it was disgusting. So, I laughed it off and acted like it wasn't a big deal. But it really made me afraid to be who I am. I've always been scared to tell my partners about my preferences because I was terrified of their reactions." She wipes the tears from her cheeks. "But then you came along. I didn't have to say anything. You just dove in head first. Learning everything you could so you could take care of me." She smiles before going on. "This all goes way beyond sex. It's you knowing the real me and loving me for it. I just— thank you."

My heart pounds in my chest, feeling like it could burst at any second with the love I feel for her. "Baby, you are fucking perfect. Thank you for letting me take care of you. I know it wasn't easy for you. But you can lay down next to me every night and sleep easy knowing that I'll always be there."

She takes a content breath before a small giggle escapes her.

"What's so funny?" I question.

"You called me your girlfriend," she replies.

I exhale a laugh. "Yeah, I did. Didn't I?"

She smiles, happiness radiating from her as she leans forward and rewards me with a deep kiss. Although Brady put a temporary damper on our evening, I refuse to let it ruin the ending for us. Instead, I take my girl home and spend the night showing her exactly how I feel about her.

THIRTY-SIX
MADS

I'VE BEEN awake for the past ten minutes, but I have yet to open my eyes. Blaze's warm body is pressed against my back and his strong arm is holding me in place. I imagine my alarm is about to go off any second, but I'm going to squeeze every moment I can out of the peace and quiet of morning before we both have to get up and get ready to go our separate ways for the day.

It's been two days since the Children's Hospital fundraiser. I still can't believe Brady had the balls to approach me and Blaze as we waited outside for our car. I've known him a long time and I've never seen him drunk like that. And the horrible things he said? It's like he was a completely different person than the one I dated in high school.

Don't get me wrong. Brady has always been spoiled and entitled. His father gave him everything he wanted growing up, which turned him into a self-centered brat. But he always put on a good front. Even I only saw bits and pieces of what he hid underneath his fake smile. The passive-aggressive way he always told me my thoughts and actions were juvenile. The way he made me feel like I should thank him for being with me. *That* is the real Brady Jones. And hopefully after Blaze's threats, I'll never have to deal with him again.

I'm broken from my thoughts when the alarm on my phone intrudes on the quiet of our bedroom. Blaze stirs behind me, tightening his hold as if I'll just give up on the day altogether to stay in bed with him. While that's not a terrible idea, I have to get in the shower or I'll be late to my internship.

Trying to pull out from his iron grip, Blaze groans into my ear. "Let's quit our jobs and become professional cuddlers." His voice is gravelly and I feel something down low squeeze inside me.

I laugh. "As amazing as that sounds, the city would be pounding your door down after a day. They wouldn't be too keen on losing their star receiver this late in the season." The Blizzard have only lost two games so far and they're currently leading the conference. They can clinch a playoff berth with a win against Tennessee this week.

"Fine," he grumbles. "But I'm showering with you."

We slip out of bed, still naked from last night. Memories flood my brain of Blaze sliding inside me while telling me how much he loved me. We made love for hours until we passed out in one another's arms. As much as I love how rough and dominating he can be, something about the sweet moments we share mean so much.

We shower as quickly as we can before heading down to eat breakfast. Thankfully, he's had his chef meal prep for us both. I was perfectly okay with my normal morning meal of absolutely nothing but coffee, but Blaze insists that I eat a well-balanced breakfast with him before work each day. We move around the kitchen seamlessly, as if we've been living like this forever. I love how comfortable all of it feels.

We grab our bags from the closet before kissing each other goodbye and getting in our cars. I'm still getting used to my new G-Wagon, but I really love it. After my meltdown on my birthday, Blaze made me realize that my old car wasn't safe and that me driving this one is just as much for him as it is for me. I'm not sure I'll ever get used to the way he cares for me. It's hard to believe that I deserve him sometimes.

I pull into a parking space at the Tailgate Media headquarters and grab my things before heading inside. I have an extra pep in my step lately knowing that the end is near. Jacob could be picking one of us to be hired on permanently any day now. He's been extremely vague about where his head is at, but I feel confident. I've been putting so much effort into creating the perfect content. Out of the four of us, I've easily had the biggest names in my interviews. And I did it all without Blaze's help. Dalton even begged me to do a full-length article on him. He recently became the number one running back in the league for touchdowns and he won't shut up about it. I told him I didn't want to interview anyone I met through Blaze until Jacob makes his final decision. I just want to prove that I have what it takes to win this job on my own merit.

When I get to my desk, I notice that Ella, Chance, and Jason are all there. That's pretty common this early in the morning as we wait to get our daily assignments from Janine, but I'm caught off guard by the fact that they're huddled together around Jason's computer. Ella notices me first and gives me a small smile that doesn't reach her eyes.

Huh. Weird.

"Morning," I say, my normal cheeriness clouded in trepidation. The guys turn, giving me a glimpse at what had their attention when I walked in. The browser is pulled up and there are paparazzi photos from the fundraiser. Blaze and I are walking down the red carpet, hand-in-hand as he looks back at me with a proud smile. I knew they only allowed certain media professionals inside, but it didn't really register that they weren't checking press passes outside the doors.

Anyone could've taken photos of us. And from what I'm seeing now, they did.

Chance stands, stalking my way. "No wonder you were able to get all those guys to do interviews with you. When you're fucking Blaze Beckham, it's pretty easy to make friends in high places." I rear back at his words, but I can't speak. I'm stunned silent.

It takes me several moments to collect my thoughts as the three of them wait for an answer. Finally, I find my voice. "I'm not— I work for him. As his assistant," I say, quietly. Insecurity takes over as their stares bore into me.

Jason laughs. "Whatever. By the looks of these pictures, there's more going on than that. Is that how you got here? Blaze told Jacob to accept your internship application? I imagine someone like him would have a lot of pull around here."

This is exactly what I was afraid of. I knew as soon as people linked me to Blaze, they'd think he was the reason I was given these opportunities. I've worked my ass off here and they all know it. But none of that matters now.

Chance continues, "I saw you on TV during the Tampa game. I thought it was weird that he ran over to you after he scored that touchdown, but there weren't that many Blizzard fans in the front row, so I figured maybe it was just a coincidence. That he was just giving a ball to a random fan. But now I see that pussy can get you anything you want. Even a job you didn't earn."

My eyes fill with tears. I want to put my fist right through his pretty-boy face. To tell him that I got here on my own. I didn't even know Blaze when I applied to be here. I have every right to compete for this position, just like the rest of them.

I look up at Ella. She doesn't look angry with me like the guys do. Pity covers her expression, but I hate that almost as much. She and I have worked closely, and I've done as much as I can to teach her how she can improve. She knows that I've worked hard to be here, but when it comes down to it, her opinion won't matter when Jacob makes his decision. And I know he'll probably consider all of this when he does.

Defeated, I sit down at my desk and try to focus on my plans for the day. Tears threaten to spill over, but I refuse to cry here. I just want Blaze. I want him to hold me and tell me it's going to be okay. But right now, I'm on my own.

As I log in to my email account, Janine comes up to my desk. Her normal, kind expression is blank. "Madison," she says. "Jacob would like to see you in his office."

Fuck. Fuck. *Fuck.* Jacob knows. There's no other reason he'd be calling me to his office this early in the day. But I haven't broken any company policies, so why does he want to see me?

"Okay," I say, nodding at her once as I stand. She puts her hand on my shoulder and squeezes as I pass by her, headed toward what could be the end of my career before it even had a chance to begin.

I step off the elevator and head toward the reception desk outside Jacob's office. "Hello, Madison. Nice to see you today," Dani says in greeting. I paste on a fake smile, but I'm terrified right now.

"Hi," I reply. "Janine said Jacob wanted to see me in his office."

She nods once before picking up her phone to let him know I've arrived. "They're ready for you," she says to me, pointing over her shoulder. "You can go right in."

They? As in, more than just Jacob?

I open the door, walking in and closing it behind me. I'm shocked when I look up and meet a familiar pair of eyes.

Brady sits across from Jacob, one ankle crossed over his knee. A smug look covers his face as he stares back at me.

"Take a seat, Madison," Jacob says.

I nod before sitting down in the only available chair. My whole body is shaking, but I'm doing my best to exude confidence. I thought I was getting called in here about the photos of Blaze, but what does that have to do with Brady? I don't have to wait long for an answer before Jacob lays it all out for me.

"It's been brought to my attention that you've been involved in some inappropriate situations here at Tailgate Media." I stare at him, completely confused, waiting for him to elaborate. My heart pounds in my chest and blood rushes to my ears as he continues. "I wanted you to be in here while Brady explained everything. I don't know the whole story, but I've been clued in on some of it." He looks at Brady. "Start from the beginning, please."

I know that look. It's the one he used to use when he wanted people to see him as a victim. It's all fucking fake, but Jacob doesn't know that.

"Well," Brady begins, "I've known Madison most of my life. We were in a relationship in high school, so when I saw her at Connor Paul's house for the podcast, I thought it would be nice to go out together and catch up." He looks at me, then to Jacob. "We were having a nice dinner. Until Madison propositioned me."

"What?" I yell, shock radiating from my words. "That's not true!"

Jacob gives me a stern look. "Let him finish, please."

"Thank you," Brady says before continuing. "She asked me to go back to my place so I could tie her up. She wanted to rekindle our old flame, but I told her I didn't feel comfortable with the things she was asking for. I'm a gentleman. I kindly declined her offer and she lost it. She started raising her voice and made a giant scene before walking out. You can ask anyone who was at Donatello's that night. They'll confirm my story."

What a crock of shit. Brady Jones is the literal opposite of a gentleman. He's a wolf in sheep's clothing. That's all he'll ever be, but he's always gotten away with it, so I know this is not going to end well for me.

He hammers the story home with a final, crushing blow. "I just don't think you want someone like Madison making clients uncomfortable if this is a regular habit of hers," he says to Jacob, a look of innocence masking his face.

Jacob takes a deep breath, exhaling harshly before addressing Brady. "I am so sorry. This behavior is not something we allow here. Thank you for bringing it to my attention."

Brady nods, reaching forward to shake Jacob's hand before exiting the room. I'm trembling with everything I want to say. I want to scream that Brady is lying. That he was the one who hit on me and got mad when I said I didn't want more than friendship. But I'm trying to stay professional, so I sit and wait for Jacob to speak.

"Madison, I don't know if all of that is true, but I can't have this kind of drama here. We just went through it with our last reporter and even if Brady is fabricating some of his story, word travels fast in this industry. I can't have the reputation of a company that I've worked so hard for tarnished by disgruntled clients."

Tears well up in my eyes. I know what's coming before he even says it. But I wait for it anyway.

"I appreciate all your hard work, but we have to let you go. I hope you understand."

And there it is. My future, ruined by someone who could care less about how hard I had to fight to get where I am. I want to rip this entire office to shreds. To take Jacob by the shoulders and shake some sense into him. For a moment, I consider trying to defend myself. But then I realize it doesn't matter. His mind is made up. Even if he believed my side of the story, the risk isn't worth it for him. Once Brady tells other clients that Tailgate is allowing this type of behavior from employees, it's only a matter of time before sponsorships start getting pulled.

I stand, shoulders slumped in defeat before reaching out my hand for him to shake. "Thank you for the opportunity," I say sadly before turning and walking out of his office.

THIRTY-SEVEN
BLAZE

I FLY up the driveway as fast as I can, heading for the house. I've been texting and calling Mads all day and she hasn't answered. It's unlike her not to at least check in, so her radio silence has me in a panic. I even texted Dia to see if she had spoken to her, but her efforts to contact Mads ended the same way mine have.

We play Tennessee at home in two days, so today's practice was a long one. By the time I arrived at the room that we use to watch practice tape and take notes on the day's performance, I was sick to my stomach with worry. I had to sit through a meeting with my wide receivers coach that seemed to go on for hours before I ran like a bat out of hell to my truck and broke every traffic law on my way home.

I've barely shifted into park before I'm flinging the door open and running inside. "Mads!" I yell in a rush as soon as I'm inside. The house is dark and eerily quiet. Something is wrong.

"Baby, are you here?" I yell, my throat beginning to tighten with anxiety. I check all the downstairs rooms first, but they're all desolate. I hit the stairs at lightning speed and stop dead in my tracks when I hear a soft sob coming from our bedroom. On one hand, I'm relieved to see her safe. But the fact that she's been here alone, crying, has me rushing to her side, ready to kill whoever hurt her.

"Baby Doll," I say, the lump in my throat catching my words as they try to make their way out. "What happened?" She continues sobbing into the pillow while I sit on the bed beside her. Whatever it is, I'll fix it. I have to. "Mads. Talk to me." I lean over, clicking on the lamp that sits on her nightstand.

Nothing prepares me for what I see when she turns to me. Her eyes are almost swollen shut from crying. Her mascara has run down her cheeks and stains the pillow where her face was pressed into it. I feel helpless, watching her body shake as she attempts to breathe.

"Shhh. It's okay," I say, even though I have no idea why she's so upset. I move onto the bed, putting my back against the headboard before pulling her into my lap. I kiss her head and gently rub my fingers along her back to soothe her. Eventually, she calms slightly, but the tears continue flowing from her beautiful green eyes.

"Can you tell me what happened?" I try again. This time, she takes a few deep breaths before speaking.

"I got to work this morning and the other interns had pulled up some photos of us from the fundraiser," she says quietly. "They said some really mean things, just like I expected." She sniffs, using the sleeve of her sweatshirt to wipe her running nose. "But I knew I didn't do anything wrong. So, when I got called up to Jacob's office, I was confused."

"Baby," I interrupt, "if he's mad at you for working for me, or being with me, I'll talk to him."

She shakes her head as more tears roll down her cheeks. "I walked into the room and Brady was there." I stiffen. "That night? When we went to Donatello's and I rejected him?"

"Yeah," I say, scared for her to continue, but knowing I need the whole story or I'm going to lose my fucking shit.

Her face twists in sadness. "He lied. He said I propositioned him to tie me up and have sex with me. He told Jacob that I made him uncomfortable, and when he told me no, I made a scene." She buries her face into my shirt, tears soaking through the fabric.

"Jacob didn't believe him, right?" He couldn't have. Mads has been a great asset to Tailgate Media. She's the first intern there every morning and the last to leave. Her assignments have been light years ahead of the others. She's gone above and beyond for that company. He can't possibly think she would sexually harass a client.

"It doesn't matter," she says, defeat evident in her voice. "They just went through a big scandal where a reporter actually did get herself into a similar situation. They won't want to go through it again, even if they don't believe Brady." She looks up at me and my heart cracks. "They let me go."

I say nothing as I hold her trembling body and try my best to soothe her. What can I say to fix this? Nothing. Because she's right. Unless we can prove Brady is lying, Tailgate won't want to risk word getting out about the whole situation. Especially when she isn't an actual employee. It'll look like they're condoning the behavior, and the court of public opinion will be calling for Jacob's head.

After what seems like hours, Mads has finally stopped crying. I push her tear-soaked hair from her beautiful face and place a soft kiss to her lips.

"I have to go home. To Chicago."

Her words are a shock to my system. My body goes rigid below her, panic settling back in as I try to figure out exactly what she means. "Baby, no. We'll figure this out."

She shakes her head as a look of sadness settles over her face. "I can't be here, Blaze. I came to Boston for this job. I was so confident that if I worked hard and showed them that I belonged there, they'd pick me. And I did all that. But it didn't matter. They tossed me aside and chose Brady's sponsorship over me."

"Mads," I plead, "let's let the dust settle. Then we can figure out a new plan. If Tailgate is dumb enough to let you go, somebody else would be lucky to have you."

"Who?" she replies. "What other media company in this city would give me a job once Brady tells everyone that story? He lives here and he'll make sure I don't get hired anywhere in Boston. I have to go back to Chicago and figure out if I can save my career."

"Okay," I relent. What choice do I have? I can't keep her here when being a journalist is all she's ever wanted. I could beg her to stay, but that would only be holding her back from achieving her dreams. I can't do that to her. I love her too much. "Just, please, stay with me one more night." Tears threaten to fill my eyes, but I do everything I can to keep them at bay. She's falling apart right now, and I need to be strong for her.

"Alright."

I carefully pull her off my lap, laying her down on the bed. This may be the last time I ever have her here, and I need to show her how much I love her. I gently run my lips down her neck, removing her shirt so I can feel her skin against mine. She trembles as I move lower, pulling down her shorts and panties. I kiss my way back up her body, stopping to pull off my clothes in the process.

I lower my naked body onto hers and she opens her legs for me. I settle between them, moving my hips gently, back and forth. She whimpers under me, waiting for me to push into her, but I can't. I know once it's over, I'll have to let her go. Maybe she'll come back to me. But what if she doesn't? What if she finds a job on the other side of the country and we can't make this work? What if she meets someone who sees her the way I do and she moves on, leaving me here knowing that I'll never love anyone this way again?

A tear slides down my cheek as I bury my face into her neck and slowly slide home. I keep a torturous pace as I move in and out of her, hoping that I can draw this out forever. I whisper over and over how I love her and how I'll never stop. That she's my whole world. That no matter where she goes, my heart will always belong to her.

We come together, our tears mixing where our faces press against each other. "I love you, Madison," I say softly as I kiss her one last time before rolling to the side and pulling her tightly into me.

"I love you too, Blaze," she whispers, her soft snores filling the room moments later. But sleep never finds me as I cling to her for what could be the last time.

MADS

"That's all of it," I say to Blaze with a shaky exhale. I woke up early this morning and packed my suitcases to head back to Chicago. I don't know if this is the right move, but I need to do it in order to clear my head. With everything that happened yesterday and getting let go from my internship, the future feels hopeless. I need to get out of Boston and make a new plan for my life. The only problem is that leaving this city means leaving Blaze behind. At least for now.

He picks up the last bag, carefully putting it into the back of my car. I tried to tell him I didn't feel comfortable taking the Mercedes since he bought it, but he insisted that I keep it. If it makes him feel better knowing I'm driving a safe, reliable vehicle, that's the least I can do when I'm the one leaving him here while I sort my life out.

He walks over to where I'm standing and pulls me into his arms. I've been doing my best not to cry today. But knowing this will be the last time I feel his embrace, at least for a little while, makes my chest ache. He loosens his hold just enough to pull back and look me in the eyes. "My Black Amex card is in the center console. Use it for whatever you need." I open my mouth to argue, but he cuts me off. "Please. Just let me do this. I'm barely holding myself together right now, knowing that when I get in bed tonight, you won't be there. Let me take care of you while you're gone."

"Alright," I relent.

"Good girl," he says with a weak smile. He drops his lips to mine in a deep kiss. It's like he's trying to commit the feeling to memory. And honestly, I'm doing the same. I don't know how I'll get through my days without this. In the short time Blaze and I have been together, he's already become the most important person in my life. Everything we share, from the passionate moments to the mundane ones, are something I'll miss dearly. I know this isn't end of us, but it really fucking feels like it right now.

We break the kiss and I lean into his chest, fisting my hands in his hoodie and letting the tears I've been holding back fall from my eyes. I just want to stay right here where I know I'm safe, but the only way to figure out where my career will lead me is to get out of Boston. To go back home and start applying for jobs in other cities. From there, Blaze and I can figure out what the future holds for us. But I can't say I'm not terrified. What if my absence makes him realize how much he loves the single life? What if he meets someone better? Someone who has a good career and can offer him all the things I can't.

"Stop it," he says, pressing his lips into my hair. "I can tell whatever you're thinking isn't good." *How does he always know?* "Everything is going to be fine. *We* are going to be fine. Go back to Chicago, take some time to reset, and we'll figure out the rest together."

I kiss him one more time before he leads me to the driver's seat, reaching over my body to buckle me in. I take a long inhale, hoping his scent will somehow stay in my nose long after I leave. He chuckles, removing his hoodie and slipping it over my head. His cologne envelops me, and I feel an immediate sense of peace. Like even though Blaze won't be with me physically, he'll always be in my corner.

"I love you, Baby Doll. Remember to use my card as often as you need. Pull over if you get tired and call me when you can." He shuts my door and takes a couple steps back as I turn the key, the engine roaring to life.

"I love you, too," I say, trying my best to keep a smile on my face, but it's fake. We both know it.

I pull down the driveway, watching in my rearview as the love of my life stands there clutching his heart, his face twisting with all the emotions he didn't want me to see. I have to believe what he said about us getting through this. I could end up getting a job in another city with a company a million times bigger than Tailgate Media, but will it really even matter in the end if I don't have Blaze to share it with?

That's the question that plagues my mind for the entire fourteen-hour ride back to Chicago.

THIRTY-EIGHT
BLAZE

A KNOCK ON MY DOOR, followed by a string of loud rings from my doorbell wake me from a dead sleep. It's been two days since Mads left. I feel like I got hit by a truck. The weekend wasn't so bad because I had a full schedule. We had a walkthrough on Saturday, followed by watching hours of game tape at the facility. Yesterday, we played Tennessee at Blizzard Stadium. We won, clinching a playoff spot, absolutely no thanks to me. I played like shit. I couldn't stop thinking about my last moments with her.

I broke down as soon as her car was out of sight, dropping to my knees in the middle of my driveway and crying like a little bitch until my head was pounding. I got it together long enough to do my job, but after my poor performance, coach suggested I take a couple days off. Normally, this is reserved for veterans who need extra recovery time after games, but he could tell that I wasn't myself. Plus, we're already guaranteed a playoff berth, so we can afford to let some of the starters rest. I climbed into bed yesterday afternoon and that's where I've stayed.

Whoever is out there lays on the doorbell again, prompting me to throw off the covers and head downstairs. I look through the peephole and swing the door open when I see Dalton on the other side. "Since when do you ring the doorbell?" I grumble, turning around and walking to the living room before plopping on the couch.

"Since you changed the lock code, apparently. You're lucky they recognized me at the gate station, or they wouldn't have let me in. Did you lose your phone?" he says, sitting down beside me.

"No," I reply. "I'm just not answering it. I don't want to talk to anyone but Mads. If she calls, I'll pick up." I talked to her yesterday after the game. She stopped at a hotel overnight, probably still tired from the emotional roller coaster she's been on these past few days, so it took her longer than expected to make it to Chicago. But she got there safely and is taking a few days to process things before she starts applying for jobs.

I miss her so goddamn much, it hurts.

Dalton kicks his feet up on the coffee table. "Well," he begins, "if you had answered any of the ninety times I called and texted, you'd know Jacob Shane is trying to get ahold of you."

I sit up straight, every muscle in my body tensing at the sound of his name. "What the fuck does he want?" I know Jacob, but not well enough for him to call me out of the blue to shoot the shit. If he's trying to get information on Mads, he can fuck right off. If he even says her name, I'll fucking end him. After all, the whole reason she isn't here in my arms like she should be is because he chose that piece of shit's sponsorship over her. I'll make sure nobody on the current Blizzard roster will work with Tailgate Media from here on out. My teammates are my brothers, and when someone fucks with one of us, they fuck with all of us.

"No idea. He called me earlier asking if I knew where you were. Said he called a bunch of times. It sounded really important," he says, raising a brow.

"Fine," I say, annoyed. "I'll check my phone." I run upstairs and grab it, noticing that I have about twenty-five missed calls from both Jacob and Dalton. Just as I go to check my voicemail, the phone rings in my hand. "Hello?" I answer.

"Blaze," he says, exhaling a breath. "It's Jacob Shane from Tailgate Media. I've been trying to get ahold of you."

This fucking guy. Just hearing him say my name makes me want to beat the shit out of him. "You have two minutes before I hang up. What do you want?" I grumble. The hand not holding my phone curls into a fist at my side as he speaks.

"I know you were involved with one of my interns, Madison Rodgers. Some things went down at the office, and I made a huge mistake. I need to get in contact with her. I tried calling the number we have on file, but it goes straight to voicemail. I was hoping you could help me."

That's laughable. Why the fuck would I help this guy when he's treated her so poorly? He didn't even give her a chance to explain her side of the story with Brady before he kicked her ass to the curb. No fucking way.

"You're goddamn right, you made a mistake. You sent the next big sports reporter out of the city to go work for someone else. You deserve whatever you get for not believing her when she told you Brady was lying."

"I know," he says, shocking me. "I should have listened to her. There have been some new developments in the story. Brady admitted to one of the other interns that he made the whole thing up and a witness heard everything. I need to get ahold of Madison to apologize. And to offer her a job. I know talent when I see it, and there was never another option for who was going to win the permanent position with us. It was always her. I'm sorry, Blaze."

Holy shit. I need to talk to her. "Don't tell me," I say. "Tell her when I bring her back home. And you better hope she accepts your apology, otherwise you can kiss working with me or my teammates in the future goodbye." I hit the end button, tossing my phone on the couch next to me.

"Was the threat necessary?" Dalton says with a smirk.

"Probably not." I shrug before getting up and heading toward the stairs.

"Where are you going?" he asks, following me.

I enter my room, throwing open the closet door and stuffing whatever I can find in my duffle bag as he stands in the doorway. "I'm going to Chicago. I'm bringing Mads home."

"Fuck yeah, baby! Throw some extra shit in there," he says, pointing to my bag. "I'm coming with you." I don't argue with him because maybe it'll be better having him there. Dalton can be a fucking clown sometimes, but he always has my back when I need him.

Twenty minutes later, he's booked our tickets and I'm driving as fast as I can toward the airport. I don't know how we managed it, but we were able to secure two first-class tickets straight to O'Hare tonight. It's like the universe wants me to go get my girl. I don't know how she'll react when she sees me, but I need to be with her. I probably could have just called, but I have a feeling it's going to take some convincing to get her back here. I know I'll have better luck if I show up at her doorstep and ask her in person to come home. Plus, I already miss holding her. So, if I'm putting forth all this effort just for a hug and she decides she wants to stay there, it's still worth it to me.

She'll always be worth it to me.

THIRTY-NINE
MADS

"I'LL FUCKING KILL HIM," my dad grumbles, standing from the couch.

"Dad!" I scold. I think I've heard him drop the f-bomb a total of three times in my whole life. But when I told him how Brady got me fired, he went into papa bear mode.

"No, Madison," he says, sternly. "That boy has made you cry too many times. He's a spoiled brat and doesn't deserve the success he has. Someone needs to teach him a lesson."

My mom walks over to stand by him, putting a calming hand on his shoulder. "Your father is right, sweetheart. You can't let him run you out of that city. You need to tell your boss the whole story. Maybe there were witnesses in the restaurant that night that heard you turn down Brady's advances."

I think back to that night. The dimly lit table in the corner. The waitress who made her judgement of my outfit very apparent. Brady voicing his disgust for the things I like in bed. I obviously can't tell my parents about all of that. "There wasn't," I say. "He reserved a secluded table. The only thing people would've been able to hear was me yelling at him when he insulted Blaze."

It's hopeless. My chances of working in Boston are zero. If I go back, I'm sure Brady will tarnish my name with his bull-shit story. I just have to focus on coming up with a new plan for my future. But how can I do that knowing wherever I end up, Blaze won't be there?

"Sorry!" Dia yells as she busts through the door without so much as a knock. "I couldn't find anyone to cover my shift at the club, so I had to tell my boss that my aunt died and that I had to leave work to go identify her body."

I scrunch my eyebrows. "Dia, you don't have an aunt," I reply.

"I know, but this is an emergency. I had to be creative." She walks over and pulls me into a tight hug. My parents head out of the room, kissing us both on the cheek as they pass by. I'm thankful that they always know what I need. And right now, that's time to sort through the things I'm feeling with my best friend. She already knows the details of what happened with Brady. We talked for a good part of my ride here. I practically had to beg her not to get on a plane to Boston and beat the shit out of him. I'm still not completely convinced that she isn't going to go rogue and do it anyway.

I motion for her to sit down on the couch. My body aches everywhere. Between all the crying I've done, the long drive from Boston, and the broken heart I'm currently nursing from being so far away from Blaze, I feel like shit. He would be coming home from practice right now to find me waiting impatiently for him in front of the TV. We'd do what we always do, changing into our pajamas before choosing a movie that we had no intentions of watching. We'd either fall asleep in each other's arms, exhausted from the day, or find some other trouble to get into together. I miss him so much, I can barely breathe.

"What are you thinking about?" Dia asks. I decide to be honest with her. And with myself.

"Ever since I was little, all I ever wanted was to be a sports reporter. I spent so much time and money learning the ins and outs of journalism so I could be the best. I was told that it wasn't the place for a girl and that I would never make it. That always fueled me to keep going. I thought it was my purpose in life." Tears threaten to fall as I try to come up with the right words to explain what's going through my head. As messy as it all is, there's one thing that I'm completely sure about. "Now I'm starting to wonder if any of that is important. If being a journalist means that I have to be away from Blaze, I'm not sure I want it anymore. I just want him."

"So, go get him." She says it so matter-of-factly. Like it's just that simple to throw away everything I've worked for and go back to Boston to be with Blaze. What would I even do there? Work for him as his assistant and have him pay me to make his daily schedules? That's a good side job, but I won't be content like that. I won't want to have him taking care of me and paying for everything. I wasn't raised that way and it's not who I am. I want to be his partner, not his problem.

"Dia, I can't just go get him. It's not that easy," I say.

"Bullshit," she replies. "You literally just said you don't know if you want to be a journalist anymore if it means being away from him. We both know damn well you won't give up on your dream, but the fact that you're even considering it an option tells me that being with Blaze is most important right now. Go get him. Worry about your career later. You can and will have *both*."

I sit there for a moment as realization hits me like a speeding bus. "I'm so stupid," I scoff. "Why did I leave him?" They say hindsight is twenty-twenty and that's never been truer than it is right now. All I've ever known is wanting to stand on the sidelines with a microphone in my hand, so when someone threatened to take that from me, I panicked. I left Boston thinking the city had nothing to offer me. But it does. It has Blaze. And that is all I need right now.

Dia is right. I don't want to give up on becoming a journalist, but I can figure out my next move with Blaze by my side. I'm stronger that way. His love and encouragement is exactly what I need to dust myself off and take the career I've earned with my middle fingers held high in the air for anyone who has told me I don't belong.

I jump up from the couch and head toward the stairs.

"Where are you going?" Dia yells from behind me.

"Getting my bags," I rush out. "I need to go to him."

She grabs me by the arm, halting me halfway up the staircase. "Bitch, are you crazy? You just drove for like, a million hours and you're running on ninety minutes of sleep and a Snickers bar. You need to chill the fuck out, get some rest, and head back tomorrow."

I scrunch my nose. "I hate when you're rational. It's annoying," I say as I make my way back down the stairs. Just as I plop back down on the couch, the doorbell rings. I'm not expecting anyone, but maybe my parents ordered some pizza since they didn't want to disturb us.

"I'll get it," Dia says, walking across the living room. She presses her face to the door, looking out the peephole. "*Holy. Fucking. Shit.*"

I turn, wondering who could be out there that would have her so surprised. But before I can ask, she swings the door open to reveal Blaze and Dalton on the other side. I don't even speak as I let out a strangled cry, hop over the back of the couch, and launch myself into his waiting arms. "You're here," I sob into his shirt. He smells so good.

"Hi, baby," he chuckles, his chest rumbling against my ear. "I missed you."

I allow myself another few seconds of just being in his arms before I pull back. "What are you doing here?" I ask, leading him further into the room.

He smiles at me. "Well, apparently, our old friend Brady

slipped up and got caught in his lie. Jacob has been trying to contact you, but I'm guessing you've been dodging his calls."

I lower my head sheepishly. "I have. I was so mad. I knew if I answered, I'd end up saying something I regretted for the way he let me go. He's too influential in the sports media industry to do that, so I was going to cool off for a few days before I returned his calls."

He sits on the couch, pulling me into his lap like he just can't get close enough. "He knows the truth. He was calling to apologize," he says with a big grin. "And to offer you a job."

"What?" Dia and I yell in unison. "I got it? I got the job?" I say, wanting to make sure I heard him right.

Blaze scoffs. "Of course you did. You earned it."

A blanket of relief flows over me as I relax into the warmth of his body. I let the situation settle in my mind for a moment. "Wait," I say, sitting up straight before turning to look at him. "You said Brady got caught in his lie. How?"

He shrugs. "I don't know the whole story. Just that he was talking to another intern about it and someone heard him."

I wonder who he was talking to. And why? How would Brady even know any of the other interns? His sponsorship of Connor's podcast didn't have anything to do with us. The only reason I went there that day was because the regular sound engineer wasn't available and the others don't have the same experience with the equipment as I do. So, where would he even have crossed paths with Ella, Chance, or Jason? I guess that's a question for Jacob when I talk to him. For now, I'm just going to enjoy knowing that the truth is out in the open.

"Hey, Wifey," Dalton says from his place next to Dia on the loveseat. "Did you hear I lead the league in touchdowns for running backs? The whole *league*." A look of confusion crosses her face because he may as well be speaking a different language. He takes her silence as an invitation to put his arm around her shoulder, which she immediately brushes off.

"Okay, I don't know what that means. And don't touch me," she says.

He pulls a throw pillow out from behind his back, placing it in his lap. "Don't get feisty with me here. It turns me on."

"*Oh my God,*" She says, disgusted. "If you're hard right now, I'm going to puke."

He scoffs, as if that's the most ridiculous thing he's ever heard. "What do you think I am? A teenager? I'm not hard. It's only a *semi*."

Her eyes go wide as Blaze and I laugh from our place across the room. I drown out their bickering and turn back to look at him. I can't believe he's here. "Come home," he whispers in my ear before pressing his lips to my neck.

I don't bother telling him I was already on my way before he got here. It doesn't really matter. All that matters is that we're back together and I have no intentions of running from him or from Boston ever again. "Okay."

He rears his head back, his brows pinched together. "Really? You're not even going to put up a little fight? Not even a fake one?" he questions sarcastically.

I wiggle my eyebrows. "Why? Are you going to punish me if I do?"

He groans, shifting me in his lap so I can feel him hardening under me. "I plan on cuffing you to the bed and spanking you for leaving me, either way. It's up to you to decide how badly you're going to get it."

I realize that his body isn't the only one reacting to our close proximity as my clit begins to throb. We need to tamp this down. At least until we're out of my parent's living room. I'm not sure they'd be happy about Blaze and I fucking on their couch. A shiver of horror runs through me at the thought of getting caught by them. No thanks.

As if I've summoned them with my mind, my parents

choose that moment to come back downstairs. "Blaze!" my mother says, a look of surprise blanketing her face. "Nice to see you again, honey. What brings you all the way out here?"

He carefully moves me off his lap before standing to give her a hug. He then turns to my father, shaking his hand. "Well," he addresses them both, "if it's alright with the both of you, I came to bring my girl home." My heart pounds in my chest. *Home*. I always thought that was here in Chicago. But as it turns out, home is wherever Blaze is.

My dad chuckles. "She's all yours, son," he says, winking at me. My mom sidles up beside him, wrapping her arms around his waist. I'm so thankful they've shown me the perfect example of why I shouldn't settle for anything less than a partner who adores me. Even after all these years, my parents are so in love. I thought I'd never find it, but I have a feeling that, twenty-five years from now, Blaze will still be by my side. Supporting me and loving me through all my failures and successes.

"Why don't you guys stay here tonight?" my mom suggests. "The couch pulls out and I can get the guest room together. We'll order some food and you guys can get a good night's rest before you head back." I love the woman, but she's crazy if she thinks I won't be sleeping in Blaze's arms tonight. No funny business, *I promise*.

"That sounds great," Blaze agrees, sitting back down next to me and lacing our fingers together.

We eat dinner and have one last makeover movie marathon before I leave Chicago for good. Dalton is easily convinced when Dia asks if she can paint his nails ice blue to match his uniform. I catch them laughing a little too hard and sitting a little too close all night, but I don't say anything. I just elbow Blaze and nod my head their way so he's in on the secret, too. If I didn't know Dia, I'd almost think she likes him. But she was right at my birthday party. She would break him. I have to admit, it might be kind of fun to watch.

We end the night falling asleep on the pull-out couch before our last movie ends. I don't know what tomorrow holds or what my career will look like five years down the road, but none of that matters right now. I have everything I need right here next to me.

FORTY
MADS

I PULL into the Tailgate Media headquarters parking lot and park my car. Blaze offered to drive me, but I wanted to do this alone. I wanted to go in there with my head held high and claim the job I rightfully earned. I don't know if the other interns will be here, but I'm glad I'm going straight to the top floor to meet with Jacob. I still don't know which one of them was involved with Brady, and to what extent, but it would be pretty awkward to have to be around them, wondering which one had a possible hand in me being let go.

I ride the elevator to the executive suites floor and walk toward the desk. Unlike our normal interactions, this time when Dani sees me, she gets up and rounds the desk before flinging her arms around me. "Oh my God, I'm so glad you're here!" she says. I can't say I'm not thoroughly confused, but this is better than the not-so-warm exit I made last time I left here.

She steps back, smoothing her skirt down on her thighs. "You can go right in. Jacob is waiting for you."

Here we go. I don't know why I'm so nervous about this meeting. He's the one who fucked up when he fired me last week. But unlike him, I plan on hearing him out completely before I decide whether or not I'll be taking his job offer.

Who am I kidding? Of course I'll accept it. But I'll make him sweat a little first. He deserves that much.

He greets me when I enter his office and motions for me to sit down. I wipe my clammy hands on my pants and wait for him to launch into his spiel. His demeanor is different than the other times I've been in here. Before, he exuded confidence. But today, he looks embarrassed and unsure.

"Before we get into things," he says, "I owe you an apology. You tried to tell me Brady was lying and I dismissed you. You never gave me a reason to not trust you and I let you down. I'm sorry, Madison."

"Okay," I say quietly. Mainly because I need to hear the whole story before I decide if I actually do accept his apology. Thankfully, he continues.

"I was unaware of this, but there's an office on the eleventh floor that employees have been sneaking into whenever they need a break. The whole floor is being remodeled, but that particular office is the only one that still has the old locking door." I definitely know about that office. Rachel and Ian from accounting used to go in there to have sex on their break at least three times a week. Or so I've heard. "Dani's boyfriend brought her lunch on Friday afternoon, shortly after I met with you and Brady, and they wanted to eat in private."

Eat? Yeah. Ok. Seems like everyone here is using the eleventh-floor office as their own sex room.

He continues. "They heard footsteps coming down the hall, so they hid behind the desk, afraid of getting in trouble for being in there. Turns out, Brady and Chance were working together to get you fired and they were discussing it privately right here in our building."

Fucking Chance. I hated him from the first day with his interrupting and mansplaining. Jason wasn't much better, but he only seemed to disrespect me after Chance had taken a shot first. He was more of a follower.

"But how did they even know each other?" I ask.

He fiddles with the pen cup on his desk. "They were in the same fantasy football league. Chance went to school with Connor Paul's brother, so when he moved to Boston for the internship, Connor asked him to join. I guess Brady was in the league, too."

That makes sense. Brady did seem very comfortable with Connor and his friends that day. I didn't even think that they could've known each other beyond recording a podcast together.

"Anyway," he goes on, "they came up with a plan to get you out of Boston. Chance knew he couldn't beat you out for the permanent position here, and Brady wanted to hurt you after you rejected him. He started with me, telling his story about how you propositioned him, knowing I wouldn't want to have another workplace scandal on my hands. He planned on telling all the other media outlets in the city so they wouldn't hire you. Then, you'd be forced to leave."

I fucking knew it.

I blow out a breath. "Wow." That's all I can say right now. I know Brady is an asshole, but he was completely ready to ruin the life I was building here just because he couldn't have me. And he almost succeeded. I had a feeling that he was going to run my name through the mud. That's why I left the way I did. I did exactly what he wanted me to do. Thank God Dani and her boyfriend couldn't wait until after work to have sex that day. I should send them a fruit basket or something.

"So," he continues, "I would like to offer you a permanent position here, if you'll take it. You have been a great asset to this company and I'm not dumb enough to let you go twice." Blood rushes to my ears. I can't believe this is happening. All the years I put into getting here. Beating every single odd as a woman in sports journalism. Keeping my eye on the prize even when I wanted to give up. I fucking did it. "If you accept my offer, we'll start with you doing interviews for social media Then, when you're ready, we'll get you on the side-lines. Maybe you can talk your boyfriend out of telling his teammates to boycott us," he jokes.

I suck my teeth, leaning back a little in my chair. "I don't know, Mr. Shane. He was pretty mad at you." I wink. "I'll see what I can do."

We end the meeting with me signing on the dotted line to become the newest member of the Tailgate Media team. I walk back to the reception desk, hoping to catch Dani so I can thank her, but she isn't there. Then again, it's lunchtime, so she may be on the eleventh floor. *Good for her.*

I leave the office for the day, rushing home to tell Blaze the good news. I'm staying in Boston for good.

FORTY-ONE
BLAZE

Super Bowl Sunday

"ALRIGHT, BOYS," Tanner says, standing in front of the group. "This is it. The day you've been dreaming of since the first time you laced up your little cleats. That day, you began a journey. And it's led you here today. To this moment. To this *game*. This is a culmination of all the years of hard work you've put in to becoming the best. There are kids at home right now, wearing their little Blizzard pajamas, hoping that one day they'll be playing in this game. They're watching you. There are men and women in the stands who would give anything to be where you are, playing the sport they love at the highest level. They're watching you. Your families and friends who supported you through bad games, good games, injuries, and all the milestones you've reached along the way. They're watching you. Let's go out there and make them proud. What do you say, boys?"

The whole locker room erupts into cheers as we gather together with our outstretched hands placed over Tanner's. "On three!" he yells. "One! Two! Three! Blizzard!" we shout in unison before storming out toward the tunnel. The excitement in the air is palpable, like I could reach out and touch it as we make our way to the field.

The last couple of months have been a whirlwind. After bringing Mads back home to Boston, she immersed herself in work as I did the same. We fought our way through playoffs, almost losing again in the Conference Championship Game. Thankfully, Ramirez came in clutch with the winning field goal that sent us to the Super Bowl. My first of many, I hope.

The lights in the stadium dim as the announcer introduces the team. It's a warm night in Los Angeles, but I'm shivering from adrenaline. I just want to get out there and win this thing. Then I want to take my girl back to the hotel and celebrate by sliding inside her and not leaving the room for the next three days. Jacob has her on assignment here, but she finished interviews before we did warm-ups, so right now she's sitting right where I want her. At the fifty-yard line behind the Blizzard benches.

We take the field as lights flash and music blares through the place, but I'm only focused on finding her. When our eyes lock, all my nerves fade away. It's just us for a moment, speaking to each other without saying a single word. I never thought I'd have this with anyone. Seven or eight months ago, if you had told me I would find the girl I planned to marry this season, I'd have told you to fuck off. I never saw her coming. My life changed the day Madison Rodgers landed on my doorstep. I still don't know if I'll ever deserve her, but I know I'll spend the rest of my life trying to be everything she needs.

"I love you," She mouths. I kiss my fingers before bringing my palm down to my heart. It's my sign to her. She hasn't been able to make it to every game after starting work, so I wanted to come up with something to let her know that she was with me, even when she wasn't. I made it my new move after every touchdown. I knew that was the only time I could bank on the cameras being on me, so I made sure to score in

every game so I could tell her I loved her on national television. The viewers may not have understood my message, but Mads did.

We win the coin toss and defer, sending our defense out on the field first. They force a three-and-out, so I buckle my helmet and follow Tanner and the rest of the offense to the line. The first pass comes my way, but the lineman gets a hand on it, making it drop short before I can make the grab. On second down, Dalton busts through for forty yards, getting tackled right as he makes it to the sideline.

Scoring on the opening drive is a rare occurrence, but it sets the tone for the whole game. I want it. I want to know what it feels like to score on the biggest stage of the season. That hunger motivates me as I line up for the play.

Tanner sees the blitz coming, so he changes the play to an out-slant combo, which will get the ball out of his hands faster, avoiding the sack. This isn't supposed to gain us a lot of yardage. I just have to get my hands on the ball and get out of bounds so we can come up with a new strategy for the next play.

The ball is snapped, and I run my route, going about five yards before cutting toward the sideline. Tanner fires the pass and I make the catch, realizing that the defenders pulled off me, assuming I was headed out of bounds. I manage to keep my feet in as I turn, running as fast as I can up the open lane. The crowd is going wild, but I swear I can hear my girl screaming over all of them as I cross the plane into the end zone.

Holy fucking shit. I just scored a touchdown on the opening drive in the Super Bowl with the love of my life watching from fifty yards away.

MADS

There are less than three minutes left in the fourth quarter and the Blizzard are beating the Dallas Sharpshooters by seven points. All we have to do is stop them from converting here, then they'll be forced to punt. Then it's up to Blaze and the offense to get one first down before they can take their victory formation.

I hold my breath as the defense goes to work, causing a loss of yardage on first down. On the next play, the running back finds a hole for a six-yard gain. *Fuck.* We have to hold them here or they'll have an opportunity to score.

The ball is snapped and our edge rusher, Maverick Moran, slips through a hole in the offensive line. He hits their quarterback at just the right angle, causing him to fumble. The stadium collectively gasps as players from both teams pile up on top of each other, arms reaching for the ball. It's too hard to see who is at the bottom, so I wait with bated breath as the referees pull players up one by one. As soon as our guys start jumping and pointing in the direction of the opposing team's end zone, I know we got it.

The refs confirm my assumption and the crowd goes nuts. All we have to do is get one first down, then we can kneel to run out the clock.

The first two downs don't go well. They try sending Dalton up the middle, not wanting to chance an interception with a pass play. They'd have no choice but to punt if this next play doesn't result in a ten-yard gain. Ramirez is good, but this is out of his target field goal range. Blaze lines up and looks back at Tanner, nodding. It's then that I realize something fishy is going on. Instead of leading with his inside foot, he puts the other one forward. I bring my hands over my mouth as he backs up, lining up parallel to Tanner, who is in the shotgun formation.

No fucking way.

I hold my breath as the ball is snapped and Tanner tosses a lateral to Blaze. The defense was expecting the pass, but by the time they realize it won't be coming from Tanner's hands, it's too late. Blaze fires the ball downfield to Dalton, who tucks it under his arm and runs at lightning speed into the end zone.

Even with time left on the clock, Dallas can't come up with two touchdowns. The Blizzard won the Super Bowl!

Ice blue and white confetti rains down on the field as players and their families rush out to celebrate. A security guard, no doubt bribed by my boyfriend, hoists me over the guardrail and I take off in his direction. I don't even slow down before launching myself into his open arms, wrapping my legs around his waist.

"You did it!" I say, covering his face in kisses. "I'm so proud of you!"

"*We* did it, Baby Doll," he says, grinning from ear to ear before setting me down and running back to his team. I'm confused for a moment, but then I realize why he took off so quickly.

I watch from afar as the Lombardi trophy makes its way through the crowd, stopping along the way for the players to kiss. It's tradition. My heart feels like it could burst as the Jumbotron zooms in on Blaze as he presses his lips to the precious piece of metal.

This season has been full of ups and downs for both of us. But we made it through. Blaze is officially a Super Bowl champion, and I'm working my way toward my dream of being a sideline reporter. Finding love was never part of my plan when I moved out to Boston, but it was inevitable. Fate brought me to Blaze that day. And I can't wait to see what the future has in store for us.

EPILOGUE

MADS

One Year Later

I SMOOTH my light blue sweater before taking my microphone back and turning it on. The Blizzard just won their second Super Bowl in as many years, and while I wish I could be running onto the field to Blaze like I did last year, I'm working.

During the last week of preseason, Jacob called me into his office and offered me a new position as Tailgate Media's official sideline reporter for the Boston Blizzard. After about one second of mulling it over, I happily accepted his offer.

Right now, I'm waiting for them to announce the Most Valuable Player. I know whose name I'm hoping they say, but Blaze and Tanner both had outstanding performances, so it could go either way.

The announcer's voice comes through the speakers and I hold my breath, waiting for the decision. "And this year's Super Bowl MVP with ten catches for one-hundred and eighty-one yards and two touchdowns...Blaze Beckham!"

The crowd goes wild as I jump up and down like a maniac, not caring in the slightest that I look unprofessional as hell. Tears of pride fill my eyes as the Commissioner hands Blaze his trophy. He worked so hard this season. After being out with a high ankle sprain for six weeks during the middle of the regular season, he somehow came back stronger and faster. Although he wasn't able to break any records this year, he made his mark. Especially today, scoring the only two Blizzard touchdowns.

I wait patiently on the sidelines as the team takes the podium, waiting for their turn to make a speech. It seems like hours have gone by before the field has cleared a bit and I see Blaze making his way toward me. My instinct is to jump on him and press my lips to his, but then I remember that I'm about to be on live television, so I settle for a hug. I'll congratulate him properly back at the hotel.

My cameraman, Danny motions to me that we're on the air and I do my best to remember all the questions I had ready for this year's MVP.

"Blaze," I begin, speaking into my microphone. "That sixty-yard touchdown late in the fourth sealed the game for the Blizzard. Tell me what was going through your mind during that play." I turn my microphone, bringing it close enough to his mouth that it'll pick up his voice over the screaming fans in front of us.

"Well, Madison," he says, winking at me. I swear he's trying to melt my panties in front of the entire country. "All I was thinking about was making a play that would be big enough to win MVP. I had to score this interview."

I laugh, trying not to swoon on camera. "And why was this interview so important to you?" I ask.

He looks back at Dalton, who is standing off to the side with something clutched in his hand that I can't make out. He tosses it to Blaze, who swipes it out of the air. "So I could do this."

I'm shocked as he drops down to one knee and opens the blue box in his hand, revealing a very large emerald cut solitaire diamond ring. My microphone drops to my feet before he picks it up, holding it in front of his face.

"Madison Rodgers, a year and a half ago, you rang my doorbell and changed my life in an instant. I knew almost immediately that I'd never let you go." I'm full-on crying at this point as he continues. "We've been through a lot since then, but one thing hasn't changed. I love you and I can't imagine my life without you in it. Will you marry me?"

"Yes!" I say without hesitation as he stands and wraps me in his arms. He drops his lips to mine in a kiss that's far too PG for my liking, but we are being broadcast live right now, so I'm glad one of us still has our good sense about us. He pulls back, reaching into the box and plucking out the ring before sliding it on my finger. I've all but abandoned the interview as the fans that are left in the stands cheer from above us.

These last couple of years have been so surreal. I started as a college graduate trying to make her way in an industry that didn't accept her. And now I'm living my dream both professionally and personally. Blaze has been my biggest cheerleader, always telling me how proud he is of what I have accomplished.

Danny cuts the camera and I finally jump into Blaze's arms, giving him the kiss I've been holding back since he came over here.

"You better watch out, dirty girl," he says quietly, so only I can hear. "If you get me hard in front of all these people, I'll have to punish you when we get back to the hotel."

My lips tip up in a devilish grin. "Can't wait," I say before grabbing my fiancée's hand and heading toward the tunnel.

ACKNOWLEDGMENTS

My husband - What a year it's been. We've experienced some of the highest highs and the lowest lows, but one thing never changed. Your love and encouragement has always made me feel like I could do anything. Even in those moments where I wanted to throw this whole book in the trash. You believed in me and I couldn't have done it without you.

My mom - I really, really hope you didn't read this book. And if you did, just know that absolutely no part of it is a reflection of your parenting. I swear you didn't raise a degenerate. But seriously, you've always been in my corner, supporting all my crazy dreams. I wouldn't be half the woman I am today if I didn't have you as my role model.

My kids - I love you, but if you are reading this, you're grounded forever.

Breanne - I can't even express how blessed I feel to have you in my life. It's hard to look back and remember a time before we were sisters; even though it's through marriage. That was just fate's way of putting us in each other's lives. I'm so thankful you allowed me to share this project with you before it went out into the world. And I really can't wait to have you with me on the rest of this journey!

Hannah Gray - My friend. My cheerleader. My editor. My sounding board. This book would not exist at all without you.

When I questioned myself about my ability to create this story, you were there with constant encouragement and support. I love you!

Lexi James - I'll never forget the first time I realized I wanted to write Blaze and Mads' story. I thought it was a pipe dream, but you gave me the courage to type out those first words. I love our friendship and I'm so thankful you are a part of my journey. Now, STFUATTDLAGG.

The team at Wordsmith Publicity - Thank you for taking on an author who claimed she could *do it all herself*. Turns out, no she can't. I'm so thankful for everything you did to help me along in the process of releasing this book.

My alpha readers, Jenn and Nicole - The two of you have been with me since day one of my Bookstagram. I knew I needed you with me while I wrote this and I can't thank you enough for taking the time to help me through this crazy process.

To my beta and ARC readers - The fact that you took a chance on a new author with a wild imagination means more to me than you'll ever know. Thank you.

To my readers - I don't even have words. If you willingly picked up this book and read it, you've changed my life. Thank you for making my dream of being an author a reality.

ABOUT THE AUTHOR

C.L. Rose is a wife and mother of two. She lives in Northeast Ohio with her husband, son, daughter, and dog, Tank. When she isn't writing, you can find her reading in front of a space heater, wrapped in a thick blanket, probably complaining that she's cold.

instagram.com/authorclrose
tiktok.com/@authorclrose
pinterest.com/authorclrose

COMING SOON IN THE BOSTON BLIZZARD SERIES

The Stunt: A Boston Blizzard Novella - February 2024

Run Game - Spring 2024

QB Keeper - Summer 2024

Printed by Amazon Italia Logistica S.r.l.
Torrazza Piemonte (TO), Italy